Sherlock Holmes
Consulting Detective

Volume Eighteen

Airship 27 Productions

AN AIRSHIP 27 PRODUCTION

Sherlock Holmes Consulting Detective Volume 18

"The Adventure of the Restless Dead" © 2022 I.A. Watson
"The Adventure of the Girl on the Black Velvet Swing" © 2022 Michael A. Black
"The Adventure of the Queen's Tiara" © 2022 Raymond Louis Lovato

Cover illustration ©2022 Warren Montgomery
Interior illustrations © 2022 Rob Davis

Editor: Ron Fortier
Associate Editor: Jonathan Sweet
Production designer: Rob Davis
Promotion and marketing manager: Michael Vance

Published by
Airship 27 Productions
www.airship27.com
www.airship27hangar.com

ISBN: 978-1-953589-40-8

Printed in the United States of America

10 9 8 7 6 5 4 3 2 1

Sherlock Holmes
Consulting Detective

Volume XVIII

TABLE OF CONTENTS

Sherlock Holmes

in

THE ADVENTURE OF THE RESTLESS DEAD

by
I.A. Watson

"These facts relate to the singular series of events which happened in connection with the vault at Christchurch, near the village of Oistin, on the south coast of Barbados."

Sir Arthur Conan Doyle introducing the mystery of the Barbados Coffins in "The Uncharted Coast—I. The Law of the Ghost", an article for *The Strand Magazine*, December 1919, collected in *The Edge of the Unknown* (1930)[1]

"I'm very glad you're arrived, Dr Watson," our landlady told me as I was admitted to my former lodgings on 221B Baker Street. "Since you moved out he's been quite impossible to restrain."

"The opium again?" I ventured. Holmes had taken to stimulating and calming himself with drug preparations when he had no work that engaged his interest, and his health suffered for it. It had been my main concern for him after I had moved out to my Kensington practice the previous November on the occasion of my marriage.[2]

Mrs Hudson gestured helplessly to the stairs up to our sitting room. "He's up there right now, sir, calculating, he says, the cubic capacity of a lead coffin."

"Very well, Mrs Hudson. I shall see to it."

"I'd be grateful as you would, doctor. It's morbid, all this funeral mathematics. I put up with the chemical smells and the scrub-kneed urchins and the occasional villain with a knife or firearm, but just sometimes I wish Mr

1   A full copy of the article, in which Doyle outlines the "known details" of the case, is available at:
https://www.arthur-conan-doyle.com/index.php?title=The_Law_of_the_Ghost

2   Watson's marital status is a source of much debate amongst Holmesians, who struggle to reconcile the clues given within his Canon statements with a coherent continuity. A tentative consensus, typified by W.S. Baring-Gould's biography *Sherlock Holmes* (1962), is that Watson married on three occasions, in November 1886, May 1889, and October 1902, and was widowed twice. Of these women the Canon supplies only the name of Mary Morstan, whom Watson met in *The Sign of Four* and who is generally accorded to be the second wife in this assumed marital history. Watson's comments in our present account would seem to place events during his first marriage; Baring-Gould identifies this wife as "Miss Constance Adams of San Francisco".

5

Holmes would find a little bit of restraint!"

"I assure you, dear lady, that any discussion of or calculation about burial caskets will be concluded as soon as feasibly possible. My word on it. I'll go up now and have a word with Holmes, shall I?"

Mollified for the present, Mrs Hudson allowed me to progress up to my old chambers and join my friend in our familiar rooms.

"Watson!" Sherlock Holmes greeted me affably as I entered. "My dear fellow, thank you for coming. And on such a wet, gloomy afternoon, too. Come in, come in, and review my diagnosis."

"You seem remarkably cheerful, Holmes. I can only hope that some new mystery or fascinating course of study has come to light. I trust that we can discuss it without further trying our hostess' patience?"

Holmes looked me over and smiled. "I perceive from the details of your attire and your choice of moustache wax that Mrs Watson is not at home presently. She is most likely visiting her friend Mrs Whitney, who is nursing her husband through opium withdrawal.[3] You are somewhat at liberty for a few days and might lapse to bachelor habits. Shall I explain what I am doing to so vex our unfortunate Mrs Hudson?"

"I should be glad to know," I agreed. I was still annotating Holmes's investigations when I could, having that very afternoon completed my initial sketch of the Reigate Puzzle and the fall of the Cunninghams.[4] "You have evidently tidied up the business after the strange disappearance of Neville St Clare, with the beggarly brotherhood deceivers' luxurious club concealed beneath that derelict warehouse?"

I have written elsewhere of the St Clare kidnapping and the remarkable involvement of the beggar Boone, an adventure that followed my retrieval of Kate Whitney's husband from the vile vice den where his addiction had dragged him. Holmes, unsatisfied with his tardiness in uncovering the truth of St Clare's situation (he had deemed himself "one of the most absolute fools in Europe" over his slowness), had continued his investigation

---

3   Watson's retrieval of Isa Whitney from the notorious Bar of Gold opium den is described in "The Man With The Twisted Lip", *The Adventures of Sherlock Holmes* (1891), and is generally held to have taken place in mid-June 1887, about three months before the present account.

4   Watson's account of "The Adventure of the Reigate Squire" debuted in Britain in *The Strand Magazine* in June 1893, appeared in the U.S. in *Harper's Weekly* on the 17th of that month, and then featured in the American version of *The Strand Magazine* the month following. It was collected in *The Memoirs of Sherlock Holmes* (1893) and reprinted in sixteen other newspapers and periodicals in the next thirty years.

and had finally uncovered the Amateur Mendicant Society, an entire club of gentleman whose income was derived from impersonating beggars or from undertaking nefarious business in such guise.[5]

"There are still some enquiries in hand before that matter may be completely settled," Holmes allowed. "I have set the case aside until investigations I have commissioned are reported back to me. But I have resolved the small matter of the Clockwork Mouse and concluded the Paradol Chamber affair[6] and am at liberty to turn my attentions to a different kind of problem."

I reached for the tantalus. "I would be pleased to hear the details."

Holmes waved a sheet of tracing-paper in the air and grinned at me. "I know you like a good ghost story," he told me. "What better for a chilly winter's entertainment with evening drawing in? Here, settle in your old place and allow me to present my present researches."

I owned that I was intrigued as to why Holmes might need to determine the volume and density of a lead-lined coffin.

"Our mystery begins with the book you see on the side-table there, Watson. The appropriate paragraphs are marked."

I picked up the rather dog-eared and foxed travelogue, an antique edition titled *Transatlantic Sketches* by one Captain James Alexander, published in 1833.[7]

"Read it out," Holmes requested, so I did.

"'It is not generally known that in Barbados there is a mysterious vault, in which no one now dares to deposit the dead. It is in a churchyard near the sea-side. In 1807 the first coffin that was deposited in it was that of a Mrs Goddard; in 1908 a Miss A.M. Chase was placed in it; and in 1912 Miss D. Chase. In the end of 1812 the vault was opened for the body of

---

5   The St Clare investigation that reveals the London businessman to be masquerading for profit as the tramp Hugh Boone forms the main narrative of "The Man With The Twisted Lip." Holmes's further exposure of "the Amateur Mendicant Society, who held a luxurious club in the lower vault of a furniture warehouse" was referenced in passing in "The Five Orange Pips", *The Adventures of Sherlock Holmes* (1891).

6   The Adventure of the Paradol Chamber is another of those untold cases mentioned in the Canon and is amongst the list of Holmes's recent accomplishments offered by Watson in "The Five Orange Pips."

7   *Transatlantic Sketches, comprising visits to the most interesting scenes in North and South America, and the West Indies* (1833) by Sir James Edward Alexander is available online at https://archive.org/details/transatlanticske01alexrich The passages quoted by Dr Watson come from pages 96 and 97 of that work.

the Honourable T. Chase; but the three first coffins were found in a confused state, having been apparently tossed from their places. Again was the vault opened to receive the body of an infant, and the four coffins, all of lead, and very heavy, were much disturbed. In 1816 a Mr. Brewster's body was placed in the vault, and again great disorder was apparent in the coffins. In 1819 a Mr. Clarke was placed in the vault, and as before, the coffins were in confusion.

"'Each time that the vault was opened the coffins were replaced in their proper situations, that is, three on the ground, side by side, and the others laid on them. The vault was then regularly closed; the door (and a massive stone that required six or seven men to move) was cemented by masons; and though the floor was of sand, there were no marks of footsteps or water.'"

I looked up from my reading. "Holmes, if the story is true then it is incredible. What are we to make of it? But it was long ago and far away, and travellers' yarns are not always to be relied upon."

"That it was a mere winter's tale was also my first assumption. The detail is somewhat convincing, but a good storyteller knows what to include for verisimilitude. You will note that the next paragraph outlines the investigations of the Governor of Barbados, Lord Combermere.[8] A proper ghost story always requires an investigator."

"'The last time the vault was opened was in 1819'," I read on. "'Lord Combermere was then present, and the coffins were found thrown confusedly about the vault; some with their heads down, and others up. What could have occasioned this phenomenon? In no other vault on the island has this ever occurred. Was it an earthquake that occasioned it, or the

---

8   Field Marshal Stapleton Cotton, 1st Viscount Combermere GCB GCH KSI PC (1773-1865) was a British Army officer, diplomat and politician, veteran of the Flanders Campaign, the Fourth Anglo-Mysore War, and the suppression of Robert Emmet's 1803 insurrection. He was Sir Arthur Wellesley's cavalry commander in the Peninsular War and later served as Commander-in-Chief, Ireland and then Commander-in-Chief, India. His governorship of Barbados and the Windward Islands was but one chapter of a long and interesting career.

Ironically given his brief role in the Affair of the Moving Coffins, the 1st Viscount Combermere is less remembered in the annals of strange events as his son, Colonel Wellington Henry Stapleton-Cotton, 2nd Viscount Combermere (1818-1891), politician and soldier, who was born during his father's time in Barbados. During the funeral of the 2nd Viscount, his sister Sybell Corbet took a long-exposure photograph of the library at Combermere Abbey that when developed seemed to show a translucent figure sitting in the deceased man's favourite chair. "Lord Combermere's Ghost Photo" was attested to be one of the best evidences for spirit photography ever produced, although Sir William Barrett, who investigated the case and reported on it in the Journal of the Society for Psychical Research (December 1895) remained sceptical.

effects of an inundation in the vault?'" I looked up. "Those seem the likely explanations to me."

"We may dismiss the earthquakes at once, Watson," Holmes advised me. "Barbados is seismically stable. No tremor of note was recorded between 1812 and 1820."

"Flooding, then? The account mentions that the vault was near the sea."

"Very near, evidently, for the chapel that the graveyard was associated with actually had to be rebuilt because it was claimed by the waves during a storm in 1669. The new Christ Church was erected in 1780 on higher ground. But the Chase vault lies thirty yards above sea level on porous Pleistocene coral reef limestone that drains very quickly. The next volume beside you includes an account of a first-hand inspection of the site by surveyor and geographer Sir Robert H. Schomburgk, sometime before 1848 when his *History of Barbados* was published. Combermere's own inspection was evidently outlined in his *Memoirs and Letters* and is much-quoted but I have so far been unable to acquire a copy of the original."[9]

I settled back into my old comfortable armchair. It was very pleasant to be ensconced again with Holmes, warming my feet at the fire-grate and discussing some intriguing problem while rain rattled the casement and runelled down the panes.

"Does the nature of the ground make the flooding theory unfeasible, then?" I wondered.

"It might not. The Chase vault lays underground, approached down eight steps into a mausoleum some thirteen feet by eight, with a low Roman barrel roof of local brick which is less than six feet high at its apex. The ornamental capping monument which overlays the site is of cemented coral blocks. The entrance-stone was a single slab of blue Devonshire marble, but that has now been removed since the vault was emptied and the coffins reburied elsewhere."

"You think that the construction might make the place a natural pooling point?"

"Barbados is known for its heavy and sudden rainfall, between forty-seven and fifty-five inches annually. A snap inundation may have caused a brief torrent to gather in the subterranean tomb and the ground beneath it could drink it up just as quickly."

"And that is why you were calculating the cubic capacity of a coffin, to

---

9   Holmes is not alone in this; there appear to be no surviving copies of *Memoirs and Letters of Lord Combermere* (1868), although it is mentioned or quoted in several other works.

our landlady's discomfit!" I realised. "You wish to know whether a sealed lead coffin can float!"

Holmes nodded acknowledgement. "We must make some assumptions, of course. Let us consider a standard box some six feet by three by two. That is the largest of the coffins; some were caskets for children, one of an infant. The largest possible sarcophagus affords us thirty-six cubic feet, displacing 224.23 gallons of water. And so to the weight of the coffin..."

"How do you know it was lead-lined?"

"There is an account of eight men being required to bear Colonel Thomas Chase's casket. Such heavy funeral constructions were commonplace amongst the better classes in Barbados at the time, as a means of excluding predators both animal and human. Colonel Chase may have wished for such protection more than most; contemporary accounts describe him as 'the most hated man on the island'."

I wondered what the chap had done that was so notably unpleasant.

"He was the worst of plantation slave owners, violent-tempered and cruel," Holmes noted. "There were evidently rumours about an unhealthy relationship with his daughter Dorcas, who died of 'decline', which some sources intimate was self-starvation to escape her domineering and brutal father's bedroom attentions."

I might have commented further on such appalling allegations, but Holmes drew me back to his sketches and calculations. "A typical lead coffin weighs around 700 lbs. Perhaps we should allow another 40 lbs for the skeleton of a large male—in life Chase weighed over sixteen stone. Now you will recall from your schooldays, Watson, that $B = \rho \times V \times g$. B is the buoyant force, ρ the fluid density, V the volume of the displaced fluid, and g the acceleration due to gravity. Now we shall assume a flood of sea water, with a fluid density of 63.99 pounds per cubic foot. That of course gives us a weight of displaced fluid of 2,305.6 pounds and a buoyant force of 2,305.65 pound-force or 74.181 poundals in the new measurements,[10] quite sufficient to overcome the weight of even the heaviest coffin. If we substitute freshwater for saltwater then the displaced fluid weight is 2,247.3 lbs, still quite adequate."

"I'm sure you're right, Holmes." I could scarcely remember a declension from my classroom years, let alone physics formulae.

---

10   Poundals were a new measurement to Holmes, having been adopted as the Imperial unit of force in 1877, replacing the older pound-force (which is still sometimes used in the U.S. as part of the "English Engineering Units" system). The International System of Units (SI) depreciated both units internationally with the adoption of the Newton in 1947. Holmes's calculation would yield an equivalent figure of 10,256 Newtons.

"However, the average annual rainfall in Bridgetown, Barbados is 50 inches a year, peaking in November at 7.1 inches for the month. Even allowing for flooding into the sunken vault during monsoon season it would require several *feet* of flooding to float the coffins from their positions. And remember that the smaller, easier-to-float caskets were stacked on top of the heavier ones." Holmes shook his head. "I'm not satisfied, Watson."[11]

"It is rather too far and rather too long ago for any other investigation," I pointed out. "The histories must be rather sketchy and the accounts second-hand." I knew how much Holmes disliked that.

"You think I have latched onto some new obsession to divert myself from ennui, to avoid the seven percent solution,[12] doctor? Well, perhaps I have, but I am not yet reduced to considering seventy-year old ghost stories from halfway around the globe. There is a present case that... No, I chide others for running ahead with their stories. Allow me to unfold this one in a logical manner. You must follow my researches."

He indicated another stack of papers for me to examine. "Burial records?"

"Burial records," Holmes boomed enthusiastically. "Here are notes taken from *The Book of Christ Church*, which includes original interment records for the churchyard where the Chase vault is located. The tomb was commissioned at significant cost for the Honourable John Elliott in 1724, who appears to have never used it. The first occupant was one Thomasina Goddard, placed there in 1807 and left there after the grave-plot was sold. The Goddards and the others who later used the burial site were all linked by family."

"Alexander's report is not quite right, then," I observed, glancing at the

---

11   The Reverend Lionel and Mrs Patricia Fanthorpe conducted an on-site investigation for a BBC radio programme in 1996 and published an account of their findings in *Fortean Times* #133 (April 2000). Of the flooding theory, the Fanthorpes wrote, "When we examined the vault and its surroundings...it seemed to us that the tomb was so close to the top of the slope on which Christchurch parish church stands—and so close to the church door that unnoticed flooding would have been impossible. No seawater from Oistins Bay could have risen that far.

"We also checked the masonry for ourselves as [parish priest] Orderson and his colleagues had done almost two centuries before. The bricks and coral-stone blocks looked solid, original, and sound; only the big blue Devonshire marble slab was missing."

12   That is a weak dose of liquid opium, a legal self-medication in Holmes's day. Watson reports Holmes becoming a "self-poisoner" in April of 1887 (according to most interpretations of Canon chronology), some five months after Watson's departure from Baker Street to married life.

detailed material that my friend had accumulated. "The vault was acquired by Colonel Chase in 1808, upon the death of his younger daughter, two-year-old Mary Ann Maria Chase. The elder sister Dorcas joined her in the tomb in 1812. Only a month after that, Thomas Chase took his own life. It was when the tomb was opened for his interment that the coffins were first found disordered. In 1816, the tomb received the remains of the infant Samuel Brewster Ames. On this occasion the coffins were particularly disturbed, with Colonel Chase's coffin leaning head-down upon a wall."

"This is a significant argument against the flooding theory, given the dimensions of the vault," Holmes interjected, "but remains just feasible. It was on that occasion that a careful search was made for hidden entrances, and sand was scattered to show intruders' footprints. The door-slab was mortared into place and several prominent men apparently placed their seals upon the entrance, including Lord Combermere."[13]

"I see that many of the Black servants were questioned, under suspicion that they were wreaking revenge upon the much-hated Thomas Chase."

"There was much dispute and suspicion at that time. Samuel Brewster senior, father of the infant who had last been interred, was himself placed in the vault a mere six weeks later. He had been murdered during a short-lived slave insurrection and feelings were running high. The seals were carefully inspected before the door-slab was opened, but found to be untouched. A crowd of sightseers had gathered to witness the event, and they were not disappointed. The interior was once again in disarray. Mrs Goddard's coffin, the only one that was not reinforced with lead, was in pieces and had to be reassembled."

"The malice of the slaves was considered a motive."

"The general view was that they were rather too terrified of the 'supernatural' events, of 'duppies', to venture anywhere near the Chase vault; but even if they did, there remain questions about how they gained entrance

---

13   Lady Combermere reportedly recorded in her diary: "In my husband's presence, every part of the floor was sounded to ascertain that no subterranean passage or entrance was concealed. It was found to be perfectly firm and solid; no crack was even apparent. The walls, when examined, proved to be perfectly secure. No fracture was visible, and the sides, together with the roof and flooring, presented a structure so solid as if formed of entire slabs of stone. The displaced coffins were rearranged, the new tenant of that dreary abode was deposited, and when the mourners retired with the funeral procession, the floor was sanded with fine white sand in the presence of Lord Combermere and the assembled crowd. The door was slid into its wonted position and, with the utmost care, the new mortar was laid on so as to secure it. When the masons had completed their task, the Governour [s.i.c.] made several impressions in the mixture with his own seal, and many of those attending added various private marks in the wet mortar..."

without trace."[14]

I read on. "The last opening of the Chase vault was in 1819, before illustrious witnesses upon the intended committal of Mrs Thomasina Clarke—or so we are told in the surviving accounts."

"And the coffins were again found displaced—there is a plan of their positions on the sideboard there, and remarkably the broken wooden Goddard casket was the only one now undisturbed. The coffins were thereafter removed from the vault and interred elsewhere."

"Thus concluding the peregrinations of the unquiet coffers."[15]

"Those unquiet coffers," Holmes responded gnomically.

I apprehended that there were other piles of documents cluttering the sitting room. The investigation evidently ranged wider than I had so far been informed. I was about to prompt my friend to explain further but Mrs Hudson knocked and entered to enquire whether I would be staying the night. If so she might have the sheets aired and warmed for me, and "So that Mr Holmes need not go on a-muttering about coffins and tombs any more."

I agreed that I would be happy for a bed and a little light supper. Holmes assured our landlady that his calculations and researches were unlikely to necessitate the appearance of any actual coffins in our quarters, "for the present."

"You should be kinder to Mrs Hudson," I chided Holmes when she had left us. "She is a jewel amongst housekeepers."

---

14   On 20th April 1820, witness the Honourable Nathan Lucas wrote, "...I examined the walls, the arch, and every part of the Vault, and found every part old and similar; and a mason in my presence struck every part of the bottom with his hammer, and all was solid. I confess myself at a loss to account for the movements of these leaden coffins..."

15   The first thorough literature investigation of the Chase Crypt mystery was presented by researcher Andrew Lang whose 1907 talk on the subject was published in *Folk-Lore: A Quarterly Review on Myth, Tradition, Institution & Custom*. It was Lang and his correspondents who cited James Alexander's *Transatlantic Sketches* volume 1, a similar early account in *The Mirror of Literature, Amusement, and Instruction*, Volume 22, J Limberg (1833), burial records in the *Book of Christ Church* that confirmed the deaths, and an account from the Governor himself in his now-lost *Memoirs and Letters of Lord Combermere*.

Lang pointed out that most of the literature on the subject appeared to originate from anecdotes by the Rector of Christchurch, Thomas H. Orderson, some versions of which were contradictory. Doyle's account, cited in footnote 1, was amongst several that summarised Lang's data.

A more recent summary and analysis of the salient points of the Barbados Coffins legend is offered by sceptical science writer and author Brian Dunning at https://skeptoid.com/episodes/4399

"She would be more disconcerted if I began to show consideration now, Watson. For the present, adduce this account from *The European Magazine and London Review* volume 68, July-December 1815."[16]

The marked article was only half a column, amidst ribald poems, a romance story, and an account of the Abbot of Baigne once creating for Louis XI of France a musical organ composed of live pigs. Here too was a report of unquiet graves, entitled "The Curious Vault at Staunton, Suffolk."

"'On opening it some years since, several lead coffins, with wooden cases, that had been fixed on biers, were found displaced, to the great astonishment of many of the inhabitants of the village. The coffins were again placed as before, and properly closed; when some time ago, another of the family dying, they were a second time found displaced; and two years after there were not only found all of the biers, but one coffin as heavy as to require eight men to raise it, was found on the fourth step that leads into the vault. —Whence arose this operation, in which, it is certain, no one had a hand?'" I looked up. "Holmes, this might be an account of the selfsame incident as was reported in Barbados, except it is placed in East Anglia!"

"The same solution was proposed too, Watson. Look at the suffix to the letter."

The correspondent had finished his monograph: "'N.B. It was occasioned by water, as is imagined, though no signs of it appeared at the different periods of time that the vault was opened.'"

"Surely some wag has come across the story at Christchurch and has transplanted it to our shores for idle amusement?" I supposed.

Holmes made a noncommittal gesture. He was not given to forming conclusions until he had tested the evidence. "The heavy coffin requiring eight bearers is a reminiscent detail," he allowed. "But come, consider this strange case of a more recent vintage: an investigation by Baron Ludwig Guldenstubbe regarding disturbances at a cemetery in Ahrensburg on the island of Oesel."[17]

He proffered yellowed clippings from American newspapers, the *Albany Evening Journal*, 6th October 1860 and *Frank Leslie's Illustrated Newspaper*, 10th March 1866. I read the first tagline. "'The Cemetery of Ahrensburg:

---

16   The full text is available at:
https://babel.hathitrust.org/cgi/pt?id=njp.32101065086736&view=1up&seq=242 on page 226.

17   Nowadays the Estonian town of Kuressaare, formerly Arensburg, on the island of Saaremaa in the Baltic Sea. At the time of Guldenstubbe's investigation he was Baron of Ahrensburg and Thale.

"Adduce this account from *The European Magazine and London Review.*"

Disturbances In A Chapel In The Island Of Oesel'."

"In brief," Holmes summarised, "in 1844 the local landowner was called in because a burial vault was opened to admit a new occupant and the lead coffins were discovered in a state of disarray. Baron Guldenstubbe created an investigation committee including the local physician and burgomeister, whose inspection of the disturbed caskets noted a curious detail; the caskets of a grandmother and of two small children were undisturbed whilst the others were 'tossed around casually'. The committee took precautions to search and seal the vault, sprinkling ash to detect intruders' footprints."

"The same story and the same precautions as were applied in Barbados."

"Very close. In Ahrensburg one of the coffers split open from its treatment and an arm was found protruding—that of a family member held to have committed suicide. A new feature of this story is the discomfit of horses tied up outside the Buxhoewden family tomb which become frantic when led close to the site. Four horses perished in their panic."

I considered the newspaper sources. American publications have sometimes been known to fabricate 'tall stories' to fill column inches with sensational events. "These clippings are from rather far away and somewhat after the fact, Holmes."

The detective acknowledged it. "They evidently both spring from the same wellsource, an account taken down by Mr. Dale Owen, an American Minister to Naples, who met Miss de Guldenstubbe and her brother in 1859 and recorded their statements.[18] And you are right to question the similarities in the accounts of claims of mysterious phenomena from five thousand miles apart. These are not the only strangely-alike accounts of moving coffins."

This time Holmes referred me to a dogeared edition of *Notes and*

---

18   The account was published in Robert Dale Owen's *Footfalls On the Boundary Of Another World* (1860), now available online at https://archive.org/details/ foot00fallsonboundowenrich. Owen and the Guldenstubbes were all ardent Spiritualists and promoted the events on Oesel as proof of their faith. It was in this context that Doyle cited their account in "The Law of the Ghost", in his own period as an evangelist for the Spiritualist movement. Subsequent researchers have bemoaned the lack of source documents and supporting evidence (c.f. Andrew Lang, "Death's Deeds: A Bilocated Story", *Folklore* vol. XVIII (1907) pg 379).

The events were written up again in *The Shadows Around Us: Authentic Tales of the Supernatural* (1891, available at http://gutenberg.net.au/ebooks15/1500011h.html#ch1) by Arthur Morrison. The author made much of an allegation that Carl Buxhoewden, one of the men to be interred in the vault, "was found weltering in blood, with his throat cut from ear to ear, and with a razor tightly clenched in his right hand, the whole family ascribed what was, of course, assumed to be suicide, to some development of the quarrel with his brother Otto."

Queries dated 1867.[19] There was a letter from an F.A. Paley whose father had been rector of the parish of Gretford near Stamford twenty years previously, where another disturbance had occurred.

"'Twice, if not thrice, the coffins in the vault were found on reopening it to have been disarranged'," he wrote. "'The matter excited some interest in the village at the time, and, of course, was a fertile theme for popular superstition, but I think it was hushed up out of respect for the family to whom the vault belonged.'"

Paley's letter included correspondence with a lady who declared, "'I remember very well the Gretford vault being opened when we were there. It was in the church and belonged to the—— Family. The churchwarden came to tell the rector, who went into the vault, and saw the coffins all in confusion; one little one on top of a large one, and some tilted on one side against the wall. They were all *lead*, but of course cased in wood. The same vault had been opened once before and was found in the same state of confusion, and set right by the churchwarden, so that his dismay was great when he found them displaced again.'"

Holmes had a layout plan of the Gretford vault, with helpful measurements.

Paley's correspondent had something to say about the impressions and investigation that she had experienced and witnessed. "'We had no doubt from the situation and nature of the soil, that it had been full of water from a flood which floated the coffins. I dare say —— is still alive, and could give the date. The vault had been walled up, so that no-one could have been in it.'"

"These troublesome flash-floods," Holmes observed, "which are so helpful as to tidy up all trace of themselves except for scattered lead coffins."

"You have some other theory?" I asked my companion.

Holmes waggled the end of his meerschaum at me. "You always seek to tease out my theories in the wrong order, doctor. Indulge me with one last tale."

I accepted the proffered dossier, recognising it as the work of one of the busy researchers whom Holmes employs to sift though countless national and international publications to keep abreast of news items of interest to him. This folder contained yet more clipped articles from a profusion of

---

19   This quarterly journal publishes short articles related to "English language and literature, lexicography, history, and scholarly antiquarianism." It was founded in 1849 and is still going, being the 250th-most-quoted source in the *Oxford English Dictionary*.

The specific edition to which Dr Watson alludes here is the 9th November 1867 issue, "Disturbances of Coffins In Vaults" pg 371.

exotic sources: The Louisiana *Times-Picayune*, the *Kalamazoo Gazette*, the *Portland Daily Press*, *The Atlantic Monthly*, the *San Francisco Bulletin*, and the *Cincinnati Daily Gazette*, all published between 23rd February 1879 and 14th May of that year; but the substance of the articles was much the same, redressed to each editor's taste.

"These stories lack the sort of detail that Sherlock Holmes might usually look for," I noted, gently twitting my friend. "Events occur at 'H-k Hall, Lincolnshire, in possession of the H- family for hundreds of years.' Our American cousins do enjoy a story about English aristocrats!"

"And their family dramas," Holmes answered me, good-humouredly. "Indulge me by recapping the yarn, my dear chap."

"Well, it appears that the venerable H-family had only two descendants remaining, a Squire and his brother, jointly occupying the hall after the death of the Squire's wife, who had evidently not got on with her brother-in-law for unknown reasons. Then the brother declined, and on his deathbed declared to the attending clergyman, 'I know that I am dying; but mark my words, if, when I am dead, you dare bury me I the same vault with that accursed woman, the living as well as the dead shall hear of me!' Dramatic penny dreadful stuff!"

"And entirely unsourced by any of the clippings you hold there. Pray continue."

"It appears that this stated wish was ignored. The deceased was interred with the Squire's wife and only daughter in the ancestral plot. That night the villagers heard shrieks and cries coming from the vault, 'a noise of strife and struggling and blows, as if of enemies engaged in a close fight'. In the morning the Squire and the parish priest took a party of fellows to examine the vault and found the coffins had moved. The wife's coffin was at the far end of the chamber, with the daughter's laid across it 'as if to protect it', and the brother's coffin stood on end close by, 'erect and menacing'."

"It would be instructive to know whether that perception was of the primary witness or added by some enthusiastic reporter after."

"Assuming any of this happened at all," I pointed out, sceptically.

Holmes pressed his index fingers to his lips, anticipating his revelation.

"You have identified H- Hall," I guessed.

"I am aware of the place and of some of the possible circumstances," he admitted.

I should have known. I referred back to the papers. "The disorder was corrected, the coffins laid back as was proper, and the vault resealed, but evidently a similar ruckus disturbed those sensitive villagers the following night, with the same chaos discovered in the morning. And so on until the pragmatic Squire erected a dividing wall to separate off wife and brother's caskets."[20]

"A fine practical solution, Watson, in the great British tradition of compromise!" Holmes helped himself to a whisky and soda, refreshed my glass, and sat back with anticipation."

"You *have* located H- Hall," I surmised from Holmes's demeanour.

"I have been consulted on the matter," my friend confirmed. "It seems that the coffins are on the move again."

I leaned forward. "Surely not. This cannot be an actual phenomenon, more than folk-tales from distant climes and bar-room yarns."

"Something is happening at Hadlingham, in Leicestershire not Lincolnshire, and it has occasioned my present attention." Holmes gestured to the files we had been considering. "The majority of this research is not mine. It belongs to a historian named Walden Stockwell, a young scholar who set out to compile a family history of the fine and noble Haddle dynasty, whose line can be traced back to William the Conqueror's invaders. Hadlingham was the family seat of the Haddles for many generations."

I was handed a wide folded-out paper containing a very complex genealogy, showing the descent of many Haddles from their first arrival on British shores.

"The Haddles are now fallen from their former fortunes and ancestral glories," Holmes told me. "Indeed they are extinct in the main line and their squireship of Hadlingham lapsed with the death of Edward Haddle in 1881.[21] A distant cousin was reluctant to retain the hall given the succession

---

20   A good summary of the various moving coffin tales, with many of the key document quotes and useful references, is offered by Theo Paijmans in "Where the Dead Do Not Rest", *Fortean Times* #347, December 2016.

21   The term *squire* evolved from its medieval usage as a knight's assistant or knight-in-training to refer to a local landowner who occupied a manor house and was the major patron of a parish church. Such an occupant gained the courtesy title Squire, although it is not a recognised rank of nobility. The Squire formed part of the local social fabric, being majority landlord of a parish, often the Justice of the Peace (local magistrate), "holding the living' of the local church (i.e. having the authority to appoint and dismiss the vicar, whose stipend he probably paid and who might well be a relative or friend), and often representing his locality as a Member of Parliament. The right to the title has sometimes been 'sold on' with the property with which it was associated and has sometimes been claimed by descendants despite no longer holding the original property, but the role and rank of Squire has now mostly lapsed.

duties now levied upon such estates and the Hall was sold."[22]

I saw the last entries on the Haddle family tree, the brothers Edward and Joshua who had latterly occupied their somewhat-decaying ancestral seat. Edward's wife Charlotte and daughter Amelia had both predeceased him; all in accordance with the American journals' sensational summaries.

"The Hall was purchased by Mr Dougal Stobard," Holmes informed me. "Stobard made his money in trams—American trolley cars to be more exact—and purchased Hadlingham Hall at auction as a home for his eventual retirement. He did not reside there until his declining health required his withdrawal from the cut-throat and hurly-burly world of New York transportation. He moved to Hadlingham Hall in November of last year, was disappointed that the locals did not recognise him as Squire as he felt they should, quarrelled with several prominent residents and neighbours, and died of apoplexy on the 12th of May this year."

"He insisted on the Squire's right to burial in the Hadlingham vault?" I guessed.

"Just so. His will was quite specific on the matter and included instructions for the old place's repair and renovation—the original fabric being long neglected and considered overdue for attention."

"Was there a dividing wall in the vault?" I enquired, remembering the newspaper reports. "Was it removed?"

Holmes ticked a finger at me to acknowledge that I had hit the mark. "The vault was opened, which required removing modern bricks and mortar from the entrance archway that had remained in place since Edward Haddle's interment beside his wife and child some thirteen years previously. Curious locals were perhaps disappointed to discover no signs of supernatural furniture-shifting. Much of the interior was repointed, and the rather shoddily and hastily erected partition that confined the coffin of Joshua Haddle was taken down as being both ugly and unsafe."

"Nobody mentioned the local superstition to Stobard's executor?"

"His widow, Mrs Deborah Stobard, was cautioned by local gossips, but she is a practical lady who was not deterred by ghost stories."

"But there was a disturbance?"

"Evidently so. The matter did not come to light until the arrival of the

---

22   From *the Succession Duty Act* 1853 onward, a series of legislative bills introduced what we would now term as inheritance tax, claiming sums of between 1% and 12% of the deceased's estate. This had the long-term effect of eroding vested land wealth and led to the decline of many well-off dynasties, with effects such as that on the impoverished Haddle family.

historian Stockwell in July. Stockwell had been commissioned by the distant cousin to undertake a history of the Haddle family, perhaps in some attempt to preserve some last vestige of a long and distinguished dynastic legacy. Naturally the researcher came to Hadlingham to consult parish records and whatever documents remained in the Hall, and to interview older residents who remembered the family, even some that had been in service to them. Mrs Stobard kindly put him up at the Hall and granted him access to the library."

"He wanted to see the vault?"

"There are evidently some features of architectural note around the burial site; medieval mason's marks suggesting the reuse of material from some older ecclesiastical construction, some superior sculpted mouldings around the door-lintel, and a pair of dedicatory plaques let into the walls of the mausoleum. And Stockwell admits in his correspondence with me that he had heard of the strange rumours about the shifting coffins and was curious to inspect the site."

"The door was unsealed, then?"

"On 18th July, in the presence of Stockwell, Mrs Stobard, the parish vicar, and three sturdy labourers who were required to unbrick the entrance for the occasion."

"And inside?"

"Chaos. Here is Stockwell's sketch of the positions in which the various coffins were found. You will see that those of Mrs and Miss Haddle were turned on their sides at the far end of the chamber. Mr Edward Haddle's coffin was leaned almost against the doorjamb. Mr Joshua Haddle's casket was again stood upright between the others. Two older coffins were pushed to one side, the one piled upon the other."

"Remarkable. And no signs of entry?"

"A search was made. The builder could find no indication of intruders, although I cannot speak to the thoroughness and competence of his investigation."

I shook my head in disbelief. The quaint spook-stories from far-off climes were one thing, but a present manifestation of the otherworldly was hard to credit. "There is some explanation," I insisted.

"Of course there is," Holmes assured me, his eyes alight with anticipation. "But what? Two subsequent tests were made on following nights, replacing the coffins *in situ* and ensuring that seals were in place. Twice the contents of the vault were disturbed by morning. Mrs Stobard elected to remove her husband's remains from the site until matters can be resolved. Joshua

Haddle's coffin has also been temporarily placed elsewhere in a chapel of rest, and the situation had quietened once more. Walden Stockwell undertook some research into the history of the coffins, made some intriguing findings, and then wrote for my opinion on the matter."

It was now four weeks since the events that Holmes had described, enough time for the correspondence the historian had gathered to come to him from across the globe.

Holmes passed me the forwarded letter with something like glee. "Stockwell has uncovered a link with the Barbados case. A Haddle was out there in the 1720s overseeing the family's sugar interests, a crony of that Honourable John Elliot who commissioned the Chase tomb in the first place and then never used it."

My brows rose. "That is a broad coincidence, if coincidence it is."

Holmes proffered another letter, and a translation of it from the German. "This is from work undertaken by scholars at the Universität Dorpat,[23] experts on the *Fratres militiæ Christi Livoniae*, the Livonian Brothers of the Sword who conquered Oesel in 1227, bringing Christianity to the island. It was they who founded Ahrensburg Castle, now the seat of the Guldenstubbes. Here is an account of Volkwin von Naumburg zu Winterstätten, Herrmeister of the Livonian Brothers from 1209 to his untimely death in 1236 at the disastrous Battle of Saule which so broke the order that they were thereafter folded into the Teutonic Knights. And this is the only mention of Volkwin's sister, whose 1208 wedding to the 1st Viscount Vaughn was delayed by the Pope's interdiction of King John of England. Her daughter wedded Sir Thomas Haidle in 1231."

"Haidle, as in Haddle?"

"So Stockwell asserts."

I sat back in my chair. "Well, this is a pretty knot of mysteries, linking moving coffin stories over sixty years than half the planet, tying them to one family tree—and now to impossible disturbances at a quiet village in the Leicestershire countryside. What are we to make of it, Holmes?"

Holmes refilled his pipe and passed me the Persian slipper to take a pinch. "Well, my dear Watson, I intend to respond to Mrs Stobard's kind invitation and go down to Hadlingham tomorrow to look at some coffins myself."

He viewed me speculatively. I nodded back. "I'd be pleased to join you,

---

23   Since 1919 this has been the Estonian University of Tartu, but the second university founded in the Swedish Empire started its long and many-named history from 1632 as the Academia Gutaviana.

old man. If Sherlock Holmes cannot lay the ghosts then no man in England can do the job, and I would be delighted to see him do it!"

We took the train from St Pancras to Leicester as soon as Holmes had dispatched his latest enquiries on the Mendicant case. "You can wire me at Hadlingham if anything breaks on the beggars, John," Holmes instructed the burly fellow who was running messages for him just then; I recognised the same man who had carried out such work for the notorious Irene Adler earlier that year.[24]

Scarcely more than an hour later we were in the old cathedral city and engaging a carriage to take us out through Thurnby and Houghton on the Hill to the picturesque village that was our destination.

Hadlingham Hall was one of those older-style two-storey country houses that are a mixture of family home and weekend shooting lodge, with a central block and stubby wings, backing onto stables and outhouses. The frontage overlooked the village green and a rather silty duckpond. The village church occupied an adjacent site to the north. Beside a private gate between the hall's grounds and the churchyard was the low mausoleum where the excitement had occurred.

Walden Stockwell was waiting for us. He bustled us inside out of the rain and made sure the servants took our things up. "Mrs Stobard asked me to make you welcome," explained the houseguest. "She's been called into town for a meeting with her estate solicitors, something about tithe shares or whatever, but she should be back this evening. In the meantime I am to show you round and introduce you to whoever you might need to talk to."

Holmes nodded, but already his attention was on the crypt we had seen on our way in. "I would like to inspect the vault site first," he declared, confirming my expectation.

We braved the country downpour, passing through a kitchen door to a pleasant kitchen garden and from there along a formal path that was the family's route into the parish church. Holmes took in the garden and house,

---

24   Scholars of the Canon, ever eager to find concurrences, were quick to note that Holmes's driver in "The Adventure of the Man With The Twisted Lip" shared a Christian name with the Woman's trusted manservant in "A Scandal in Bohemia", and to speculate that Holmes might well have found work for a man whom Miss Adler had found useful and who now needed other employment.

the condition of the restored paving slabs on our route, and all the other evidence that a once-neglected house had been put back into order during its most recent ownership.

Stockwell followed Holmes's thinking. "The Haddles were scarcely able to maintain the place by the end," he admitted. "Edward and Joshua's father made some unwise investments that was hit badly by the Panic of 1847, when speculative railway stocks crashed so hard. Edward's alliance with Miss Charlotte deVere-Leverstone brought some much-needed money, but some of her income was only 'for life' and was lost after her untimely passing in 1867. The Hall was sadly neglected during the latter time that Edward and Joshua dwelled here together and moreso when Edward lived here alone in his last days, served by a single retainer."

"Do you believe that Mrs Stobard will remain at Hadlingham after the present unpleasantness?" I wondered. The house was too large for a lone widow, just as it had been for the widower Edward Haddle.

"I suspect she will return to the United States," Stockwell confided. "After Mr Stobard's death the domestic staff was reduced to just three, and even they have now been replaced with newcomers. I think that Mrs Stobard wanted no associations that might remind her of her grief. In any case, I am hastening to complete my own studies whilst it is possible for me to access the Haddle family papers retained here."

We arrived at the mysterious vault. It was a gloomy-looking construction of old weathered granite, built from massive bricks some two feet in length and a foot deep. It must have taken four burly labourers to set each in place. The mausoleum was accessed down four outer stairs to an ornate lintel with carved side-pillars and a sculpted archivolt. Above the doorway was a rather weathered relief of a shield with triangles on it.

"The materials for the Haddle tomb were acquired from nearby Grace Dieu Priory after Henry VIII's abolition of the monasteries," Stockwell lectured us. "The vault here was probably erected around 1616 and partially rebuilt again using much of the same materials in the mid-eighteenth century. At that time the parish church was much refurbished and the Haddles interred in the former vault were buried under the floor of the nave; you may still read some of the inscriptions written on the paved cover slabs there. The new vault was not brought into use to hold coffins until 1799."

"Rather like the long disuse of the Chase vault in Barbados," I noted.

Stockwell perked up. "You are familiar with the history? Yes, it was very much like that. The similarities between the two sites are striking. Apart from having similar internal dimensions, and of course the Haddle

It was a gloomy-looking construction of old weathered granite.

connection, they were both erected at considerable expense and then left unused for many years."

"Unoccupied," Holmes corrected the researcher. He cupped a hand to shelter his eyes from the drizzle and looked at the carvings. "That shield appears to depict three sets of callipers and a square, which are Masonic symbols. The worn marks at the base of the wall are also reminiscent of old Freemasonry."

"The Masonic Guilds built all the monasteries," Stockwell pointed out. "The Augustinian nunnery at Grace Dieu would be no exception."

"The lintel carving is not of an age for that," Holmes judged. "I would need to refer to textbooks to be certain, but I would place that style in the early eighteenth century. Freemasonry was then becoming a fashionable pursuit for the landed gentry, the so-called 'accepted masons' who did not earn their living cutting stone or carving it. At that time the 'operative' Masonic lodges were being overtaken by the 'speculative' ones. The Grand Lodge of London and Westminster was founded in 1717."

It was evident that mortared bricks had once sealed the low stone entranceway, but after the most recent disturbances a temporary panel of thick wood planks had been cobbled together to fill the gap. Large flat frames were pressed against each side of the entrance arch then pinned together by bolts that held each frame tight against the jamb. A metalwork brace held the whole construction in place and allowed for a heavy padlock to be attached to seal the barrier.

Holmes inspected the padlock with his magnifying lens before allowing Stockwell to release the hasp. Holmes and I had to assist shouldering the wooden flats aside; they were heavy and cumbersome but a lot less trouble than removing a wall each time entry was required.

There were four more internal steps, bringing the floor level down to six feet below ground. The roof was vaulted in the medieval style but with smaller bricks.

Holmes paused again under the lintel to inspect the old crumbled cement that had held the original brick barrier in place. "There are several kinds of mortar here, consistent with the stones that blocked the door being removed and reset on different occasions."

"I was here when the workmen chiselled out the bricks last time," Stockwell testified. "Those are the stones there, piled in the corner of the vault."

Holmes went to examine the evidence. I counted the coffins. There were six of them. "Both Haddle brothers are here," I saw. "Along with the late Mrs Charlotte Haddle, her daughter, and Edward and Joshua's parents."

"The vicar kindly allowed us to lodge the brothers' caskets in the Lady Chapel for a time after the...difficulties occurred. Mr Stockwell is presently in a chapel of rest at an undertaker's parlour while his coffin is being repaired. It was a stout oak box but it was not strong enough to survive undamaged whatever forces threw these heavy lead-lined coffers about."

Holmes moved on to viewing the walls of the vault, shining a hand-lamp on the battered plaster, reading every dent and crack upon it. The low roof required him to crouch.

I ventured to test the coffins themselves. None of the lead caskets were constructed in the now-customary lozenge shape which is wider at the shoulders and tapers to the feet. The newly-returned Haddle brothers' boxes were simple rectangular affairs, six-foot-two in length, three feet wide and three feet deep. They had been set down upon thick wooden beams much like railway sleepers. I could not lift even a corner of one of the caskets unaided.

The oak and teak panelling of the coffins was scratched and defaced, as if by careless handling. In particular the brass covers at the corners were dented and pitted. The nameplate of Joshua Haddle's coffin seemed to have been defaced by a heavy blow as from a hammer.

Holmes questioned Stockwell. "You mentioned in your written account of finding the disturbed vault that this casket was upright; but the roof is lower than the coffin is high."

"The box was wedged at an angle," the historian explained. "You see the mark in the roof brickwork there? That was where the casket was embedded—leaning—looming. It took all three of our labourers to knock the coffin free."

Holmes gave him a disapproving frown. He does not like imprecise accounts.

"These coffins have been recently opened. The lead seals are broken."

A lead-lined coffin is intended to preserve its occupant from decay and the vicissitudes of insects and vermin. It is designed to be airtight. When it is closed, the top of the box is often fixed with molten lead all around, to ensure a complete seal. So it had been with these caskets, but someone had used a cutting tool to break in.

"We did that," Stockwell confessed. "The vicar was keen to see that the bodies were laid out reverently again, not crumpled into whatever position they had been tossed by their... unusual movements. The labourers heated a knife and sawed their way in."

In addition to the lead seal they must also have prised open the heavy metal clasps that had held the lids in place. It was these bulky clamps that must have prevented the moving coffins from spilling open as they were shifted about. Holmes ran his finger over one of the hinges that had been recently oiled to allow it to unfasten.

"What was the condition of the corpses?" I ventured.

"Mr Edward Haddle is still relatively intact, though much desiccated," Stockwell reported. "He died only six years ago. James Haddle has been in his box for thirteen years and the lead seal must have been incomplete, for he is nothing but unarticulated bones."

I remembered the solution that Lord Combermere had come up with to resolve the Barbados case. "Was no thought given to siting these coffins elsewhere? Cremation, even?"

"I have seen the deed of transfer for the Hadlingham estate, with the terms of purchase. These bodies cannot legally be removed from the Haddle vault. They have a right of tenancy."

Holmes rapped his knuckles on the lid of Joshua's casket. "We will need to inspect the contents," he decided. "A review of the interior of the caskets will be quite instructive."

"Labourers will be required to help port off the lids," I pointed out. "These box-tops, latched and unsealed as they are, must still weigh upwards of two hundred pounds, and they sit in a groove that will benefit from the application of crowbars."

"I can arrange for the local workmen who restored the caskets to the vault to return before evening," Stockwell offered. "It may be that Mrs Stobard will be back before that and can instruct her footman and gardener to assist, but I lack the authority to set them to such work."

We thanked the historian for his aid, but Holmes dismissed him before returning to a more detailed examination.

"Have you any theory as to how such remarkable occurrences might have happened without the intervention of spectres?" I asked the detective.

Holmes wagged his finger at me, reminding me that I should know better by now than to seek revelations from him while he was still working.

He went back to examining the vault floor, the entrance arch, and the sombre haunted coffins.

"We shall take a late lunch in the local coaching inn, I fancy," my friend told me at last. "There is nothing like a country pub for picking up on country gossip."

We did not have to walk far. Just across the village green lay the Mason's Arms, a pleasant old establishment with Tudor-style windows and a pleasing orange tile roof, wreathed in variegated ivy.

Holmes pointed the pub sign out to me, a faded old image of a coat of arms not unlike the crest above the Haddle vault, showing compasses and set square in a coat of arms shield. He traced his fingers over some old marks cut in the foundation stone beside the public house's main entrance and looked satisfied.

We hastened inside, shaking off our umbrellas, and found a suitable place near the snug where Holmes could observe the passing trade. Most of the rural locals who came for their shepherd's pie or mixed grill had already returned to work, but there were a few stalwart village elders to talk with as we waited for our ham, cheese, and pickles to arrive.

"You're over at the Hall," one such ancient told us; little happens in a small English village that is not noticed and remarked. "Looking at that there tomb-vault."

"Unnatural, that hole," another complained. "Asking for trouble it is, to mess about with that place again. No good'll come of it."

"Makes sense Old Josh w'un't be happy," a third opined. "If he di'n't like sharing with his brother's missus he w'un't want an American in there, would he?"

"Ah, but he di'n't have a grudge against the American, did he? It were her ladyship what he detested, and she him."

Since Charlotte Haddle had not had any formal rank except Squire's wife, I concluded that she had been dubbed with the title out of respect or irony. From the speaker's tones it was the latter.

"Mrs Haddle had a good opinion of her class, then?" Holmes prodded.

"She were a woman who enjoyed her rights. Thought herself a better class than others. But she came with money, not breeding." He pulled at his cider mug and added, "You can't buy breeding."

"You can buy breeding stock, though," another argued. "Her father did for her, d'in't he?"

"She brought money to the Haddle family again," I recognised.

"Not enough," an old fellow by the hearth insisted. "When I were a lad there were a score or two dozen folks working at the big house or on the grounds, without you count the farm hands and field men. Right busy place it was, back in the Earlies.[25] But when she come, even with all her

---

25   That is, the first years of the nineteenth century.

la-de-dah money, there weren't but ten servants brought back to the hall."

"My mam was in service there before she got married," one geriatric commentator confided. "If she could see how run down it got, she'd turn in her grave like Old Josh. Even now them Americans has tarted it up, it's naught on what it were once."

"Our Effie was day-maid there until Mrs American decided to change all her staff," the cider drinker mentioned, and prominently set down his now-empty tankard.

Holmes obligingly bought a round for the house. When they had toasted his very good health, he led the old man to expand on the theme of Effie.

"She's my sister's daughter's youngest," he explained as if it was evident to any but the most ignorant of outsiders. "Went in Mondays, Wednesdays, and Fridays, and sometimes when more help was required. General cleaning and carrying, laundry and ironing, and a bit of helping Cook out when needed. It's a good thing for a young lass to have a bit of service behind her afore she weds; knocks some common sense into her, fits her for a wife with a household of her own."

"She was at the Hall recently? Until Mrs Stobard decided upon a complete change of staff?"

"Aye. Well almost. That American might be rich as Mrs Her Ladyship Haddle, but she pays no better wages. That's why most of the staff drifted off to work for Colonel Savage over at Stenton-On-The-Hill. He expanded his staff and was happy to take on most of the people who were fed up of working in a house of mourning."

"A haunted house of mourning," the chap by the hearth insisted. "Who'd want to be in service at a place as is cursed by restless spirits of the wronged?"

"Not our Effie, for one. 'Gloomy', that's how she described the atmosphere at Hadlingham Hall. She were well out of there when they had to poke about in that vault again and wake up the old feud that we'd all hoped settled."

Through skilful leading of the conversation, Holmes gleaned from the habitués of the Mason's Arms that the sensational newspaper accounts of the original incident were not quite as blatant as had been printed. The succession of events was reasonably accurate; Joshua Haddle had feuded with his sister-in-law in life and had wished not to be buried with her in death. Thereafter there had been disturbances in the supposedly-sealed vault. Many had witnessed the disarray of the coffins on the mornings after and one old fellow had a son who had been one of the labourers called in to set things straight. But the loud crashing and screams that had reportedly woken the whole village were a journalist's fancy. The first report that had led to the tomb being reopened had come from the vicar's adolescent son, who had heard something as he had walked his spaniel past the monument that night.

The locals confirmed that a wall had been erected to bisect the vault, with Joshua's coffin in the further part and the others in the nearer to the entrance, and that that had been the end of it, "a three-days-wonder." The rest was idle chatter and a tale growing as it was retold.

The old men also allowed that the vault had been refurbished as part of the Stobards' general renovation of their retirement home, and that a disturbance had been discovered recently that had shocked "new Vicar" and brought back memories of the mysteries of thirteen years before.

Holmes pressed them for information about Mrs Haddle and her feud with the brother Joshua.

"Oh, there's plenty of stories," our cider-drinker admitted when his mug was again replenished. "Tongues will always wag, and nasty minds'll make up what they don't know. Yea, I'm looking at thee, Howard Wallys, with your thee-ories about an affair betwixt the two and him fathering poor little Amelia on her. Or about him a-forcing himself on her."

"It's true that Old Josh was a threat around lasses," the hearth-hugger admitted.

"Might as well chew out that old saw about Squire Edward wanting him to help father an heir, so as to keep that legacy if aught happened to the missus. Or the story about Her Ladyship and Old Vicar, or that nasty spec-u-lation about him and the little girl. But it's all just dirty minds, 'cause there's no facts at all."

"What do you say it was then, Hosiah?" the landlord asked from the bar. "For they did mislike each other mightily."

"If you were to ask me to guess, I'd say as it was money. Nine out of ten its always money. Squire Edward reckoned as his ship had come in when he got his hands on a deVere, but her father was too smart to hand over the bank-book. It was money, you mark my words."

"Many people quarrel over money," I pointed out. "Not all of them start hurling their coffins at each other."

"Ah, well," the ancient by the hearth chuckled, tapping his nose, "not all of them is squared away in that there Haddle vault."

Holmes looked up sharply. "They were put there but they were not on the level?" he asked.

"That'd be it, aye."

Holmes asked about the old vicar's son and his hearing some noise in the tomb. The former parish incumbent had vacated his position when his health declined in 1882 and had evidently passed away a short time after. Since the post and role of squire had then lapsed and no contribution or patronage had been given to the parish church for many years, the vacancy had been filled by the Diocese and 'New Vicar' had been installed.

"The old vicar did not receive his stipend from Squire Edward?" Holmes checked.

"Well, he would have done once, I suppose," one of the elders considered. "I mean, he come to the village back in Old Squire's day, same year as old Wellington and Peel got rid of them wicked old Corn Laws, and good riddance says I. To them laws, I means, and woe to the bad men what profited by them!"

It was clear that the fellow must have been a political firebrand back in 1846 when the old price-fixing mercantile system had been abolished in favour of free trade, and the domestic tariff price of wheat, oats, barley, and all kinds of cereals was no longer artificially inflated to squeeze the poor.

"There was naught wrong with Old Vicar, except as he jawed on a lot a-Sundays, preaching on for over an hour when you just wanted to be home and have your dinner."

"Squire Edward should have paid his due, though, to upkeep the parish," the old chap at the fire-grate insisted. "If there was aught they all argued about, it were that. Old Vicar and Sir Edward often rowed over it. Why, Squire even threatened to dismiss Vicar a time or two. But it all settled down after Mr Joshua's death and the strangeness of the dancing coffins."

The landlord called last orders and we returned to the Hall to see if Stockwell had assembled his workforce.

The Haddle vault was west-facing, so the low evening sun shone directly into it, washing the inside with an orange glow. Holmes used the improved lighting to point out to me some of the old carvings on the tomb's interior. Amongst the most striking were a G inside a rectangle and a cross flanked by the letter H.[26]

Mrs Stockwell was expected to join us, but Holmes was unwilling to

---

26   In Masonic symbolism these are held to represent God, "the grand geometer of the universe", and mankind within the compass of God's creation.

delay his inspection to wait for her. "Opening coffins is no occupation for a lady," I agreed.

Stockwell had acquired four farm labourers, strapping fellows well used to manual work, and had brought the portable pulley that had been used last time to lift the casket lids. Once the apparatus was set up around Edward Haddle's coffin it was only a matter of straining hard to raise the lead-lined top and look inside.

There was the cadaver of the late Squire, well preserved for its age, the features more-or-less recognisable for the man in the portrait that Stockwell had shown us. The corpse had been laid out again, its hands crossed over the chest, his cuffs pinned together to keep his arms in position—an old undertaker's trick, evidently. The cadaver showed some signs of previous rough handling, doubtless from the coffin being shifted in its midnight perambulations.

Holmes was more interested in the box in which he lay. "Lead caskets are expensive items," he pointed out, "yet the impoverished Haddles all used them. Now I apprehend why."

He had the lids raised on the other coffins and continued his investigation. Mrs Haddles's body was now a dried-out husk. Joshua Haddle's body was a mere random pile of stripped bones.

"Why, then?" Stockwell asked Holmes, unable to restrain his curiosity.

Holmes rapped his knuckles on Mrs Haddles' box. "It is obvious. Look at the style of the woodwork. Compare it to the methods of welding used for the leadwork. Note the oxidisation levels of the interior, and the wire-brush marks where it has been polished up."

"You will have to explain further, Holmes," I warned the detective.

Holmes slapped the coffin lid in exasperation. Sometimes the whole world thinks too slowly for him. "Squire Haddle was poor. But there were already in his mostly-unused vault unused lead coffins. All that was required was for a modern outer sheath of cedar, oak, and mahogany to be constructed around them and they would become perfectly acceptable sepulchres—the best of caskets at a fraction of the cost."

"These coffins are reused!" Stockwell realised. His scholarly interest flared. "These were part of the older vault, from before its adoption by the old Squire and his wife. They were left over from the 1799 works, when the seventeenth century tomb was brought into use." He smoothed his hand along Joshua's casket. "The original bodies were probably taken out and reburied elsewhere when the vault was reconsecrated. I never thought that the lead coffins might be retained and later adopted."

"The interiors of the box have been cleaned down with wire brushes or steel wool as part of their recommissioning," Holmes noted, "but there are still discernable traces of the original engravings on the inside surfaces. These are also mason marks."

I thought of the crest over the door, and of the name of the village pub. "The Haddles have evidently had significant Masonic connections once upon a time."

Holmes grunted but did not comment on my assertion. He turned his attention to the vault entrance; that carved arch with its supporting pillars and heavy architrave. "The Masonic connection is the solution, of course," he told us. "You must remember that all of this was put in place long before the standardisation of Masonic tradition to just a few feuding grand lodges, dating to an era when Masons were still very much a practical trade guild."

Stockwell confessed himself puzzled and I echoed him.

"Modern Masonic rites include initiations to each successive rank," Holmes reminded us. "The actual rites are closely-guarded secrets. Those admitted to the fellowship are sworn to secrecy by terrible oaths—which admittedly are probably more colourful than serious. But there was a time when the professional secrets of the guild were very closely guarded, as a means to retain a monopoly on the knowledge of their craft. The modern initiation 'ordeals', the descent through three pits, the test of swords and whatever else has been 'rediscovered' by our present Freemasons, are echoes of older traditions. I believe I have discerned one variant here."

"In what way?" Stockwell demanded. He seemed slightly nervous, and I wondered if the historian was perhaps a Mason himself.

"We were told that the feuding Haddles had been 'squared away' here. When I responded that they had not been 'on the level' my assertion was affirmed. These are Masonic terms, recognition codewords from building terminology. This tomb was never built as a resting place for the Haddle family. This is a Masonic vault."

"It was unoccupied for many years after it was erected," I remembered. "Like the Chase vault in Christchurch."

"Imagine an initiation ceremony, Watson. A young man is brought by night, blindfolded and guarded, to a dark vault. He is laid in a coffin, given dire warnings that this is his future if ever he speaks the secrets he is to be taught. He is left there, the door sealed shut, literally entombed."

"You believe that the Chase vault and this one were originally used for this purpose?"

"I shall prove it, Watson. You see, this was not just an ordeal test, it was a practical one. Had the young apprentice been diligent in his learning of the craft? Could he read the marks on the walls, the banners that covered them? I presume them to have been instructions. They are reminiscent of the chiselled glyphs that medieval builders placed on stones to inform other workers how and where they should be placed. The neophyte was expected to overcome his fright, gather his wits, and prove his mastery."

"That is speculation, not proof," Walden Stockwell objected.

"Ah, but wait. You see, the initiate would move over to this door, reading the marks placed about it. He would locate this brick, and a trowel left for him to find, and he would lever it out like so."

Holmes moved one small exposed brick on the third interior step. There was a heavy crack of stone hitting stone.

"That is the clue that the young mason would be expected to find. It would drop the internal counterweight hidden inside the wall beside that lintel column. Then he need only place his shoulder here and...heave."

Holmes applied his weight to one of the side columns about the entrance. To my astonishment the whole stone doorjamb swivelled inwards, like a door itself, grinding open on granite pivots.

"This is how the vault was entered without the bricked-up portal being touched!" I gasped. "The door itself was set in a larger hidden door! Masons' secrets indeed!"

"This is remarkable," Stockwell declared. "The frame is so well made that it is impossible to discern."

Holmes was satisfied. "The whole apparatus can be reset, manhandled back into place to be reused again. The secret was perhaps forgotten in the decades after the vault was originally made, its purpose neglected except in local folk tradition. But someone remembered, or rediscovered the hidden entrance. I would speculate that Old Vicar probably heard about it from some aged parishioner and his son from him."

"The son who so conveniently overheard the shifting coffins," I mentioned.

"Yes. Edward Haddle had previously quarrelled with the vicar, withholding due stipend and threatening his living. Moreover, this was at a time when political feelings were running high between the rich landowners like Haddle who supported the Corn Laws and those economic and social reformers who wanted an Importation Bill. A fiery young hothead of a lad and his rowdy comrades might well seek some petty revenge or mysterious diversion from a serious feud. Of course, this can only be speculation now, but there is your means of accessing the vault. Equipment such as that brought today by Mr Stockwell might well achieve the supposedly-disarrayed scene that dismayed observers until part of the vault was bricked off."

"Might similar vaults have been made elsewhere, accounting for the parallel legends?" Stockwell posited. "In the West Indies, Colonel Chase had quite enough enemies who would exploit some hidden knowledge to his disadvantage or disgrace. If there were Freemason traditions on Barbados…"

"St Michael's Lodge No. 186 was founded in 1740 by Mr Alexander Irvine, under the Premier Grand Lodge. Thomas Baxter was issued with the appropriate patent to be Provincial Grand Master of the Provincial Grand Lodge of Barbados. But of course, the Honourable Thomas Elliott was an active Mason of sorts in 1724 when he built what would become the Chase tomb, before a formal Lodge imposed approved practices upon the rites."

I realised that Holmes must have looked this up before coming to Hadlingham. "You suspected a Masonic link."

"You will recall that the Barbados documents recorded that after it was reordered, the vault was closed and the stone door 'cemented' by 'Masons'—*cement* in Masonic parlance being that which unites the brethren.[27] At least two of the men involved in the case were high-ranking Freemasons. I cannot assert with confidence that the later troubles of the moving Chase coffins was caused by those who knew the secret of accessing the tomb, but the possibility is attractive."

"And they were all linked by the Haddle lineage," Stockwell added.

"Perhaps," Holmes responded. "It is impossible without further investigation to verify the provenance of the correspondence that drew such connections."

The historian cavilled at the suggestion. "Are you questioning my diligence?"

"No. I am certain that you have undertaken your tasks extremely assiduously."

A problem occurred to me. "Holmes, if we accept for now that the original supposedly-supernatural disturbances in this vault were mischief caused by the vicar's son or some other radical or prankster, what of the disturbance that was discovered when Stockwell convinced Mrs Stobard to reopen the place two months ago? Surely the perpetrators cannot be the same?"

"Indeed not, doctor. We must interview Mrs Deborah Stobard on that point. And here comes the lady, if I am not mistaken."

---

27   C.f. *A Dictionary of Freemasonry*, Robert McCoy (1869), a textbook to which Holmes would undoubtedly have had access.

There were footfalls on the path, and the shadow of people approaching. An unhappy-looking lady of middle years, clad in mourning weeds, climbed down to join us in the vault, accompanied by two staff of her household.

The staff were bearing firearms, and they pointed them at Holmes and I.

"You have walked into a trap," the lady told us.

Holmes did not seem as surprised as I at this sudden twist. He looked Mrs Stobard up and down, reading her as another man might scan a document for vital information. "You are a captive," he surmised. "Your new staff have held you against your will."

"What?" I blurted. "What's the meaning of this?" I would have shifted forward to remonstrate more, but the newcomers held their weapons steadily and were ready to use them.

"Ah," Holmes breathed. "I understand now. I need no longer await replies to my telegrams."

"You won't be getting replies," one of the servants answered; this was the fellow Holmes had dispatched to the Post Office in nearby Stenton-on-the-Hill—or had expected he had dispatched.

"Not responses to the messages I sent off via you today," Holmes scorned. "To previous enquiries about my ongoing investigation into your covert double lives and the unscrupulous businesses you conduct in them." He snorted. "Did you really expect me to be fooled again? I may have made an ass of myself with Hugh Boone, not recognising immediately that the apparent tramp was actually a gentleman in disguise. Now that I am taking the trouble to review the lack of callosities on your hands, the telltale marks of a businessman, your unservantlike posture, the difficulties you have had shining your own boots, and a dozen other betraying signs, I know you for mere amateur mendicants."

"The Amateur Mendicant Society!" I recognised. "I thought they were finished."

"Significantly inconvenienced," the faux-servant snarled at us. "Not done."

"Not yet," Holmes retorted. "The net is closing in. Soon Inspector Bradstreet will haul the rest of you up entire."

The other armed man chuckled. "Not without help from the meddling Sherlock Holmes, he won't. Not when you are vanished."

Mrs Stobard quivered between her captors, close to collapse. I ignored the pistols pointed at me and moved to support her. "Never fear," I told her. "Holmes and I will resolve this matter."

"I cannot help but fear," she answered me. "They have made me sign

"You have walked into a trap," the lady told us.

papers, write letters. I am supposed by those documents to be returning to America to escape my grief at Dougal's passing, leaving my business interests and property here in charge of a manager."

"But actually in control of this Mendicant's Society," I supposed. Neville St Clair's ruse to make a good living as an apparent beggar seemed quite innocent compared to these, his darker brethren. Some of the abuses that Holmes had uncovered in his investigation of that hidden luxury club beneath the abandoned warehouse in Limehouse had been quite disgusting.

And now we were caught in this dingy vault, surrounded by the false servants and burly labourers who had come to lift the coffins.

"And so you crafted a puzzle that would lure me in," Holmes said to our captors. "A most convoluted and cunning one too. Elaborate enough to keep me chasing details, well-planned enough to withstand my investigation. Worthy of the beggar-king, Mr Stockwell."

I looked over at the historian and saw the look of triumph upon his face.

"You are a clever man, Mr Holmes," Stockwell confessed. "The work you did to uncover us was inspired. We, who make our living disguised as beggars, never saw through your portrayal. But we have used that cleverness against you."

Holmes shook his head. "You stitched together various old ghost stories, ill-reported half-forgotten mysteries, to feed to me like a baited hook. You came into Mrs Stobard's life at a time when she was grieving and vulnerable, and perpetrated the latest performance of the dancing coffins to draw me in here. It is a very elaborate way to lure me to my murder."

"You have cost us dearly," the man calling himself Stockwell retorted. "Your murder must be very elaborate."

"You cannot think that Sherlock Holmes can be done away with and there be no outcry," I protested. "There will be the most thorough and active of investigations."

"I'm sure there will," the beggar-king agreed. "There will be many clues to follow. From his sojourn here, Holmes will apparently travel post-haste to Southampton and make urgent enquiries there. He will dispatch a slew of telegrams that suggest he is pursuing this coffins case overseas. He will depart for Constantinople, and thence to the Isle of Oesel on the steamer *Polydore*. Witnesses will see him board. Others will speak with him on the voyage. You will be with him, Dr Watson."

"You mean my impersonator will be with him," I understood.

"Just so. It is on Oesel that you will seem to disappear—until suitable corpses are discovered on the far tip of the island many months from now."

"You are ambitious in your plans," Holmes remarked.

"We are *comprehensive* in them. Shortly after you depart these shores tomorrow there will be an unfortunate fire at your lodgings in Baker Street. Your housekeeper and page boy will perish in the conflagration, along with all your notes and evidence regarding the Amateur Mendicants."

"You would harm a woman and a boy?" I thundered.

"I assure you they are not the first."

"You intend to threaten Mrs Stobard and Dr Watson until I write whatever correspondence you require to simulate my journey," Holmes surmised.

"And to make similar menaces to Dr Watson to produce similar missives to his wife and colleagues," Stockwell confirmed. "Be of good cheer, doctor. We could not be certain whether you would accompany Sherlock Holmes to Hadlingham or not. Had you not come here to be taken with your dear friend there would have had to be another tragic accident for you and your wife. This way her life is saved—but not yours."

"You must do as they say," Deborah Stobard warned us, her voice quivering. "Otherwise they...they hurt you."

"Control your chivalry, doctor," Stockwell warned. "You can write letters just as well with a new bullet in your bad leg."[28]

The Mendicants and their thugs took the precautions they described. Holmes and I were made to turn out our pockets. Our hats and overcoats were appropriated for our disguised duplicates to wear to Southampton. We were given documents to sign and others to copy out in our own hands word-perfectly.

"This is most through," Holmes noted to Stockwell. "You must congratulate the architect of this. He has done his job very effectively.

---

28   Watson's wound is a fertile source of debate for Holmesian scholars. In his initial account, *A Study In Scarlet*, he is quite explicit about the injury that pensioned him from army service: "I was removed from my brigade and attached to the Berkshires, with whom I served at the fatal battle of Maiwand. There I was struck on the shoulder by a Jezail bullet, which shattered the bone and grazed the subclavian artery." However, in *The Sign of Four* Watson is "nursing my wounded leg. I had had a jezail bullet through it some time before." This raises the possibility of Watson been hit by bullets from a Jezail rifle *twice* in his career, or of a single bullet at Maiwand ricocheting from shoulder-bone to leg, or of the bullet passing through a crouching body twice. Recently the psychosomatic argument has gained popularity, entertaining the possibility of Watson suffering from what we would now term post-traumatic stress disorder. Perhaps the most creative theory is that Watson died at Maiwand and his orderly Murray took his identity before Holmes ever met him; therefore his war wound may have been entirely faked.

It seems, however, that for at least some of Watson's time with Holmes, Watson had a leg injury, probably from gunfire. Readers are at liberty to read in 'Watsonian misdirection' and substitute their favoured explanation of the present comment.

"Why should the plan not be mine?" the beggar-king insisted. He sounded almost defensive.

"The vocabulary of the reports you sent me on the various moving coffins cases is at odds with your oral content. Those documents were rather too scholarly and grammatical for your speech patterns. The syntax and word choices of those letters was far superior to those you command in conversation, and the collation of data was a masterclass in organising a thesis. You are a relatively cunning fellow, Stockwell, but I cannot rank your mind sufficiently highly to be the author or those documents or of this plot."

Stockwell glanced at his fellow gentleman-beggars, who had heard Holmes's scornful indictment. "We Mendicants are accustomed to using whatever we have at hand," he replied. "If necessary, we can hire expertise."

"A consultant," my friend pondered. "One with sufficient wit to prepare documents for me to copy that perfectly match my own style, with a shrewd enough grasp of my character to know what would provoke my imagination and interest, with the skill to anticipate what lines of enquiry I might pursue and lay evidence for me to find; someone who solved the mystery of this vault before me and decided it would make a suitable rat-trap for an overcurious consulting detective. I am flattered by his attention."

"It is me and the Mendicants who have overcome you," Stockwell insisted. "The victory is ours.

"Your plan is already crumbling without external supervision," Holmes critiqued the men holding guns on us. "You were surprised, I think, Stockwell, when I uncovered the secret way into the Haddle vault? You had expected to pen Watson and I up here, locked in this lightless tomb until we could be spirited off to some other final destination. You had not expected me to read the mason's marks and find an escape."

Stockwell did not deny it, but he was still triumphant. "You may have found the way to open the door, but we have other ways of confining you, Sherlock Holmes." He gestured with his weapon. "Climb into Joshua Haddle's coffin with him."

The men who flanked Mrs Stobard and I flexed their pistols. Holmes scowled but complied with the demand, folding his long body into the lead box.

"Now you, Dr Watson," Stockwell insisted. "Climb in atop him. Move now or it is the lady who will suffer for it."

I had no choice. I clambered into the casket and lay atop Holmes.

Stockwell added a flask of water to the box. "I would not wish you to perish of thirst," he sneered. "You shall starve instead. A beggar's death, Mr

Holmes, slow and terrible, proper payment for the damage you have caused."

"Wait...!" I called out.

"Lower the lid," the beggar-king told his Mendicants.

That heavy lead sheet was cranked into place. The side-clasps snapped shut, making an almost-airtight seal; I knew it could not be absolute for insects had crawled in before to devour Joshua's cadaver.

We were in complete darkness, Holmes and I, so close-pressed that we could hardly breathe, sealed in with the mortal remains of Joshua Haddle.

"Crank Edward's coffin atop that one, to be sure," I heard Stockwell order, through the muffled sheeting. There was a long period of squeaking pulleys and huffing men, and then a thump on the lid that pressed down on me.

Mrs Stobard was sobbing. "It is time for you to go now, too, Deborah," Stockwell told her. "Place her in with Edward for company. Then lock her down."

The lady screamed and struggled, but we could no nothing to help her. At last we heard the clack of the clasps on the coffin in which she had been confined, and her terrified howls became muted breathless sobs. Edward's coffin was properly airtight.

Stockwell rapped on the side of our casket. "You can be as clever as you like now, Mr Holmes. You are cramped into a metal box under half a ton of lead. Your mighty brain means nothing. You will die a mean, slow death with your friend atop you. At the last you may go mad, fighting each other for space or air or water. I hope you do."

Holmes made no reply, so I stayed silent also.

"Presently tonight we will brick the doorway up again," Stockwell went on. "We shall seal the tomb until such time as arrangements can be made to have your caskets moved to a different location where they will never be found. So ends the last investigation of Sherlock Holmes. These coffins will not dance you to freedom."

He rapped a victorious farewell tattoo on our coffin-side. And then we were left to confined crushing darkness and slow death.

Holmes and I lay silent for a time, scarcely able to breathe let alone move in a coffin designed for a sole occupant. At last I found my voice. "Mrs Stobard. It is Dr Watson. Do not despair!"

"Stout old Watson!" Holmes cheered me. "I should have known that confinement in the grave would not daunt your courage or decency. Although

I might have wished you to be slightly less stout."

No answer came from the imprisoned lady. "How are we to escape?" I asked my coffin-mate.

"You are so certain, then, that we are not doomed in this miserable box?"

"I have hope. You always calculate the odds, Holmes. When we were accosted by the Mendicants with their weapons and hostage, you considered whether to make one last mad attempt to overthrow our enemies. If you had decided that there was nothing to lose you would have hurled yourself into the thousand-to-one chance that might save Mrs Stobard. That you did not suggests that you apprehended some other course that offered improved odds of survival."

"Even though it caught us in this unpleasant predicament?"

"Even so. You would have fought, and I with you, had you not determined a better plan."

Holmes snorted, which crushed us even worse inside that claustrophobic container. "Stockwell did not properly understand the plan to neutralise me," he declared. "Watson, you must shift your arm so you can feel along the middle-left ridge of the casket, where the side touches the lid. Feel for a stud about the size of your smallest fingertip and depress it."

I found the button and slid it flat. There was a clunk from within the side of the box.

"You must endure my wriggling now," Holmes warned. "The apprentice locked in here would have had more room to reach about him, and possibly a candle-stub."

"An apprentice?"

"You did not recognise the purpose of the casket? The Masonic test? Possibly an allegory of some sort, but that is of little interest to me. Not only was the aspiring Mason expected to find the door mechanism, he was first supposed to discover his way out of the coffin in which he was buried—a sort of resurrection into his new degree, I suppose. Why else was this coffin left with a concealed air vent?"

Holmes struggled to read the carvings on the lead by touch alone, and to shift his hands into the right position. At last he flexed hard and gasped. There was another clack.

"How many of these hidden buttons did the old Masons put on this casket?" I demanded.

"Four, as I read it, as there are four cardinal points and four sides to a square. You should find a third stud on the upper rim by your head," my friend told me.

That was the hardest to reach, for my arms were mostly pinned by our close confinement. It took me the best part of an hour of swearing and grunting to twist so I could finger the button.

There was a third sound. Holmes gave a gasp of satisfaction—or I may have laid my weight on the wrong soft spot—and depressed a fourth and final stud. The head-end of the casket hinged open and clattered to the flagstones.

I slithered out, then helped Holmes free. His body was suffering badly from pins and needles.

We had little time to recover, though. We immediately turned our efforts to rescuing Mrs Stobard, using the block and tackle arrangement that the Mendicants had left in place to shift our coffins elsewhere. With just two of us, in absolute darkness, it took all our strength and ingenuity to pull open Edward's casket lid.

"There now," I comforted the wild-eyed and distraught lady. "The worst is over. Now all that is left is the resolution."

We felt for the door, and found it blocked with newly-relaid slabs. Though the mortar was not quite dry it would have been impossible for us to force our way through without sledgehammers and crowbars. Fortunately, Holmes could find the cobble that triggered the hinge counterweight to open the wider doorframe, sealing blocks and all.

"There may be a guard outside the vault," Holmes considered. "If so, I shall distract him while you grapple him, Watson. Do not feel the need to adhere to the Marquis of Queensbury's rules."

I assured Holmes that after our close encounter with the coffin I had no qualms about overcoming our captors by whatever means was necessary. But our precaution was unneeded. The Mendicants were confident of their triumph and had left no sentry.

"You must take Mrs Stobard to safety at the vicarage and send word for the constabulary," Holmes told me. "Have them contact Bradstreet at Scotland Yard and tell him that his Amateur Mendicants have made an amateur error."

"And what of you, Holmes?" I worried.

"I shall be making up for my professional error. Someone has anticipated me quite handily and I must improve my game accordingly." He shivered in the light downpour, for we had lost our coats. "We cannot allow 'Stockwell' and his cronies to disperse. They may not all be assembled again in so opportune a manner. Fortunately we can be sure of one thing."

I enquired what that might be.

"They will return to the Haddle vault with enough men and equipment to haul our coffin away to some oubliette that we are not known to have visited. You may be certain that the architect of the plot that brought us here also made provision for us to vanish without trace. The Amateur Mendicants will come to get us."

"You cannot face them all alone, Holmes."

"I will not be alone," Holmes promised. "I will be aided by the restless dead."

I carried out my part of the work, bestowing the American widow with the new vicar and his wife, hiking over to Stenton-on-the-Hill to knock up the postmaster and send an urgent telegram to the Criminal Investigation Division at Scotland Yard, then waiting as a local force consisting of whatever officers might be scrambled from Leicester arrived by police coach to reinforce us.

Still, a dull dawn had broken over the Rutland hills by the time we were confident in our numbers and assured that our approach might not be seen by some supposed hedge-tramp who was actually a lookout for the villains. Bradstreet was on his way from the capital but would not arrive in time for the action, so precedence went to the local Assistant Chief Constable, who directed his men with a commendable military precision.

"What might we expect?" he asked me as we travelled into Hadlingham.

"If things have gone badly for Holmes, these men might have fled after committing murder. But I daresay that things will have turned out for them differently than they expect."

A heavy covered dray stood on the road beside the village duckpond, its team of four Shire horses unattended but content with their feedbags. I feared that the beggars might have received reinforcements.

We approached the Hall with caution, from both sides at once, but found it open and empty. Holmes awaited us on the path beside the vault, sheltering under a borrowed coat and umbrella. He tossed a heavy shaped masonry wedge in his hand, catching it over and over.

"Holmes!" I cried. "You are unharmed!"

"Quite unharmed, Watson, and all the more refreshed by enjoying this little adventure. The Barbados coffins have been a joy from start to finish, with only the exception of our somewhat uncomfortable first-hand encounter with the grave."

"The Mendicants, though. They have fled the Hall!"

"Not fled, Watson. They came to do what they boasted of, to remove our casket to a place where we could be left to starve with no hope of rescue. But they are beggars, not Masons."

He handed me the stonework he was carrying. It was ancient but well preserved, cunningly carved into a tapered shape with a groove and notch at one end. "This is what they'll be missing."

A suspicion crept upon me. "Holmes... is this the brick you moved in the third step to unfasten the secret door-frame?"

"Indeed it is. I fear that, if a number of men have swarmed into the vault to manhandle Joshua Haddle's coffin out to a waiting cart and the trap-door was closed on them, there might be no way to reopen it from that side."

"Stockwell is in there?"

"Along with all the so-called servants who had such dire plans to rob and murder Deborah Stobard. Nine fellows in all and from them we will find the last few of their sordid little cabal."

Stockwell was not so jubilant when Holmes triggered the mechanism that reopened the vault and allowed the men in there to be dragged out by armed police. He relied upon his right to remain silent, and I mentioned to him that he might have used it earlier to save us his ineffective jawing.

None of the prisoners would name the 'expert' who had advised them for a handsome fee on how to dispose of Mr Sherlock Holmes; I would not hear the name of that consulting criminal for a little while longer.

"Do you believe the Masonic theory to be the proper explanation for the haunted tombs, then?" I asked Holmes as we travelled back to wet, smoky London. "That there was a sect of primitive Freemasons who had some kind of rite that required a prepared coffin and rigged vault, and that some of their places were later reused to scare or to gain revenge upon others?"

"We will never know, Watson. An expert mind has turned to knotting the stories into an intellectual trap for me, and that may have destroyed whatever traces remained to reach the real truth. The whole narrative might have been spun from pure fiction. Or it might be an allegorical tale meant to be interpreted by the cognoscenti. Or perhaps your friend Doyle might yet be proved right against all the laws of established science."[29] He sat back on his seat and touched his fingertips together. "With your kind permission I will stick to the facts."

THE END

---

[29] It was in 1887, shortly before the time of this account, that Arthur Conan Doyle encountered Major-General Alfred Wilks Drayson, a member of the Portsmouth Literary and Philosophical Society, and began with him a series of 'psychic investigations' including experiments in telepathy, sittings with mediums, and a score of séances. He wrote up his experiences for the Spiritualist journal *Light* and declared himself a believer.

THE UPRIGHT HOLMES AND THE HAUNTED WATSON

A post-graveyard reflection by I. A. Watson

Sir Arthur Conan Doyle was a complicated man, of much greater depth than the Nigel Bruce-like stereotypical Englishman he resembles in photographs. He was far more than the somewhat-gullible bereaved Spiritualist seeker he is sometimes depicted as in his latter years.

He was born in Scotland of an Irish mother and an English father. When he was seven his parents temporarily separated because of his father's alcoholism; readers of *A Study in Scarlet* may recall Holmes's observations about Watson's alcoholic brother's watch. Doyle's[30] education was paid for by wealthy uncles, but he disliked his first alma mater Stonyhurst College and "did not have any fond memories since the school was run on medieval principles". He spent a year in Jesuit School at Feldkirch in Austria but later renounced his family's Catholic faith.

He studied medicine at the University of Edinburgh, botany at the Royal Botanic Garden, and failed to get his first writing efforts published. He served as ship's doctor on the Greenland whaler *Hope of Peterhead* and, after graduating as Bachelor of Medicine and Master of Surgery, he was ship's surgeon for a voyage to the West African coast on the SS *Mayumba*. He gained his Doctor of Medicine degree with a dissertation on *tabes dorsalis*, a late consequence of neurosyphilis.

After failed attempts at running a general medical practice (like Dr Watson his efforts were intermittent and mostly unsatisfactory) he went to Vienna to study ophthalmology, but failed due to difficulties with the German in which it was taught; he spent much of his time there ice skating. Returning via Venice, Milan, and Paris, he opened an ophthalmology

---

30   Not actually Conan Doyle. Conan was his middle name, though in later years he sometimes used it as a double-barrelled surname. When he was knighted he was gazetted as Doyle.

47

consulting practice in London which faltered for lack of patients—any patients at all!

Fortunately by then his literary endeavours were beginning to earn him income, although he was compelled by poverty to surrender the rights to his first Sherlock Holmes work *A Study in Scarlet*, for just £25—all the money he ever made from that book.

He was an amateur boxer (like Holmes), goalkeeper for Portsmouth Association Football Club under the pseudonym A. C. Smith, played ten first-class matches for the Marylebone Cricket Club, was elected captain of the Crowborough Beacon Golf Club, and entered the English Amateur billiards championship in 1913. He married twice and had five children (but no grandchildren; the Doyle line died out). He argued in defence of the Boer War and the government's choices in it, publishing articles and books on the topic that probably won him his knighthood.[31] He failed twice to be elected to Parliament.

Doyle personally investigated two closed-case crimes and exonerated two falsely-accused men.

I cite all this, and could have mentioned a lot more, to illustrate that Doyle was anything but a caricature. I envy him the breadth of his experience and the sheer energy by which he acquired it. Much of his travels, his reading, his adventures, and even his tragedies fuelled his writing and inspired some of the most prominent literature of the Victorian age.

Doyle became a Spiritualist in 1887 at the age of 28, and for some of his life he was a Freemason. He was initiated at Phoenix Lodge No. 257 in Southsea on the 26th January 1887, resigned from the Lodge in 1889, and returned from 1902 to 1911.

Doyle the Freemason has prompted some enthusiasts to look for hidden Masonic meanings in his published fiction. The charge is led by Joe Nickell, who wrote in *Real-Life X-Files: Investigating the Paranormal* (2001):

"For instance, Holmes uncovers dark secrets in 'The Adventure of Shoscombe Old Place.' Beneath an old chapel on the Shoscombe property, accessed by stumbling through 'loose masonry' (an obvious pun) and proceeding down a steep stairway, Holmes finds himself in a crypt with an 'arched ... roof' (evoking the Royal Arch degree of Masonry). Accompanied by his client—a 'Mr Mason'!—Holmes finds the key to a series of strange mysteries. Similarly allusive Holmes stories are 'The Red-Headed League' (featuring a client who sports a Masonic breastpin), and the suggestively titled 'The Musgrave Ritual'."

31   For further discussion of this by I.A. Watson refer to his novel *Holmes and Houdini* (2017), ISBN 10: 0997786809 ISBN 13: 978-0997786804

Nickell developed his theme from his article "Barbados Restless Coffins Laid To Rest", *FATE*, April & May 1982, pp 50-56, 79-86, which proposed the Masonic allegory solution and is supported by sceptical investigators such as Robert Dale Owen and Brian Dunning who question the mystery's initial sources.

As the opening tag for "The Adventure of the Restless Dead" demonstrates, the Barbados Coffins mystery drew the attention of Arthur Conan Doyle, who cited the 1907 researches of folklorist Andrew Lang. It was Lang who first noted the similarities between cases across the planet. Doyle mentions three of them in his *Strand* article "The Law of the Ghost" (1919).

And so, by a roundabout route, we illustrate that Doyle drew upon a rich menu of experiences, and that his interests in Freemasonry and in Spiritualism informed some of his fiction. The modern author who seeks to present a Sherlock Holmes pastiche—and especially one who must find a fresh theme for this *twenty-eighth* Holmes pastiche—must similarly delve into Doyle's life to offer stories that are both *authentic* and *new*.

Note to self: work in the word *Saxe* to Holmes' speech. That is an old term for "except" that Doyle himself uses in his "Law of the Ghost" article, and is undoubtedly the sort of vocabulary that he would place upon the erudite tongue of his great detective: "We might have neglected the clue, Watson, saxe the curious coincidence."

Few of Holmes's modern authors can match Doyle's rich life experiences, but to attempt the kind of stories that he produced we must dig similarly deep to find some narrative hook. One source of inspiration for several of my tales has been the writings of criminologist, journalist, and editor Richard Whittington-Egan (1924-2016), to whom I should really dedicate a book sometime since he has provided me with so many leads.

In the 1970s and 80s, *Weekend* was a cheap magazine given away with a national newspaper Sunday edition. It was full of things that were of no interest to a juvenile Ian Watson—celebrity gossip, cookery, gardening, fashion, knitting—except for a regular column about some gruesome murder or world mystery. *Those* caught my attention. The best of them were written by lead writer Whittington-Egan; he was probably one of the first authors whose name I noted and looked for.

In 1975, the teenaged Ian was delighted to discover a cheap compilation volume of many of these articles, *The Weekend Book of Ghosts*, edited by Richard Whittington-Egan. He purchased it with his own money, for 60p; I am looking at the much-read, dog-eared old thing right now. Other volumes were released in 1978, 1981, 1982, and 1985.

These short articles have served me well. My Holmes stories "Spring-Heeled Jack", "The Scotland Yard Murder", "The Adventure of the Failing Light", and "The Lucky Leprechaun" all started with subject matter I first encountered there. Peter Rogers's "The Awful Riddle of the Restless Coffins" in the *Weekend Book of Ghosts and Horror No. 2* (1982)[32] pp 106-109 started me on the long road that has led me to produce "The Adventure of the Restless Dead" in this present volume.

The *Weekend* series has also pointed me towards various ghostly tales that I have appropriated for other things I've written. Not bad value for 60p to £2.25 a volume.

Sherlock Holmes's departure from that course of study and direction of life that had been planned for him began with his encounter with Oxford friend Victor Trevor's father and his investigation into a secret past that had doomed the old man.[33] That mystery led him to many others and a lifetime of chasing them. I must at least part-credit Whittington-Egan and his *Weekend* confederates for likewise inculcating in me an enthusiasm that led me thereafter to discover Sherlock Holmes and other investigators of the macabre.

IW
May 2020
Under lockdown, as restless as a moving coffin.

---

32   That work had a cover photograph of a young lady with inspiring décolletage shying away from phantom writing on her bedroom wall. For some reason at the time this caught my purchasing interest, and now offers a valuable lesson in the marketing mysteries to the heterosexual teenage male.

33   Holmes's narration to Watson of his first case is recorded in "The Adventure of the *Gloria Scott*" in *The Memoirs of Sherlock Holmes* (1893).

I.A. WATSON—doesn't have a middle name. He adopted the initial for marketing reasons and to baffle his enemies.

Robin Hood: King of Sherwood was his first full-length novel, written to order for a publisher who whom he'd previously produced *Sherlock Holmes* anthology stories. Each of the Hood volumes and most of the Holmes stories were nominated for Best Pulp Novel or Best Pulp Short Story of the year; one short story got him an actual trophy. Since 2009 he has written twenty novels, nine novellas, three compilation editions, and one non-fiction book, and contributed to over fifty multi-author anthologies. Quite a bit more is heading to print soon. A full list is online at **http://www.chillwater.org.uk/writing/iawatsonhome.htm** Robin Hood-specific material is at **http://www.chillwater.org.uk/writing/robinhome.htm**

Sherlock Holmes

in

THE ADVENTURE OF THE GIRL ON THE BLACK VELVET SWING

by
Michael A. Black

"A preposterous contrivance masquerading as literature," I said, hurling the cheaply printed booklet toward the fireplace. It missed going into the aperture, bouncing against the hearth and skittering across the floor. Sherlock Holmes strode across the room with a look of amusement on his face and retrieved it, smoothing it out as he glanced through the pages. The two of us were alone in our Baker's Street lodging preparing for the violinist's recital that evening.

"I should think you need to practice on your aim a bit more, old boy," he said, placing it on the mantel. "And as for this, I shall look forward to reviewing it later with interest."

"What? Why would you waste your time doing such a thing?"

He arched a querulous eyebrow.

"Anything that could elicit such an extreme reaction from you," he said, "is worth a perusal."

"You read a novella?" I answered, scoffing. "Although describing it as such is flattery, it hardly seems in keeping with your interests. And it's a penny dreadful at that. A waste of a shilling if you ask me."

"And why pray tell is that, my dear Watson?"

Holmes's thin visage twitched with a slight smile. It was obvious that he was enjoying himself at my expense.

"Take my word on it," I replied. "The author's premise is preposterous. The protagonist is a *doctor*, for heaven's sake. Poppycock."

"Your ire has made you a bit redundant, old boy." The smile widened as he grabbed one of his pipes from his desk and began looking around for the Persian slipper that contained his tobacco. Spying it on the mantel where he'd set the penny dreadful, he once again picked it up. "*The Strange Case of Dr. Jekyll and Mr. Hyde*," he read. "By Robert Louis Stevenson. " He raised an eyebrow momentarily, then peered at me with those piercing eyes of his. "And what, pray tell, is this outlandish premise that has you in such a tizzy?"

"A tizzy," I remarked. "Hardly. The man's no better than a charlatan. He's written a piece in which he has a doctor, a doctor, mind you, cast as this duplicitous villain most foul."

Holmes continued to page through the cheap, yellowish pages.

"This Dr. Jekyll," I continued, "is a physician who drinks this concoction he's prepared which turns him into this blackguard who goes by the name, Edward Hyde. He then proceeds to commit all sorts of heinous acts. It's pure debauchery."

"Interesting premise," Holmes said.

"Hardly. He then imbibes another dose of the concoction and reverts back to his mild mannered self. Eventually, the dominant Hyde personality keeps reasserting itself and Jekyll is then forced to commit suicide to keep his darker self at bay." I snorted and shook my head. "A dreadful excuse for a story."

Holmes set the booklet on top of the mantel again and retrieved the Persian slipper. He spoke as he packed a scoop of tobacco into the bowl of his pipe. This particular one was from India and the outside of the bowl had an intricate carving of a bearded man's face. His hollow turban formed the circular expanse for the tobacco. I'd always admired the pipe, but Holmes had never shared with me how he'd acquired it.

"But isn't this Jekyll something of noble figure as well?" Holmes asked, holding a match over the top to ignite the tobacco. "Choosing to end his life rather than allowing his baser instincts to become dominant?" He drew in on the stem and blew out a few puffs as the tobacco began to burn. "Rather like a new version of the classic Aristotelian tragic figure. A noble man with a fatal flaw who ultimately triumphs over evil, but at the cost of his own existence."

"I must admit, I hadn't actually thought of it that way," I said.

Holmes blew out a plume of smoke. "Or perhaps it's a commentary on the duality of man, each of us, no matter how altruistic our motive, must face those darker thoughts that linger in the deeper recesses of our consciousness."

"I think you're giving this so called author much more credit than he deserves," I said. "I'd like to give that Stevenson fellow a piece of my mind."

"A mind, especially a most capable one as yours, dear fellow, should not be divided up like a mince pie." Holmes chuckled and the smoke drifted out of his mouth as he spoke. "Besides the fact that to do so, old boy, you would have to travel to Samoa. I read in the newspaper that the author's going there for his health. It seems he's a consumptive."

The thought of the poor soul being afflicted with that wretched disease softened my outrage a bit.

"Well," I said. "It's not worth consternation it's causing. And we'll be late for the concert if we don't get moving."

"Quite right," he said. "I am so looking forward to hearing this young Mister Woodward. He's purported to be a prodigy."

"Let's hope his talent isn't overrated," I said, picking up my hat and overcoat. It was mid-October and there was a bit of winter's chill in the air. "Like Mister Stevenson's."

Holmes gathered up his top hat and overcoat as well.

"Don't be too hard on poor Robert, Watson. After all, you and he both share a common fondness for our late First Earl of Beaconsfield, whom he openly supported over Carlyle in the last election."

"As well he should have," I said. "Not that it made any difference. And that still doesn't excuse his deplorable story. Using a chemical to service one's baser desires. Why I would venture to say that—"

I stopped talking because I suddenly realized that my comparison could be drawn between the fictional Dr. Jekyll's dalliances with chemical concoctions to escape the doldrums of a proper existence with Holmes's own pernicious excursions with the seven percent solution of cocaine and distilled water. He continued to indulge in this destructive habit periodically, despite my continual precautionary harangues. Of late, however, he'd seemed to have weaned himself away from the noxious habit somewhat, for which I was very grateful, but for how long I did not know.

"What were you saying, old boy?" Holmes asked, picking up his walking stick.

"Nothing," I said. "Consider yourself forewarned. If you decide to read it, do so at your own risk."

"Perhaps I shall," he said. "But now, the concert awaits."

The commencement of the concert was unfortunately delayed in that we were forced to wait for the arrival of the Queen and an undercurrent of unrest began to travel through the audience. I felt particularly bad for the parents of young Colby Woodward, who had to wait to be officially recognized until after her Majesties presentments. Finally, the Queen, Prince Edward, and the Princess arrived and we all stood and applauded. The accolade for the Prince, who appeared in the upper booth after her Majesty, was appreciably less than that for Queen Victoria. Prince Edward, or Bertie, as he was less than affectionately known, had sullied the royal reputation with his dalliances, which had tragically affected the Royal Family. Nonetheless, shouts of "God save her Majesty, the Queen" arose and the applause resumed as the orchestra began to play "God Save the Queen." After the royal introductions had been completed, Lady Beth Covington, formerly Woodward, mother of the prodigy, was allowed to stand along with her new husband, Lord Earle Covington. He'd served with distinction in the Fifth Northumberland Fusiliers in India, and had returned to England to woo and married the beautiful, and wealthy widow, Lady Beth Woodward one year ago.

"Rumor has it that now that he's in the running to be appointed Chancellor to India," I whispered to Holmes as the handsome couple stood. He looked resplendent in his bright red dress uniform, despite having retired from her Majesty's Service, and still maintained the proper bearing of a military man. "Although, I do hear he's got some rather stiff competition for the position. Edmund Hillary. He has a distinguished military career as well. Was awarded the Victoria Cross for his valor in the Battle of Inkermann. He was a sergeant in the Forty-First Regiment."

"Certainly a more fortuitous position than that of an officer with the Light Dragoons," Holmes whispered back. "But one less likely to have been eulogized by Tennyson."

"Quite," I said, feeling some irritation at his capriciousness.

Holmes seemed to care little for topics such as Empire and politics, although sometimes his interest was piqued should the matters be of concern to one of his cases. Tonight, however, we were both there to assess and appreciate young Woodward's purported mastery of the violin.

The concert was wonderful, and at the prescribed time the young prodigy stepped forward to play his solo of Mendelsshon's *Leider*. I was particularly taken with the melody, and must say that he performed it with the artistry of a new Paganini. Holmes seemed to enjoy the performance even more than I. He sat with eyes closed, as if he were savoring every note. After finishing with an artful sweep of his bow, the young master lifted his right arm upward, as if he were brandishing Excalibur, in acknowledgment of the sweeping applause that welled up from the audience. He was indeed a handsome looking lad with the same auburn hair that graced his mother's fair head and a full beard even though he couldn't have been more than nineteen, if he was a day. Although the full beard he was sporting was an effete attempt to make him appear older, it did little to offset the almost cherubic face and rather slender frame.

At the completion of the concert, we joined the mass exodus from the music hall and I happened to spy some of the Royal Guards ushering young master Woodward, Lady Beth, and Lord Earle Covington into an anteroom. Sir Earle was busily straightening the agglomeration of ribbons on his chest. A swarthy looking fellow with a turban and a black beard, whom

I took to be the Colonel's Indian manservant, followed along.

I turned to mention this sighting to Holmes, but it became immediately apparent that he had already noticed the special, ongoing segregation.

"Obviously," he said, "her Royal Highness was impressed with the performance and wishes to convey her appreciation to the young prodigy."

"Looks like Lord Covington's going to try to ride on the boy's coattails," I said with amusement. "A bit of a reversal of roles, eh?"

"No doubt," Holmes said. "Whom did you say was in competition for the Chancellorship?"

"Edmund Hillary," I answered.

"Tough Eddie?" Holmes said with a smile.

"One and the same. And he's purportedly a favorite of the Foreign Office. Word is that he has the inside track. He was awarded the Victoria Cross, you know."

"For his distinguished service during the Battle of Inkmann," he said. "You're starting to repeat yourself, old chum."

I flushed at my redundancy. Perhaps Holmes earlier comment was more apropos than I'd realized.

As if sensing the sting of his remark, he placed a hand on my arm and smiled.

"An interesting dichotomy indeed," he said. "The valiant sergeant against the officer-aristocrat in a politician's duel."

I found it shocking that he knew this. Usually, his knowledge of politics was described as "feeble."

"Yes," I said. "I'll be curious to see which of them does get the nod."

"Better you than I, Watson." He smiled. "As you have often pointed out in your written accounts of my cases, I find the politics of the day so uttering meaningless and boring," Holmes said. "I find the public's fascination with those matters reminiscent of a litter of curs scurrying about trying to gain access to a vacant teat."

I snorted at his outrageous metaphor, but that was Holmes, always expressing his disdain for the mundane social interactions.

We took an open carriage back to Baker Street despite the rather inclement early November temperature. Holmes seemed invigorated by the coolness of the night air, but I wrapped my scarf once again around my throat.

"We should have elected for a closed carriage," I said. "We're likely to catch our death."

"Not likely, Watson," he said, breathing deeply. "Enjoy the clean, evening air while you can. Guy Fawkes Day is almost upon us and the bonfires will be taking over soon enough."

"A despicable custom," I said, referring to the annual riotous celebrations and open burnings that inevitably ensued every November the fifth.

At Baker Street whilst I readied myself for bed I caught the fragrance of some strong tobacco. I dried my face and stepped into the sitting room only to be surprised at the darkness. Then I saw Holmes still fully dressed in his evening wear, standing by the window. He hadn't even turned on the gaslight.

"I say, Holmes, is everything all right?"

He removed his pipe from his mouth and half-turned, the moonlight illuminating his silhouette with a silver resonance.

"Quite right, old boy," he said. "Don't mind me. I'm still appreciating the rapture of young Master Woodward's performance."

I turned and went into my room. I drew the bed covers over me and lay there worrying that he was going to seek solace with the infernal cocaine once more. After a fashion, I heard the melancholy melody of Holmes's violin. As I drifted off into sleep, I reflected that he was playing Mendelsshon's *Leider*.

Neither of us spoke any more of Young Master Woodward or the concert for two days and we went about our regular business. I had several rounds to make seeing my regular patients, and Holmes was embroiled in a peculiar, but not particularly challenging, case of a woman who was disturbed that someone had been vandalizing her flower garden. The culprit, Holmes deduced without so much as leaving our abode, was found to be the woman's next door neighbor, or, more specifically, the goat that he had recently purchased. When I returned in the late afternoon, Holmes began relating the particulars of the case to me with the customary twinkle in his eye when he suddenly stopped and raised an eyebrow.

"What is it?" I asked.

"The bell, Watson." He sat silent for a moment more, and then rose from his chair and strode toward the door, pulling it open. "And Mrs. Hudson's assiduous approach."

Mrs. Hudson gave a start as Holmes greeted her.

"My apologies if I happened to startle you, my dear," Holmes said. "But I couldn't help be hear your distinctive pattern of footfalls as you ascended the stairs. I take it I have a visitor?"

"You do, Mr. Holmes," she said, her hand still resting on her bodice. "A lady. A very fine lady, wishes to speak with you."

"Then, by all means," Holmes said. "Send her up."

Mrs. Hudson vanished from sight and I then heard those distinctive footfalls going down the stairs, followed by a murmur of voices.

"Curious," Holmes said, going to the mantel and retrieving his pipe and the Persian slipper.

"What's that?" I asked.

"It seems Lady Beth Covington is about to pay us a visit, old boy." He packed the bowl of his black clay pipe and held a match over it.

"Lady Beth Covington?" I said in surprise. "How the devil do know it is she?"

"Elementary," Holmes said, emitting tiny puffs of smoke as the flame from the match flickered over the bowl. "I caught a glimpse of her distinctive red hair when I was speaking to Mrs. Hudson a few moments ago."

I huffed a response, amused that I had grown so used to his elaborate and extraordinary deductions that such an obvious explanation seemed incongruous. A few moments later Mrs. Hudson's familiar knock sounded and Holmes strode to the door and opened it. Lady Covington was dressed in an elegant looking blue dress, her red hair pulled up under a hat, and a lace vale shielding her face. Despite the pungency of Holmes's powerful tobacco, I detected a wisp of French perfume as she entered.

"Won't you come in, Lady Covington," Holmes said, bowing slightly and holding out his hand. "This is my friend and associate, Dr. John H. Watson."

As she looked at me I couldn't help but notice that her beautiful face appeared a bit puffy, along with a distinct redness about her eyes. She had greenish irises and long, luxuriant lashes. Despite the obvious fact that she'd been crying did nothing to offset her stunning beauty. Holmes ushered her over to one of the chairs in the sitting room and held her hand as she lowered herself onto the seat. Then the detective stepped back and said, "Why don't you tell us about the problem that's brought you here."

Before she could answer, Holmes turned to me and snapped his fingers.

"Quickly, Watson. A glass of sherry for our guest."

"Certainly." I stepped over to the cabinet and took out the decanter. As I poured, Holmes continued.

"Watson and I had the uncommon pleasure of seeing your son perform two nights ago," he said. "I must say, his talent is enviable. You should be very proud."

"I am, Mr. Holmes." Her voice sounded brittle.

I handed her the sherry and she stared at it without drinking.

"Please," Holmes said. "Do tell us what type of trouble young Master Woodward has gotten into."

Lady Covington looked startled.

"How did you know?" she said with an accompanying gasp.

"You've been holding your body stiffly since entering the quarters," Holmes said, "indicating that you're harboring a considerable amount of anxiety. And my pronouncement about your son brought a slight and involuntary narrowing of your eyes. This connoted your concern for your son's wellbeing. The logical deduction is that he's in some sort of trouble. And you've obviously been crying, despite your attempt to conceal your visage with the vale, so whatever situation your son is involved in, it portends to be of a most serious nature."

Lady Covington seemed stunned, which was the normal reaction the first time people were confronted with the detective's amazing powers of deduction.

"Perhaps a sip of the sherry might make you feel more at ease," I said.

Holmes nodded in agreement.

She brought the glass to her lips and drank a tiny bit, then heaved a sigh.

"Colby's been arrested, Mr. Holmes," she said, a tear winding its way down her cheek. "They're charging him with murder."

It took Lady Covington less than ten minutes to relate the sordid details. Her son had been ebullient after his special audience with her Highness and the Prince. After they'd arrived home that same evening, her husband, Earle Covington, had insisted on taking young Colby out for a bit of celebration.

"As you may be aware," she said, dabbing at her cheek with a white handkerchief, my husband's under consideration for a very important governmental position. Meeting her Majesty was very fortuitous."

"The Chancellorship to India, I believe," Holmes said, casting a slight wink in my direction. "We are very aware of such, madam. But do, pray tell, go on."

"Since it was already getting late, and I was a bit fatigued, I retired and went to sleep. What time they arrived back, I do not know, but I know it was late." She paused and compressed her lips. "The next morning, when I arose, I went down to breakfast and found Collin and Earle already at the table. Collin had a rather unseemly bruise on the side of his face." Her hand rose to rest briefly against her left cheek. "When I inquired as to the circumstance, he immediately got up and left the table. Earle attempted to dismiss the matter, but I pressed him. He then admitted that he'd committed a bit of a gaff. It seems he brought Collin to a—" She paused and I detected a bit of a flush creeping upward along her slim neck and settling in her flawless cheekbones.

"A gentleman's club?" Holmes inferred.

The way he'd said it made it obvious that his phraseology was euphemistic.

She nodded, seeming a bit shocked.

"How ever did you know?" she asked.

"That doesn't matter," he said. "Please, go on with your story, and leave out nothing, no matter how inconsequential it may seem."

The greenish eyes closed momentarily, then opened and she began again.

"It seems that at this…club, Collin began imbibing a bit." She leaned forward slightly, her hands clenching into fists on her lap. "Mr. Holmes, I assure you that Collin is not a rowdy young man at all. Why, I have no doubt that his imprudent dalliance with the liquor brought on this entire matter."

"No doubt," Holmes said. "Please continue."

He was sitting across from her, the still-full glass of sherry resting on the small oval wooden table between them.

"Earle told me that this particular club has a series of swings suspended from the ceiling," she said. "These swings are covered in various colors of velvet, and each has a young lady sitting on it, swinging back and forth over the heads of the gentlemen in attendance. There's a bucket attached to each of the swings, and it's customary for the men in attendance to place coins into them to get them to stop their perpetual motion and engage in… social intercourse."

Although I daresay I didn't admit it, I knew the name of this establishment close to the East End. It was known as The Velvet Slipper.

The blush on her cheeks deepened and she drew in a long breath.

"You see, Collin's always been a rather frail youth," she said. "He seems to have taken after my side of the family rather than that of his father, my late husband, Gerald. His interest was always more of the arts, especially music, than the more robust activities. Earle has been harping on him to enlist in the army, but I wouldn't hear of it."

"So your new husband took him to the Velvet Slipper?" Holmes said, prodding her forward. "And?"

I must admit, I was a bit taken aback that Holmes would make mention of such a place by name in front of someone one as proper as Lady Woodward, but it seemed to propel her narrative forward.

"Yes," she said. "It was certainly not something of which I would have approved, and Earle made it perfectly clear to me that he realized it was a severe error in his judgment." She stopped and took in another deep breath. "It seems that Collin was quite taken with one of this young woman and was enjoying her company when another man approached and dropped sixpence into the girl's bucket, demanding that she grant him an immediate audience up in her room, rather than be with Collin. Apparently, he and she were mutually acquainted from previous occasions." Her eyes closed, as if relating the next part as a painful process. "A bit of a row began between this man and Collin, escalating into a physical altercation."

Holmes raised an eyebrow. "And that accounted for the bruise on his cheek that you observed?"

It was less a question than an affirmation, and I had no doubt that Holmes only said it to prod her into continuing without trying to justify her son's actions once again.

Lady Covington nodded.

"Were the police notified?" Holmes asked.

"Yes. But only after the fight had been broken up. And from what Earle said, it wasn't much of dispute. You've seen Collin. You know how young and slender he is. Hardly more than a youth. This other man was older and quite burly."

"So I take it no charges were preferred?" Holmes asked.

She shook her head. "The proprietor's men broke them apart, and several patrons claimed that it had been Collin who'd struck the first blow. Earle said it was all he could do to persuade this other man not to prefer charges. It was most embarrassing."

"Quite," said Holmes, "And this other man, was he known to you."

Again Lady Woodward closed both eyes and sat in prim silence for several seconds before answering. "He was known to my husband. His name was Edmund Hillary."

"Who's also being considered for the chancellorship," I interjected.

Holmes cast me a harsh look and I said nothing more, but my

"So your new husband took him to the Velvet Slipper?"

astonishment was growing. The nature of her earlier admission, along with her reason for being here, made the next question all too obvious.

"And last night, over your objections, Collin returned to the Velvet Slipper?" Holmes asked.

"Yes." Her voice cracked a bit in response.

"Did your husband accompany him this time?"

She shook her head with a negative response.

"And now Mr. Hillary has been murdered," Holmes said.

Another nod, another tear.

I was astounded. Although I'd heard the newsboys yelling earlier about an extra news edition, I had no idea it was this sensational event. And, I wondered, how had Holmes known it involved Hillary?

"This is the murder with which your son's been charged?" he asked.

She nodded again, her eyes still closed.

We sat in silence for the better part of a minute. I knew from experience that the detective was taking it all in, analyzing what he'd been told and making inferences and deductions at lightning speed. I know better than to interrupt this process.

"What else is there that you're not telling us?" Holmes finally asked.

Her white teeth clasped over her exquisite lower lip with a brief biting action, then she straightened up.

"They're claiming to have several witnesses from the scene placing Collin there," she said. "He was apprehended a few blocks away, covered in blood."

After assuring Lady Woodward that he would look into the matter, Holmes advised her that she and her husband in the meantime should engage the services of a good legal representative.

"But with any luck," he said, holding her elbow as he walked with her to the door, "you shan't need his services. I should be able to rectify this matter forthwith."

After the lady had left he rushed to the window and pulled back the curtains. Curious as to what had caused his hasty movements, I joined him and looked down on the street below only to see the swarthy Indian servant who had been in attendance at the concert assist Lady Covington into a carriage, after which he closed the door and assumed his position as driver.

I stepped away from the window, leaving him there to continue perusing the scene. Removing my pipe from the humidor, I began packing it with tobacco from my pouch. When Holmes turned back to face me I raised both of my eyebrows in reproach.

"I must say, Holmes, at times I find your conduct rather perplexing. I thought it was never your common practice to issue such an assurance of solvability before the investigation's been completed."

"Quite right, old chum," he said, reaching for his hat and cloak. "I'm deliberately violating my code of deductive ethics based upon the firm belief that such a prodigious talent as young Collin Woodward possesses would not be congruent with the propensity to commit such a heinous act."

"Balderdash," I blurted, holding the match above my pipe and watching the crumbled tobacco leaf fragments igniting with a red glow. "You merely told her that to give her a bit of hope."

"My, my, old boy," he said. "You are getting more and more perceptive by the day." Holmes smiled as he slipped on his cloak, wrapped a long scarf about his neck, and then picked up his tweed deerstalker hat.

"Isn't that hat a bit out of fashion for the streets of London?" I remarked.

"On the contrary. It's totally apropos. After all, we are going hunting, old chum. Are we not? Hunting for the truth. But do come along now. We have much work to do and the game's afoot." Pausing, he glanced toward the late morning sunlight shining through the window pane. "And do bring along your service revolver. We may find need of it."

As we went out onto Baker Street there were two men wearing newspaper placards and waving the latest edition in the air.

"Tough Eddie Hillary murdered," one of them yelled. "Read all about it."

I glanced at Holmes, who gave his head a minute shake.

"Really, Watson. You know I prefer to draw my own conclusions in my investigation free from any biased sensationalism designed not to present the facts, but rather to sell newspapers."

"Quite right," I said.

We hailed a Hanson almost immediately and Holmes shoved a bit of extra coinage into the driver's hand telling him we needed to get to Scotland Yard posthaste. The man's gap-toothed grin, visible through the open slot, told us we'd be there shortly and we were both set back against the carriage wall as the driver cracked his whip. The slot closed above our heads and Holmes began a rapid discourse.

"I should like to speak with young Collin as soon as possible. There were too many gaps in his mother's account that need to be filled in before I can get a sense of the full picture. We also need to pay a visit to the city morgue, hopefully before any autopsy has been performed, so that I may view the body in its recumbent state."

"Shouldn't we be going there first?" I asked.

"Ordinarily, we would," he answered. "But I fear in a case involving such potentially high-strung political considerations, we'll first need to obtain the authorization from Scotland Yard. Additionally, the summary of events we got from Lady Covington was mostly hearsay. It would be well to speak with young Collin to hear what actually occurred."

This all made perfect sense, as usual. With Tough Eddie Hillary being in line for the chancellorship, the urgency in the investigation of his untimely death would no doubt be fraught with restrictions from the police. And we were, after all, operating with the assumptions presented by the arrested man's mother, which was, to say the least, not the most unbiased of sources. Once again, Holmes was right. His ability to foresee the various potential hurdles in a potential case, such as those erected by the London Police or maternal prejudice, were always circumspect.

"In the meantime," he went on, taking out his black clay pipe, his "thinking pipe," which was already packed with tobacco. "I need to review what we've been told."

"Quite right." I took out my own cherrywood, which I'd prepared back in our room, and placed the stem in my mouth. Holmes shook out the match he'd used to light his own, and struck a new one to hand over to me. We both sat and smoked in silence as the brisk air flowed through the open windows. The cab shook a bit and the driver swore. A muffled cry came from outside and I glanced outward, seeing a bunch of reprobates tossing dried tree limbs and pieces of discarded lumber on what would soon be a gathering bonfire. The significance of the date, November the fifth, reasserted itself in my cognizance.

Guy Fawkes Day, I thought, dreading the inevitable open fires that would dot the nighttime sky. Was this reprehensible celebration really necessary?

"It appears that this night's celebrations have already commenced," Holmes said.

"A most disgraceful custom," I added. "Certainly indicative of the lower social classes."

"Of which we must always be aware," Holmes said. "Poverty breeds crimes as certainly as the rainfall feeds the crops. But it is also well to remember that crimes cross all social strata and harbors no such class distinctions."

The clip-clopping cadence of the horse's hooves slowed and the Hanson came to a stop. The slot popped open and the driver's bearded visage was visible once more.

"Here we are, gents. Scotland Yard."

"And in record time, as well," Holmes said, lifting his hand toward the slot to give the driver a stack of shillings. He was always very generous with the common man.

We exited the cab and approached the large, foreboding structure of the Yard. A barefoot urchin ran up to us offering boxes of matches. I shook my head, empathetically shuddering at the boy's bare soles on the cold cobblestones. Holmes, however, opened his purse and withdrew another stack of coinage.

"Here you go, young man. That should be enough for you to buy yourself a good pair of shoes."

The youth's lips drew back exhibiting some dreadful dentition, and he scooped up three small boxes of matches from his crate and handed them to the detective before scampering off.

"That boy will be lucky if he doesn't catch his death out here," I commented. "In weather such as this."

"Inclement temperatures for sure, Watson." Once again his thin face reflected a lips-only smile. "Let's hope Inspector Lestrade's heart is a bit warmer."

Inspector G. Lestrade sat behind his desk smoking a cigar and staring at a page of messy scribbling. A half-eaten apple was next to his tablet. He looked up in surprise as Holmes and I walked in, then his mouth edged into a smile that was reminiscent of the Cheshire Cat.

"I was wondering how long it was going to take for tough Eddie's family to enlist your services, Mr. Holmes." He brought the cigar to his lips, drew upon it, and exhaled a copious cloud of smoke. "But you're too late. We've already got this one wrapped up tighter than a harlot's girdle."

"A most intriguing choice of words, Lestrade," Holmes said, stepping forward. "However, I have been summoned by Lady Beth Covington to look into the particulars of this matter."

Lestrade's brow furrowed momentarily, then his expression seemed to wilt.

"Ah, I can't be blaming the lady in that case," he admitted. "But it'll do little good. We've got this one nailed shut and her son's only a few steps away from the gallows."

"Then you wouldn't mind us having a few words with the lad," Holmes suggested with a smile. "Would you?"

Lestrade brought the cigar to his lips again and blew out more odiferous smoke.

"I suppose that would be all right. But you'll be wasting your time. It's like I was telling you, we've got this one sewn up." He squinted through the haze of smoke and leaned forward. "Want me to tell you the particulars?"

"Most definitely," Holmes concurred. "That way I might explain the futility of any further investigation to my client."

Lestrade leaned back and clasped his hands behind his head. "Open and shut, it is. Plain as a bed bug running across a white sheet."

His repulsive similes were starting to grate on me, but I held my tongue. Holmes always stressed that when dealing with a blowhard, such as Lestrade, it was far better to cater to his vanity than to point out the folly of his theories.

"I'm assuming you've heard of The Velvet Slipper?" he asked.

"We have," Holmes replied. "Not the most reputable of social clubs in the city, but hardly a den of iniquity."

"I'll have to agree with you there," Lestrade said. "If you was to overlook what goes on in the upstairs portion of the establishment, it has a veil of what you could almost call respectability."

"And if you pulled back the curtain," Holmes continued, "you'd no doubt find some of the rather unlikely clientele."

Lestrade's mouth twisted into a sly grin.

"That you would. But just the same, when somebody as popular as Tough Eddie Hillary gets murdered, you can't expect he Yard to stand idly by. Especially when there's half a dozen eye witnesses."

"Eye witnesses?" Holmes repeated.

"Right as the mail," Lestrade beamed. "Young Mister Woodward and Tough Eddie were after the same bird on the black velvet swing. They came to blows two nights ago in front of a dozen witnesses, and then the young dandy came back last night and murdered his rival."

"And what type of proof do you have that this occurred?" Holmes asked.

"He was seen running from the room where it happened by a dozen witnesses." Lestrade pursed his lips and nodded, as if to reassure himself. "And then he was found lying in an alley a block or so away, passed out and dead drunk."

"Passed out?" Holmes raised an eyebrow. "Do you mean to say he was unconscious?"

Lestrade nodded emphatically and thrust his body forward, his forearms slamming onto the desk top. "And the front of his shirt was all covered with blood, and it wasn't his."

"What was the manner of death?" Holmes inquired.

"Hillary was stabbed. Once in the back and twice in the chest."

Holmes considered this. "Did you recover the weapon?"

Lestrade's brow furrowed again and he shook his head.

"I got a squad of men searching for it as we speak. No telling what he did with it, but my best guess is he flung it somewhere. We'll find it."

"May I see this shirt with the blood stains?" Holmes requested.

Lestrade grunted and stood up, stubbing the cigar out in an ashtray on the side of the desk.

Thank heavens, I thought. The odor from the stogie had been utterly unbearable.

He walked across the room, pulled open a cabinet, and removed a burlap sack. He undid the drawstring on the sack and took out a white shirt with the same fancy ruffles that young Collin had worn the night of the recital.

"Lestrade," Holmes said as he watched the Inspector unroll the garment. "You do realize that by bundling the shirt in such a manner that you've virtually destroyed any discernible pattern of the bloodstains."

Lestrade rolled his eyes. "Oh, please forgive me for not adhering to the strict and meaningless dictates of the great Sherlock Holmes." His voice was laden with sarcasm and derision. "But we been solving murders here at the Yard longer than you been in business, Mr. Holmes." He turned his baleful glare my way. "And we don't appreciate being portrayed as a bunch of bumbling incompetents in those supposed literary accounts you're so fond of writing, Doctor."

We stood facing one another, the blood soaked shirt lying in a wrinkled bundle on the desk between us. The stains had dried to the color of burnt auburn.

Holmes used his walking stick to unroll the garment and hoisted it upward, the empty sleeves drooping downward and displaying a plethora of gore.

He then lowered the stick causing the shirt to drop onto the desk.

"There's little to be gained from this," he declared. "I take it young Woodward was wearing it when he was arrested."

"Peeled it off him my very self," Lestrade said. "I know how to gather evidence when I see it."

Holmes didn't reply to the taunt. "Tell me, Lestrade, did young Woodward make a statement?"

Lestrade leaned back slightly with another frown.

"He was smart enough to keep his mouth shut about what he'd done.

Claims he don't remember anything about it."

"I see. May we see the contents of his pockets? And those of Mr. Hillary, as well?"

Lestrade heaved another heavy sigh before returning to the cabinet and taking out two large envelopes. He glanced at each and then tossed them onto the table next to the shirt.

Each had a string securing it. Holmes first picked up the one marked as marked *E H*.

After carefully undoing the string, he poured the contents out onto the table top and began sorting through it. I looked on with interest, intent of trying to match my powers of observation against those of Holmes. There was a large roll of currency and several coins, a book of matches, a box of cigarettes, and the usual assortment of gentleman's paraphernalia. Unfortunately, I saw nothing in the way of interest save for a perfumed card with the number *8* written on it by in apparent feminine cursive, an elaborate gold timepiece, and a spade-like bronze medallion.

"The Victoria Cross," I said in a tone of hushed reverence.

Holmes picked up the medallion, studied it for several seconds, and then replaced it in the envelope along with the other sundries.

"An appropriate enough memento to be carried on or about November the fifth," he said. "The anniversary date of the Battle of Inkermann."

After resealing it, he gazed toward Lestrade. "I'm certain you'll see the timepiece and the medal are returned to Mr. Hillary's family forthwith."

"Of course," Lestrade frowned. "I just haven't gotten around to it. I've been a tad busy writing my report, *Mr. Holmes*."

His tone lilted toward sarcasm once again as he uttered the detective's name.

Holmes ignored this taunt as well and opened the envelope with Collin Woodward's belongings. These proved even less informative than Hillary's had: a wad of currency, assorted coins, a ring with the family crest, a pocket watch, and a musical tuning fork.

After replacing these items, Holmes said, "May we speak to him now?"

Lestrade's mouth puckered into a knot as he considered the request.

"Perhaps we can help him regain his lost memory," Holmes offered.

"It might go better for him to express some remorse," Lestrade opined. "Standing there saying he can't recall anything in the face of all this evidence is bound to infuriate the magistrate." He stopped and squinted. "But don't you be putting any fancy ideas into his head, now."

"We wouldn't dream of it, Inspector. Now, if we may…"

Lestrade had a uniformed officer escort us back to the cell area in a remote part of the jail.

"He's a bit of a dinky bloke, if you know what I mean," the jailer said with a smirk. "We been keeping him in isolation, away from the burly boys we got locked up in here. Wouldn't do to let him get buggered before his trial now, would it?"

"Quite thoughtful," Holmes said. "I'm sure Lady Covington will be appreciative of the care her son is receiving."

The jailer looked a bit perplexed as he stopped in front of a solid looking door and slipped a huge skeleton key into the lock. He pulled open the door and stepped aside. The fading afternoon light entered the room by virtue of a barred window high up on the solid brick and mortar wall. The room was a scant eight by eleven, with a straw mattress on the floor and a bucket that had a putrid smell. Holmes strode over, looked in the bucket, and then picked it up.

"Would you be so kind as to empty this and see that he's given a clean one?" He extended the bucket toward the jailer, who accepted it with a frown. He held it at arm's length as he turned and locked the door, leaving the three of us alone in the small room.

I was taken aback by the lugubrious contrast of the robust young man we'd seen at the concert only two nights ago and the wretched creature who lay before us. He got up slowly from the straw bed and stood. He was wearing a striped prison garb that appeared much too big for him. His face had a haggard look to it, and I immediately took note of the swelling and discoloration on the left side of his face. His whole body seemed somehow shrunken and attenuated.

"Collin, I am Sherlock Holmes and this is my associate, Dr. Watson. We're here at the behest of your mother."

The young man appeared shocked.

"Quickly," Holmes urged, "before the guard returns, tell us everything you remember about the altercation last night between you and Tough Eddie Hillary."

Collin's dumbfounded expression didn't alter. Just as Holmes was about to give him another rebuke, the young man emitted a pitiful sobbing sound.

"But that's just it," he said between gasps. "I don't remember."

"Don't remember?" I echoed. "Are you saying you can't recall any of the particulars?"

Holmes shot me a look of rebuke, raising his left eyebrow to signal that I was not to intrude upon his questioning.

I took a step back, yielding to his superiority. Investigation was, after all, his forte.

"What is the last thing you do remember?" Holmes queried. "Prior to the police finding you."

Collin's eyes sought the floor. "I'm ashamed to say that I went back to the Velvet Slipper that evening. To see Jenny."

"Jenny?" Holmes' tone was interrogatory. "And she is… ?"

"The girl on the black velvet swing," the lad clarified. "It's short for Jennifer."

For a brief moment I saw a flash of brightness return to his eyes, but it quickly vanished.

"She's one of the entertainers at the club," Collin explained. "She's beautiful."

"I'm sure," Holmes nodded. "She is the same girl with whom you were spending time when the row between you and Edmond Hillary erupted the previous night?"

"Yes, the big lout. He was saying the worst things about her, and directed some insults my way as well."

"This was the previous evening?" Holmes asked. "When you and your step-father went there after the concert?"

"Yes."

"And the same night that you and Hillary engaged in some fisticuffs?"

"Quite right."

"Tell me what you recall about this first encounter between the two of you."

The youth took in a deep breath and I was suddenly aware just how willowy he was. His chest seemed to be but a sliver inside the baggy prisoner garb.

"We were there and Jenny swung up next to us," he said. "Earle, my step-father, put a few shillings into her bucket and we began talking. The longer the girl stays with you conversing, the more money you're expected to drop in her bucket. I'd had a bit too much to drink. I'm not used to consuming alcohol at all, but my step-father insisted. Kept saying that it was high time I engaged in a manly sort of behavior."

"And Hillary arrived and interceded?"

"Yes. He came striding over and grabbed the line of her swing, saying it was high time she swung over to him for a slap and tickle."

"A slap and tickle?" Holmes arched an eyebrow. "Those were the words he used?"

Collin's lips drew tight. "I believe it was."

"Although it's rather crudely put, Holmes," I said. "It does make perfect sense. Tough Eddie Hillary was a sergeant in the Forty-First Regiment during the Crimean War before he entered politics. A rough hewn bunch, those infantry men."

"Yes, Watson." His tone was dour. "I know." He focused his intense stare at Collin. "And the fisticuffs, do you recall who said what in the way of provocation?"

Collin's gaze once again returned to the floor of his cell.

"Not really, Mr. Holmes. As I said, I'd been imbibing, at the behest of my step-father, and my recollection of things is a bit foggy."

"And what of your step-father?" Holmes asked. "What action did he take during this altercation?"

"He wasn't there," Collin replied. "He'd excused himself to visit the loo right before Hillary sauntered over. Naturally, when he returned he stepped between us and warned him away. We left after that."

"Do you recall Hillary striking you?"

He pursed his lips, and then shook his head. "Not really. It's all just a bit of a fog. I do recall that he struck the first blow, but before I could retaliate, I was grabbed by several hands."

"And you say you returned there last night?"

"Yes, but it was by Jenny's invitation. She sent me a note. It was delivered to our house."

"A note?" Holmes lifted an eyebrow. "What did it say?"

"Just how regrettable the previous evening's incident had been and that I should come to her room at the Slipper at a quarter to eight that evening."

"A quarter to eight," Holmes repeated. "That was specified."

"It was. Along with her room number. It's on the second floor."

Holmes nodded.

"What did you do with this invitation?"

"I put it in my pocket."

"Did you show it to the police after they brought you here?"

He shook his head. "I told them about it, that Inspector Lestrade, but he said there was no note."

"And what happened after you arrived in the girl's room?"

The space between his eyebrows showed twin creases. "It's rather a blur. When I arrived she made a show of taking me upstairs. I recall being very excited. She was still wearing her performing costume." He paused and appeared to blush slightly. "Well, at least most of it. She has such a lovely

"A slap and tickle?" Holmes arched an eyebrow. "Those were the words he used?"

form." His tongue traced over his lips.

"And then what happened?"

"There was a bottle there. And two glasses. She was so easy to converse with, we laughed and I made a few jokes. We drank some of the wine together."

"Wine? You're certain it was wine?"

Collin nodded again.

"Was it white or red?" Holmes asked specifically.

"Eh?" The youth's brow furrowed at the question.

"The wine," Holmes repeated. "It was undoubtedly red, correct?"

"Yes, I believe it was. Why? Is that important?"

"Everything, at this point, has importance."

Collin's expression was one of confusion.

"And then Hillary arrived?" Holmes continued.

Collin's brow furrowed. "I can't honestly recall. I'm afraid I rather blanked out. The next I remember there were two policemen accosting me in the alleyway."

"Do you recall how the blood got onto your shirt?"

He shook his head.

"And when these policemen found you, is your recollection of this clear or nebulous?"

Collin's face twisted as if someone were applying a thumbscrew. "It's all a bit of a blur."

The light from the window was fading somewhat and Holmes told me to strike a match for more light. I took out my box of matches and lighted one.

"Let me examine your hands," Holmes said.

Collin extended his arms toward the detective, who clasped both of the other man's wrists. He rotated the limbs as he studied them and then released his clasp and stepped back.

The match was burning down and almost seared my fingers. I immediately dropped it and Holmes jumped over and stomped on it. He flashed a sly grin at me.

"Careful, old boy. We shouldn't want to set that straw on fire, would we?"

I glanced down at the straw-filled mattress and shuddered at my stupidity: dropping a lighted match in the presence of broken, bundled straw, while in a locked room with no water.

"Very well, Collin. Watson here is a doctor. Slip out of your clothes and let him examine you."

The youth pursed his lips, but complied.

Although the lighting was now poor, I did a cursory examination and found the boy to be without any serious maladies. As he was getting dressed I heard the sound of a key being placed in the lock. The door opened and the guard came in holding what I assumed to be a now-empty bucket and a bowl of gruel. I shuddered at the close proximity of the two, and was immediately reminded of the similar hardships I'd experienced in Afghanistan.

"Here's your—" the guard started to say. He canted his head slightly to the side and asked, "Here now, just what's going on?"

"I'm a physician, sir," I explained turning toward him. "And I was just giving this young man an examination."

"An examination?" the guard uttered.

"Quite right," Holmes added. "And my esteemed colleague is going to write up a full report on his findings for documentation purposes."

The guard's mouth twisted down at the corners. "Now see here, I already told you we was taking good care of him, didn't I?"

"That you did," Holmes recalled. "And I fully expect that care to continue. That would include providing the proper nourishment."

"I brought him his supper." The guard held up the bowl of gruel.

"Isn't it customary to provide a slice of bread as well?" Holmes remarked.

"Right in here," the guard said, tipping the empty waste bucket to the side to display a hunk of bread at the bottom. "We treats everybody in here with the utmost respect, and nobody better not say different."

I was mortified at the unsanitary act, but Holmes merely gave a curt nod and turned back to face Collin.

"Make the best of your short stay here," Holmes advised. "We shall return."

With that, we strode past the guard and out of the depressing cell.

We were fortunate enough to wave down a passing Hansom as we left the Yard. Once inside I took out my cigarette case and offered one to Holmes, who shook his head. I plucked one from the row, closed the case, and took out my box of matches. Holmes already had his out, as well, and struck a match against the primer of the box. He held the flame outward with an extended hand. I leaned forward to place the tip of my cigarette into the flickering yellow flame and drew in some of the smoke.

Anything to get the wretched stench of that cell out of my nasal cavities, I thought.

Holmes seemed to read my thoughts and smiled.

"A most inhospitable abode, eh, Watson?"

"Quite," I agreed, not wishing to dwell upon the embellishments.

"Where to, gentlemen?" the driver asked through the open slot.

"The City Morgue," Holmes directed and handed up some coins.

The driver grabbed them and slid the slot closed. The carriage lurched forward.

The cigarette smoke was doing little to offset the residual memory. I could have almost tasted the bitterness of the bowl of gruel, and the thoughts of that bread being in the same bucket as one used for excrement...

"Observations?" I asked, looking at Holmes through the tobacco-induced haziness.

"Our friend Lestrade has the unfortunate tenacity of a bulldog chewing on a leather shoe. He's reluctant to let go, even when he becomes cognizant that the taste is all but absent."

Once again I found myself chuckling at my friend's felicitous usage of metaphor.

"But what do you make of Collin's story? Seems a bit thin in parts."

"Attenuated for sure," Holmes admitted. "But only because the boy was giving some sort of intoxicant to induce unconsciousness. Probably chloral hydrate."

"The girl gave it to him?"

"Most likely she's involved to some degree. Which is why the wine was red instead of white, the scarlet color more adept at masking any suspicious discoloration. It's safe to conjecture that he was given the drink to place him in a compliant and stuporous condition, after which this nefarious plan was unfolded."

"So, may I assume that we're going to talk to this Jenny after we view the body?"

"Right again, Watson. Your investigative abilities are improving with each new outing. But she is obviously no more than a supernumerary in this particular play."

I was secretly pleased by the compliment. Although I harbored no misgivings that my own cognitive abilities were in the same league as his, I did fashion myself a pretty fair investigator, having been with Holmes on so many occasions, not to mention my frequent chronicling of his cases.

"Do you want to fashion a guess as to who might be behind all this?" I asked.

Holmes raised an eyebrow. "Watson, you know I never guess. It's an appalling habit that is inimical to one's logical faculties."

He took out the black clay pipe once again and held a lighted match over the still-packed bowl. We rode the rest of the way to the City Morgue in silence.

I must admit that despite having gone through medical school and having served in both India and Afghanistan under the worst of circumstances, the occasional trips I'd made to the City Morgue with Holmes always were disconcerting. The particular design of the cold, cavernous building with its white tiled walls, rough cement floors, and blood-stained metal tables was eerie enough, but the overwhelming odor of decaying bodies was most disturbing. I often remarked that one could smell the place a few blocks away, and Holmes seemed to take particular delight in pointing out the accuracy of my pronouncement.

"Ah, Watson." He raised his hand with his index finger extended. "Your perspicacious prediction about the odiferous aspect of our destination has once again proven correct." He tapped his index finger on the side of his aquiline nose. "It seems we are almost there."

And soon we were. After disembarking from the cab, we hustled up the steps and into the foyer and requested an immediate audience with the chief coroner. The meek looking clerk gazed up at us in astonishment from behind a long wooden counter.

"And whom shall I say is calling?" he asked. He was bald, save for a fringe of white hair above his ears, and he wore a set of pince-nez glasses perched on a nose that had obviously been broken and not properly reset.

"Tell the chief coroner that Mr. Sherlock Holmes wishes to see him regarding an urgent matter of the utmost importance," I said.

The little man's eyes widened and he scurried off through a door like a rat in search of a butcher tossing out the scraps.

Holmes canted his head and smiled at me.

"Well done, dear fellow."

"It wasn't me." I smiled. "Your reputation precedes you."

Presently the mousy man returned and pointed to a solid wooden door on the opposite side of the room.

"He's waiting for you in his office," he said.

Holmes thanked the little man and we made our way over to the door. He raised his walking stick and tapped three times on the mahogany surface.

"Come," a gruff voice said from the other side.

We went in and were treated to the rather unfamiliar sight of a rather short, rotund man standing next to a desk clad in brown tweed trousers, a ruffled white shirt, and a full apron that was streaked with ribbon-like stains of crimson. His bushy head of hair seemed to coat his head like a bronze helmet and extended down in front of each ear to join with an equally hirsute mustache. I hadn't seen this gentleman before, but apparently Holmes had.

"Ah, Mr. Slacker," he said. "So nice of you to see us. I assume Mr. Brownlow is predisposed?"

"'e's out with the croup." Slacker's accent was pure Cockney. "What can I do *fer* you, Mr. 'olmes?"

"May I first present my friend and associate, Dr. John H. Watson, M.D. Watson, this is Mr. Browlow's first chief assistant, Mr. Orlmand Slacker."

"Pleased to meet you," Slacker said. He made no offer to shake hands, which suited me perfectly well. I returned the salutation.

"Inspector Lestrade requested that we review the body of Mr. Edmund Hillary," Holmes said, "whom I believe you have in one of your examination rooms."

Slacker fished in his pocket, withdrew a half-burnt cigar, and began patting himself.

"Please," Holmes offered. "Allow me."

The detective took out a book of matches and struck one, holding it in front of the stout man's jowly face. Slacker leaned forward so that the tip of his cigar met the flame.

I must admit, even the noxious odor of the man's foul smelling tobacco was welcome in the putrescent atmosphere.

"What's Lestrade want with 'im?" Slacker asked. "I already sent 'im the bloody report. The bugger was stabbed to death."

Holmes smiled in a disarming fashion.

"There seems to be a bit of concern regarding the murder weapon. We may need to match it to one that was recently recovered."

Slacker blew out a plume of smoke and cocked his head for us to follow. He went through a door on the side wall and we followed him down a long corridor. I felt like pulling my scarf over my nose, but knew it would do little good. At the end of the corridor Slacker turned sharply to his left and we entered a large room with half a dozen rows of tables with metal tops set on sturdy wooden legs. The walls were white tiles, except for the outer wall, which was composed of undecorated bricks. At least half a dozen of the tables were covered with gray sheets, each of which covered a cadaver.

Slacker strode to one in the second row, pulled up the coarse covering, checked a paper tag affixed to a human toe, and then whipped the material off, exposing the body.

"'ere 'e is."

We stepped forward and peered down at the supine figure. Tough Eddie Hillary had been a large, robust man in life, and his corpse was already showing signs of bloating. His chest was massive and covered with a heavy matt of gray hair. I estimated his age to be approximately fifty-five to fifty-seven, based on my knowledge of his military service during the Crimean War. He had a faded tattoo on his left forearm commemorating the campaign. His skin was now the color of curdled milk, the eyes open and veiled with the murky curtain of death, and his mouth fixed in a rictus grin. There were two large gashes on the front of the torso, one on the side of his substantial abdomen, and the other just under his mandible.

"Gutted and throttled," Slacker said. "Got another one of them on 'is back."

Holmes removed a measuring tape and his pocket magnifier and leaned forward, first studying the wounds with his magnifier, and then pressing the measuring tape alongside. I saw an ever-so-slight twitching of his right eyebrow and then he straightened up.

"May I view that one on his dorsal side as well? Watson, give him a hand. This elevation looks as though it will require a somewhat substantial effort."

Slacker heaved a sigh and shifted the cigar to the left side of his mouth and gripped the right arm of the corpse. He gestured with his head for me to do so with the leg. I stepped forward, my nostrils flaring from the pugnacious assault of the cigar smoke and the unpleasant odor of decay, and seized Tough Eddie's right calf. The effects of rigor mortis had already commenced, and my fingers sunk into the desiccated flesh.

"Yer gonna 'ave to grab 'is arse, mate," Slacker indicated. "'e's a big bugger."

With the utmost reluctance, I placed my left hand under the dead man's buttocks and hoped he hadn't voided upon sustaining his death wounds. After a count of three we managed to flip the body over. It made a solid, plopping sound and it flipped completely face-down, the rigor mortis-stiffened limbs remaining as solid as a statue.

I saw another large gash on the right side of the back, in the approximate area of the kidney. Just as the one on the front side, this one showed a wide entry through the flesh. Holmes repeated his examination and measurement, but then replaced the measuring tape in his pocket and removed a small pen knife. He extracted the blade and poked the tip into the wound, lifting the ragged flap of skin. He brought the magnifier to play again, and leaned closer. After perhaps a minute or more of studying and occasional poking, he straightened up, folded the blade of the knife back, and put both items back into his pocket.

"Inspector Lestrade sends his gratitude," he said. "I'll be certain to convey a report of your invaluable assistance."

Slacker snorted and grabbed the coarse sheet, pulling it over the corpse.

"Aren't you going to right him?" I asked. "Roll him onto his back again?"

"What the 'ell for?" Slacker expelled an effluvium of smoke into the air. "This way 'e can be telling the world to lay a kiss on 'is arse."

Darkness had fully descended as we rode in yet another Hanson cab toward our next destination. I tried to review all of the discrete facts that we had come across thus far, but none of them lent themselves to any possible conjectures. To me, it all seemed like a bunch of disparate instances strung together without any overall definition. The cab swerved and I felt a blast of heat radiating from a large bonfire in the street. Several hooligans, obviously plied with too much liquor, tossed a broken chair onto the conflagration. Although it seemed more peaceful than the street demonstrations of the past, I wondered how much longer the authorities could afford to allow this wild behavior to endure.

Presently I felt the coach drawing to a halt. The slot popped open and driver's gnarly face presented itself with a lecherous grin.

"Here it is, gents," he announced. "The Velvet Slipper. Enjoy yourselves."

"Most assuredly," Holmes slipped him the payment.

Periodic fires in the street dotted the night a bit farther down the block and the scent of acrid smoke hung in the air like a perverse fog. As we walked toward the club a voice called out to us.

"Mr. Holmes."

We turned and I saw Lord Covington approaching. He'd traded his resplendent uniform for a plain brown suit and a gray overcoat. The hairs of his substantial mustache were heavily peppered with gray.

"Lord Covington," Holmes said, turning. "May we be of assistance?"

"I've been searching for you. My wife told me that she'd hired you to look into this matter concerning Collin."

"That is correct."

"Well. What have you found out?"

Holmes didn't reply immediately and I assumed he was choosing his words carefully, given that the Colonel's stepson was facing a charge of murder.

"At this point, I am still assembling the facts of the case. I make it a point not to engage in speculation until I have a full grasp of all the elements."

"But have you found anything pertinent?" Covington pressed. "Anything that might clear him? My wife's in an extremely delicate state with worry. Collin is her only son."

"Please inform her that I am diligently investigating the matter, and I shall contact her as soon as I find anything of significance."

The Colonel's face became furrowed with deep creases of concern and his gaze turned downward.

"Very well. I was just hoping for better news."

Holmes regarded him closely. "As I told you, we are diligently investigating."

"I'm prepared to pay you whatever you wish. If you can prove my step-son's innocence."

"We can settle upon my fee later. Now, we must be going, but is it possible that you might remain in the vicinity hereabouts so that we may converse with you after we complete our interrogation at the Velvet Slipper?"

Lord Covington pulled out his watch, flipped it open, and then shook his head.

"I'm afraid I really must be getting back to my wife. I've been trying to find you for the better part of the afternoon. If he goes to the gallows, she may not survive the strain. I'm very concerned for her health."

"As are we all, sir," Holmes said. "Rest assured I shall be in touch as soon as I have something to report."

Covington nodded with the curtness of a former military man and thanked us for our efforts, reaffirming that money was no object. The smoke in the air had grown thicker as he walked away, providing an almost ghostly aura as he hailed a cab.

"Poor chap," I observed. "He seems a bit overwrought. I do hope that Lady Covington is all right. Do you think I should make a house call to check on her?"

"Possibly. But not now."

"Well, from the sound of it, Holmes, this could be quite lucrative for you, should you be able to clear the boy."

"Watson, you of all people should know that I seldom venture these mean streets in search monetary rewards."

His eyes narrowed and he suddenly strode forward toward a gaslight lamppost and then stopped.

I quickly followed.

Holmes bent down and studied the area by the curbside for several seconds, then retrieved something from the ground. As I drew closer, I saw that it was a partially burned cigar.

"What's this?" I asked.

"A cigar, Watson." He rotated the disgusting item in his fingers, then brought it to his nose and sniffed.

"Holmes, please."

He laughed and tossed it away, but not before dragging his walking stick among the cobblestones a few times. "Come, Watson, let us not dally. We've an appointment to keep. But you do recall that I have done quite a comprehensive study of the various types of cigar, cigarette, and pipe ashes."

"One hundred and forty different types," I answered recalling one of his pronouncements.

"One hundred-forty-two, to be exact," he elaborated. "And that one is of an Indian tobacco variety."

"Indian? I wonder if Covington's manservant was with him?"

We'd reached the double-storied structure with a large sign featuring a lady's elegant shoe painted on a large sign fastened perpendicular to the building. Inside there was a glow from numerous lamplights that shone through a large, plate-glass window. Holmes pulled open the door and allowed me to enter first.

Although I'd heard a few members of my social club speak of the Velvet Slipper in hushed tones, I must admit I was hardly prepared for the rather garish opulence. A long, polished bar was set against one wall and curved out onto the floor in the shape of a horseshoe. Mirrors were fixed on all of the walls, giving the illusion that the room itself was larger than it actually was. There were numerous tables and chairs spaced in columns along the open part of the floor, and comely hostesses busied themselves bringing glasses of ale and plates of roasted chicken to the ready customers. Perhaps most startling of all were the various swings that were suspended from an enormous wheel-like contraption affixed to and running parallel to the ceiling, each part moving independently from the other, like the gears of an enormous watch. It slowly rotated, in the fashion of a horizontal windmill, and suspended from each of these separate section was a long

Holmes allowed me to enter first.

velvet-covered swing, upon which sat a pretty girl clad in a revealing bodice and colored silk stockings. The velvet on each swing was a different color, and the perching girl's costume corresponded to it. I saw girls on swings of red, green, blue, and orange.

The black velvet swing, however, was empty.

We moved to the bar and shouldered a place against the finely polished mahogany. Holmes placed his deerstalker hat on the bar and ordered us two stouts. When the bartender set them down in front of us, Holmes slipped him what was obviously an overpayment.

"Thank you, sir," the barman said, pocketing the coins.

"We heard you had a bit of trouble here last night," Holmes said.

"I'll say," the barman replied, settling both of his burly forearms on the polished surface and leaning toward us. He placed a cigarette between his lips and struck a match to light it. "One of our best customers was murdered right up there." He pointed to a staircase leading to the second floor. His lips peeled back showing a craggy set of substantially gapped teeth.

"Tough Eddie Hillary, I hear," Holmes prodded.

The bartender gave a definitive nod with his head.

"A good bloke, he was, gov'nur. Always made sure he took good care of me and the other barmen. And the girls."

The gap-toothed grin reappeared with a lascivious twist.

"And you actually saw the murder take place?" Holmes asked.

The barman's cheeks hollowed momentarily as he drew on his cigarette. When he started speaking the smoke seemed to embrace each exiting word.

"Not directly. We was all down here, hard at work. Jenny, that's his regular girl, was upstairs entertaining. She'd taken this red-headed young bloke upstairs with her. Then Tough Eddie, that's what we called him, comes waltzing in asking for her. Now, not wanting any trouble, I says to him that she's busy fixing herself and why don't he have a drink to loosen himself a tad." He drew upon the cigarette once again and blew out a cloud of smoke. "Well, Eddie looks at his watch and says to me, 'She told me to be here at eight sharp, so I guess she's fixing herself for me.' And then he goes traipsing up the stairs, he does. I signaled Mick, he's that big bloke standing over in the corner that takes care of any trouble makers, to stand ready, just in case." The tip of the cigarette glowed again. "Now, Eddie's been coming here for years, and he's no fop, mind you. Not only is he a big fellow, but he's strong as a bloody bull. Won the Victoria Cross, he did, back in the Crimean War."

"The Battle of Inkermann," Holmes added.

The barman snapped his fingers. "It was. And the little titmouse that had come to see Jenny not fifteen to twenty minutes before looked like a cousin to Oscar Wilde. I didn't think he'd give Eddie no guff, so I didn't try to stop him when he went on up." He shook his head and withdrew the cigarette, now a tiny stub, and tossed it down behind the bar. I could tell he used his foot to grind it out. When he looked up, his expression was animated. "Then all of a sudden I hear this commotion going on upstairs, and I hear a woman screaming. As Mick's running up the stairs, Eddie comes staggering out of Jenny's room holding his throat, blood just pouring out of him, and he falls pell-mell down the steps, knocking old Mick off his feet. Little Lord Fauntleroy, the bloke who went to see Jenny first, comes running up to the top of the stairs, looks down at us over his shoulder, and then disappears. He went out the back way."

"The back way?" Holmes asked. "There's another door?"

The barman gave a slight nod and showed us his awful dentition once again.

"For the gentlemen callers, like Eddie, to leave by. There's a set of stairs that leads down to the alley."

"I think we should like to speak with Jenny." Holmes pushed some more coins across the top of the bar. "Is she available? Her swing seems to be vacant."

Just then the buxom girl on the red velvet swing swung by. She was a fetching, dark haired wench with a lot of rouge and an expertly placed patch.

"Hey, Angie," the barman called out. "Where's Jenny? These gents want to buy her a drink."

Angie raised a bare shoulder in a demur gesture and shrugged. "She's probably upstairs, but she ain't with nobody. Said she was feeling a bit off, on account of her monthly."

"It would be worth your while to escort us up there." Holmes peeled some bills off his roll of currency and handing one to the barman and one to Angie. "We'd like to speak with her."

Her dark eyes flashed from Holmes to me with a glint of avarice, and she quickly grabbed the bill and stuffed it down between a substantial bit of cleavage at the front of her bodice. Then she gripped the red velvet strands suspending the swing and edged off of it. I noticed sweaty tuffs of dark stubble on her underarms, and caught the distinct odor of pungent, feminine perspiration.

"Come on." She waved at is. "I'll show you. I got to use the chamber pot anyway."

The barman winked at us and moved away, digging into his pocket for another cigarette.

We followed the girl's ample, swinging hips as she led us up the staircase to the second floor. I couldn't help but notice that the wooden steps were dappled with spots of dark brownish stains, which I took to be Hillary's blood.

"Did you know the man who was murdered here last night?" Holmes exhibited his customary quickness of foot stepping up beside her as we ascended. My war wound to my leg kept me from taking the other side of her, but I was still close enough to overhear.

"Oh, sure," she said. "He was one of her regulars. I was with him a few times, but he settled on her, which is fine with me. She's got a real pretty shape, and sometimes we'd…"

She left the rest to our imaginations.

"How about the other man she saw last night?" Holmes questioned. "Had he been in here before as well?"

"The young duffer?" Her pert nose crinkled and she shook her head. "Didn't seem like it. Maybe once."

We arrived at the top of the stairs and she led us down the hall. I peered toward the far end and saw a lighted gaslight attached to the wall next to a banister. I assumed that was the staircase to the back exit.

Angie pushed open a door and went inside, beckoning us to follow. The room had a dresser, a bed, and three wooden chairs. A basin and pitcher sat upon the dresser. She turned and smiled and I was pleasantly surprised to see that she had nice teeth.

"I was telling a bit of a fib downstairs. Jenny ain't up here. She went out to see her new fellow, but I guarantee you I'm twice as good as she is."

With that she began to pull open her bodice, as if to verify her claim.

Holmes reached up and seized her wrist with his left hand.

"Stop. We're not interested in pulchritude. We want information."

With that his right hand came up with a pound note.

Angie eyed the bill and then dropped her hands from her breast. Her smile dissipated and she was suddenly transformed from the alluring wench to an avaricious one. She reached for the pound note, but Holmes drew his hand back with his customary innate quickness.

"Not quite yet, madam. First, our questions."

Her full lips drew into a pout, but then she tilted her head to the side and the exquisite smile resumed.

"All right, love. What is it you want to know?"

"Jenny. How long ago did she leave?"

"We was up here fixing ourselves just a bit before you two came in. I was just getting on my swing when you was talking to Kips. The barman."

"And she was going out to meet someone?"

"That's what she said."

"And whom might that be?"

Her shapely bare shoulders shrugged. "Her new fellow. I don't know his name. She never told me. Been seeing him lately, when Eddie wasn't around."

Holmes raised an eyebrow. "What did he look like?"

"Don't know that neither." Her eyes were glued on the note. "She never saw him up here. Always at her place. But I don't think it was for..." Her full lips pursed as she shrugged once again. "Anything romantic, if you know what I mean. I asked her about it and she just laughed and said it wasn't nothing that would wear out the bedsprings."

Holmes thought for a moment, and then his eyes narrowed.

"Give me her address."

"What?" Her voluptuous mouth twisted downward and she uttered a vulgarity.

Holmes stared at her intently. "Now."

Angie leaned back, arms akimbo. "You ain't figuring on going over there to start something, are you? I don't want to be getting in no trouble the likes of last night."

"The address," Holmes handed her the note and withdrawing another from his pocket. "Be quick about it, girl. Your friend's life may be at stake."

Her dark eyes widened and she rattled off the address.

"Did you get that Watson?" He gave her the bill and pivoted toward the door. "Come. We have no time to lose. I pray that we're not too late."

Instead of going back down the stairs to the front of the club, Holmes turned left and literally ran down the hallway toward the rear exit. I followed, lagging a bit behind because of my leg. When I finally descended the stairs and went out the rear door, I glanced toward the street and saw Holmes frantically waving to me. He'd flagged down a passing cab and was holding the door open.

I was out of breath as I arrived at the side of the cab. Holmes assisted my assent inside and then stepped up himself, pausing to give the driver the address.

"That's just down the street," the driver said. "You could walk it in five minutes."

"Then make it in two." Holmes handed the fellow the fare and then some.

The driver grinned and nodded.

Holmes threw himself inside and slammed the door. I was still trying to recover my breath.

"A nefarious plot, Watson. We've not a moment to spare."

We passed another bonfire in the street, surrounded by a rowdy group, and the cab swerved causing me to bump into Holmes, who was half-leaning out the window.

"Will you please tell me whom we're looking for?" I said, finally recovering enough to speak without respiratory distress.

Holmes ignored my query, his head still out the window. I leaned out my side, trying to get a glimpse of what was taking all of his attention.

"Load your revolver, Watson," he ordered, partially turning back to me, "If you haven't done so already."

I felt for the Webley Mark III in my coat pocket and took it out, pulling on the release to allow access to the unloaded cylinder. I had the six shells in my separate pocket and thrust my fingers into it to retrieve them. The cab swerved again, I assumed to avoid more of the meddlesome revelers, causing me to drop all but one of the cartridges. I swore and bent over feeling around the area by my feet for them.

"Hullo," Holmes exclaimed. "Driver, stop. Stop immediately."

We'd been traveling at a pretty fast rate and the driver's sudden restriction on the reins caused me to be thrust back against the seat.

"I say, Holmes, will you please tell me what's going on, for God's sake."

But he was pushing open the door as I spoke, before the carriage had even come to a complete stop. Holmes bounded through the door and into the smoke-laden night. I snapped the Webley closed and scrambled out as well, having only successfully loaded one chamber of the revolver.

"I say," I yelled up to the driver. "Can you pass down your lantern?"

"Huh? What for?"

"I believe I left my cartridges in your cab."

"Your what?"

"My cartridges. My bullets, man." I held up the weapon. "For my service revolver."

The driver's eyes got as wide as a pair of saucers and he cracked the whip over the poor horse's flank. The animal surged away, and the open door of the cab struck my shoulder, knocking me to the cobblestones.

"Blast it all," I shouted, picking myself up. I looked about in the murky, smoke-filled air, searching for Holmes, but didn't see him among the scattered crowds of wretched topers bandying about in profligate dances among the burning stacks.

"Holmes," I called out.

His voice rang out in the squalid haziness. "Here, Watson. Quickly."

I waved my hand in front of my face in an effete gesture to clear my view. Then I saw his lithe figure loping after a burly man in a black overcoat carrying a rolled up carpet over his shoulder. It appeared to be a rather heavy load. Lambent shadows flickered over his form giving him a specter-like appearance in the haze as he walked toward a large bonfire.

I ran toward them just as Holmes reached him, grabbed the man, and spun him around. The rolled-up burden tumbled from his shoulder and fell to the street with a sodden thud. Two ne'-do-wells approached the fallen bundle with glee and picked it up, carrying it toward a near-by bonfire.

"That rug," Holmes yelled as he struggled with the burly figure. "Don't let them take it. Stop them, Watson."

I pointed the Webley at them. "Put that down!"

Their eyes widened and they dropped the load and scampered off.

I ran to it and then looked back to see Holmes backing away from his redoubtable opponent, who was now holding a horrendous looking knife like a miniature scythe. I recognized it immediately as an *akuhkun*, an Indian weapon. He swung the blade at Holmes, who slipped out of range while unwinding his scarf from around his neck. The burly knave advanced, the wisps of smoke evaporating enough for me to discern a swarthy complexion and a full, dark beard. The fearsome visage had the ring of familiarity as well.

It was the Indian manservant of Lord Covington.

Holmes took two more large steps back, and at the same time began whirling the scarf over his head. It spun around like a whirling gyre for several seconds, and then he released it. The scarf cut through the air and wound around the Indian's neck with the alacrity and precision of a boa constrictor. A row of white teeth flashed a grimace between the hirsute jaws, and he dropped the *akuhkun* as his hands tore at the material. Holmes jumped forward and kicked the large knife out of reach. I raised the Webley and pointed it at the Indian.

"Halt," I shouted. "Or I'll shoot."

He surged forward, his breath coming in ragged gasps, his massive hands reaching out toward me.

"Shoot him, Watson," Holmes yelled. "Don't let him get his hands on you. He's incredibly powerful."

I fired and once again the gashing teeth flashed, appearing like an exposed whiteness of bone showing through an open wound.

The Indian jerked slightly, but continued to advance, albeit at a slower pace than before. I squeezed the trigger, but heard only a clicking sound as the hammer fell upon an empty chamber.

Just as the brute's hand seized my sleeve, I tried to pull away but he moved with a preternatural quickness and his other hand encircled my throat. I gripped his hand with both of mine, trying in vain to dislodge his iron grip as the smoky darkness seemed to eclipse before me.

Holmes appeared over the Indian's back and drove the tip of the large knife into my attacker's back. He stiffened, the vise-like grip on my throat dissipating, and then he dropped.

"Hoisted on his own petard," Holmes said with a smile.

"My Lord," I gasped. "He was a tough bugger."

"He was a *Gurka*, Watson. I'm sure you have heard of them."

I knew what he meant. When I'd been in India, legend had it that if a man doesn't fear death, he's either a fool or a *Gurka*.

"Certainly." I said. "I was stationed over there, you know."

"And equally appropriate that I was able to initially subdue him using a *rumal*," Holmes said, unwinding the scarf from the man's neck and jingling the weighted coins in a pocket at one end.

The *rumal*, I thought. The preferred weapon of the *Phansigar* strangling cult of India.

"Now, Watson, let us check on the misfortunate Jenny, whom we saved from certain immolation."

"Eh?"

Holmes squatted next to the bundled carpet and pushed, causing it to unroll. As it unfolded the body of a young woman suddenly became visible.

"Great Scott." I knelt beside her to assess her condition.

"Does she live?" Holmes asked.

I placed my palm on her chest and felt the rise of her breathing. Her pulse seemed strong as well, although she had a vicious looking bruise forming on the side of her face.

"I think she'll be all right. But we need to get her to a hospital to be certain."

"An excellent suggestion," Holmes agreed. "And then we can proceed to Scotland Yard to speak with Lestrade and tell him to issue a warrant for the arrest of Sir Earle Covington and the immediate release of Collin Woodward."

I was aghast. "Lord Covington? He's involved in this?"

Holmes lifted his hand and clapped me on the shoulder. "I'm afraid so, old fellow. Despite his military service, he engineered the murder of his chief political rival, Tough Eddie Hillary, and then framed his stepson. I don't doubt that Lady Beth Covington would have been next. You recall how he mentioned her distraught condition over the arrest of her son, and his comment that he worried she may not survive the strain. Add to that the marital discord between them. You'll recall that she came to us singularly, independent of her husband. What dedicated mate would allow such an absence, and what wife would not wish her husband to be by her side in such a time of strife?"

I did remember that. "But how did you know he was involved?"

"I suspected as much when Lord Covington accosted us outside of the Velvet Slipper, claiming to have been searching for us. There was no conceivable way he could have traced our movements to locate us there, so his unexpected appearance had to have had another, more logical explanation. The Indian cigar led me to suspect that his manservant was in the vicinity as well, but if you recall, Lord Covington hailed a cab upon his departure. And you recall it was he who brought young Collin to the club and introduced him to Jenny."

"Obviously," I theorized, "he was setting the stage. Then he was Jenny's other fellow?"

"Precisely. And no doubt he used the girl on the black velvet swing to seduce, and then drug his stepson while his *Gurka* assassin did the dirty work. I suspected as much when I saw the nature of the wounds on Tough Eddie's body. They were obviously made by a *akuhkun*."

"But the witnesses to the crime," I stammered. "Didn't they say they saw Collin leaving the scene?"

"They saw what they *thought* was Collin," Holmes corrected. "And that was at a distance. I believe that once we examine the *Gurka's* hair and beard, we'll find traces that it was chemically altered to give it the reddish appearance consistent with Collin's auburn mane. Provide a collection of drunkards with a deception, and they are usually susceptible to whatever prompt is projected."

He turned and went to summon a passing policeman.

I stared down at the two bodies lying at my feet, grateful that one was dead and the other still breathing.

As we ate breakfast the next morning at Baker Street I was very forlorn over the preceding evening's events, despite the successful conclusion of Holmes's case. I caught him staring at me over the rim of his teacup.

"Well, Watson," he said. "Have you come upon a title for your pending literary detailing of our last case?

"Hardly." I pushed my scrambled eggs around on the plate.

"May I suggest The Adventure of the Girl on the Black Velvet Swing?"

I managed to emit a not-so-hardy chuckle.

"Truthfully, I doubt I should write about this one, Holmes. I mean think of the harm to be done to Lady Beth and her son, not to mention the stain on the memory of an officer in the Fifth Northumberland Fusiliers. Disgraceful conduct, if I may say so."

"Lord Covington's distinguished military exploits on behalf of King and Country will be remembered for their own merit, but notwithstanding, the man is guilty of several heinous crimes. Unfortunately, following his hero-ics, he was subsequently debased by one of the seven deadly sins. Greed." He leaned back in his chair and placed his fingers together in his familiar steeple-like gesture. "A motive as old as civilization itself and one which has sorely corrupted many a once-noble man."

"I'm simply amazed that he almost got away with it," I confessed. "And, despite the newspapers giving all the credit to Lestrade once again, he would have succeeded, too, had not you interceded and discovered the nefarious duplicity."

"As we had been discussing not too long ago," he said, setting his tea cup down. "The duality of man and the internal struggle of virtue over vice, is often a strange and troubling journey."

"Quite."

Holmes smiled. "That reminds me, I have a bit of recreational reading for you that will hopefully take your mind away from those imponderable questions." He slid the penny dreadful featuring the Stevenson novella across the table.

I frowned down at it. "But I've already read this drivel."

"Only the strange story of Dr. Jekyll and Mr. Hyde. There's second story in it that merits your attention."

"There is? Which one?"

Holmes rose from his chair and strode to the window. "It's called 'Markheim.' Do give it reading. It's quite entertaining, but now I perceive we have guests."

"Guests? Who is it?"

"Lady Beth and Collin," he went to the door. "Are you ready to receive them?"

I arose and covered my plate with a napkin just as he opened the door. The two of them were ushered inside by Mrs. Hudson and Holmes escorted them past our breakfast dishes and into the sitting room. Despite the dour news regarding her husband's treachery, I must say she looked exceptionally radiant. Collin, save for his discolored eye and swollen cheek, looked ebullient as well as they expressed their appreciation to Holmes and myself.

Lady Beth pulled open the handbag she had been holding on her lap and withdrew a checkbook.

"Mr. Holmes, I'm afraid we never discussed your fee. If I may use your pen, I'll write you a check to cover it."

Holmes smiled. "It is reward enough that a grievous wrong was averted."

"But your fee—" Lady Beth protested. "You did so much. We could hardly expect you to work for nothing. You must accept some just reward. I insist."

Holmes gave a small nod of his head, then got up and moved over to the mantel. "I did incur some minor investigative expenses, all of which can be easily rectified." He removed his violin from its case and handed it to Collin. "My fee will be having the distinct pleasure of once again hearing Collin play Mendelsshon's *Leider*."

The young man smiled and removed the tuning fork from his pocket, struck it on his knee, and plunked the violin string in melodic accompaniment.

Holmes smiled and handed him the bow, and then strode over to his most comfortable chair and sat down, placing the first two fingers of each hand upon his temple. I sat down as well, and the room was suddenly filled with the exquisite notes of the enthralling rhapsody.

THE END

WRITING THE HOLMES ADVENTURE

Back in my undergrad days in college I was an English major, and one of my areas of specialty was the literature of the Victorian Age. While I enjoyed the essays of John Stuart Mills and Thomas Carlyle, as well as the poetry of Robert Browning, I was a bit dismayed that the academics ignored the works of some of the best writers of the time. These professors not only failed to include these authors in their curriculums, they tended to look down their noses at them. My retort then, as it is now, was, "Let's ask the reading public if they're familiar with Mills or Carlyle, and see if anybody's reading them." It's my guess that they'd probably ask if they're the guys who work down at the local Home Depot. But even today if you ask them if they've heard of H.G. Wells or Sir Arthur Conan Doyle or Robert Louis Stevenson and you'll see an instant recognition flicker in their eyes. These were the preeminent writers of the period and are the ones who have survived the test of time. So when the opportunity to write another Sherlock Holmes story for Airship 27 presented itself, I once again jumped at the chance to pay homage to the greatest detective of them all.

I've been a life-long fan of Holmes and Watson and of Robert Louis Stevenson as well. I can remember the first time I read *The Strange Case of Dr. Jekyll and Mr. Hyde* as a youth. The story fascinated me, and later, when I reread it as an adult, I saw the nuances that Stevenson imbued into the plot. It was a classic examination of the duality of man. His short story, "Markheim," which I also reference in "The Adventure of the Girl on the Black Velvet Swing," is another examination of this same theme, which I hope is somewhat echoed in my own story.

My original idea was to do a version of Holmes vs. Dr. Jekyll and Mr. Hyde, but that had already been done in a novel many years ago. Additionally, Stevenson's story is so well known, it would impinge upon the mystery in the plot, and the Holmes stories were known for that feature. The recent riots that swept our nation this past spring and summer, and in some cities still continue as I write this, also weighed heavily on me as I struggled to concentrate on writing. Then I recalled the annual Guy Fawkes Day, and the riots that afflicted England during the Nineteenth Century, and I knew I had to include some of that and give Watson a

95

chance to comment. Guy Fawkes was a radical Englishman who orchestrated the failed "Gunpowder Plot," a plan to blow up Parliament back on November 5, 1605.

All of these elements went into my writing of "The Girl on the Black Velvet Swing," but my greatest motivation came from working in tandem with my friend, Ray Lovato, who was also working on his own Sherlock Holmes story, "The Adventure of the Queen's Tiara," as I was writing mine. I knew I had to finish it, because he was working so diligently on finishing his. It's my sincere hope that both of our stories (his is actually a novella and it's really good) will appear in the same Airship 27 anthology. Once again, I'd like to thank Captain Ron Fortier and art master, Rob Davis, for making these great tributes to the world's greatest consulting detective possible.

MICHAEL A. BLACK - is the author of forty-eight books and over one hundred short stories and articles. His latest novel is *Devil's Vendetta* and he is also writing the Mack Bolan Executioner series as Don Pendleton (*Stealth Assassin, Dying Art, Cold Fury*). Being in this anthology once again fulfills his lifelong ambition to write a Sherlock Holmes story.

Sherlock Holmes

in

THE ADVENTURE OF THE QUEEN'S TIARA

by
Raymond Louis Lovato

It was approximately ten o'clock in the morning when I climbed up the seventeen steps to the second-floor apartment on 221 B Baker Street to join my companion Sherlock Holmes. It was a hazy Monday morning as the heat was already rising from the cobblestone pavement promising a warm autumn day. As I was about to knock I heard, "Come in, Watson," from behind the closed door.

I opened the door and stepped in saying, "How the deuce did you know it was me, Holmes?"

"Quite elementary, old friend. I recognized the steady footfalls on the stairs as I have heard them hundreds of times before. Your rhythmic knock is distinctive. And through my opened window I heard you bid the driver 'good day' as you disembarked from your Hansom," he smiled.

"That is cheating," I smiled back and entered the study finding my high backed chair directly across from him. He was sitting in his familiar purple dressing gown, a cigarette clutched between his slender fingers, holding out the *Daily Mail* in front of him.

"And what brings the newly-wed doctor out here on such a fine morning?"

"I have just finished my few calls for the day and thought I'd drop in on you and see how you're faring. My Mary left Sunday for the North Country to visit her mother, a touch of the sniffles it seems."

"So, you have already been deserted by your lovely bride, I see." He took a draw of his cigarette and flicked the ash into his alabaster ashtray on the side table next to him.

"Yes, you could call it a reprieve," I chuckled. "And how have you been these past days?"

"Quite well, thank you. Solved a minor case of a string of burglaries of bakeries in the Kensington district for Lestrade. Very quiet since then. But I am intrigued by the strange occurrence of bells tolling at midnight in an old abbey in Suffux."

"And what's so odd about that?" I inquired.

"Well, the bell tower is locked. And it has even been guarded the past couple of nights. It has been covered in the *Daily Mail* and the *Strand*. I was thinking about—"

But before he could finish his sentence he stiffened in his chair and stared at the door. Suddenly there came a slight knocking.

"Now who the devil might that be?" I said.

98

"I heard Mrs. Hudson come up the stairs at a rather quick pace," Holmes said. "Do come in."

Mrs. Hudson walked in and bade me hullo and I promptly returned the greeting. "You have a guest requesting an urgent audience with you."

"Then by all means, please show him up," Holmes smiled.

Within moments a rather tall gentleman entered the study, impeccably dressed with his bowler under his arm, and stood in front of me.

"Mr. Holmes, I'm—" he began.

"I'll have to stop you right there, sir," said I, "for I am Dr. John H. Watson. Mr. Sherlock Holmes is seated over there."

"My humblest apologies. I am from—"

"The obvious fact is that you are from a branch of the military judging by the stiff way you strode into the room and stood erect when you paused and you are holding your hat rather smartly tucked under your arm. Your shoes are immaculately shined; your trouser length is also perfect. Your moustache is clipped symmetrically and you are freshly shaven. You have been dispatched by the Admiralty, or possibly by my brother, Mycroft, as the crest on your suit pocket makes that abundantly obvious. I don't know your name, but you're now free to tell me that." Holmes folded the newspaper into his lap.

The man stood there speechless for several seconds.

"Well, go on, man," Holmes said. "It's your turn."

"Um, yes, sir," the man's voice finally returned," I am Robert Smytherton serving with the Civilian Service of the Fifteenth Royal Guard Battalion assigned to Mycroft Holmes. I was dispatched here to summon you with all haste to an urgent meeting with Mr. Mycroft Holmes at the Carlton. I have a coach waiting downstairs."

"Really? An urgent meeting with Mycroft Holmes. And what might this urgent meeting be about, Mr. Smytherton?"

"I...I have no idea, sir. I was simply sent here to fetch you."

"To fetch me, you say? Am I now my brother's pet? Is there a bone involved?"

I chuckled at the jest.

"No, sir, I meant no—"

"Of course you didn't Mr. Smytherton," my companion continued. "What could be so urgent that my dear brother would send a carriage for me? This is most intriguing. I suppose we should indulge the old man, Watson. Is it possible that you might be able to accompany me, good doctor?"

"Well, yes, Holmes. As I said, I have finished my rounds for the day and

Mary is to stay the entire week up in the country, so I would like nothing more than to go along."

"Splendid. We shall have our lunch at the Carlton, compliments of my brother. Now, Mr. Smytherton, if you would be so kind to as wait here while I put on proper attire, we shall join you in a carriage ride on this beautiful morning."

And with that, Holmes retreated to put on a jacket and his hat and we proceeded downstairs for the ride to the Carlton.

It was a slow ride through the mid-day traffic from Baker Street past Oxford Circus onto Piccadilly Circus then to Charring Cross and finally to Westminster. There on the north side of Chelsea was 10 Carlton House Terrace. It was almost directly across the way from the Diagones Club, the usual spot that Mycroft Holmes, one of its founders, would spend much of his free time. But since absolute silence was the rule of the club, except for the Stranger's Room, carrying on private conversations were difficult to have.

It was approximately eleven-thirty when we arrived at the Carlton.

The Carlton was a magnificent classical building, four stories tall with impressive pillars guarding its entrance, housing a conservative club of government members who would meet to coordinate the party business of the realm. It opened up to a rotunda with a sweeping staircase on its left side made all the more regal by the brilliant blue carpeting throughout which led to a second floor hallway where we were greeted by the mounted heads of majestic lions, their awe invoking manes jutting outwards like royal crowns. Next affixed to the shellacked walls were elks horns and boars heads, their vicious tusks protruding between their dark snouts. The heavy walnut panels were accented with square walnut columns supporting exquisite candelabra made out of stag's horns.

The end of the hallway opened up to a grand, spacious dining area teeming with an abundance of tropical ferns and palms. On either side of the entrance were silver-plated suits of armor standing guard as silent sentinels protecting us from the savage beasts above. Mr. Smytherton introduced us to the maitre d' and then bade us good day, leaving us with the elderly gentleman dressed in a fine black suit. He said that the elder Holmes was expecting us and motioned to the furthest corner of the exquisite cherry wood room lit by the noon-day sun that shone in through tall, elegant windows. Segregated by several tables from all other members, Mycroft

Holmes had commandeered his own private dining nook.

After handing our hats to an attendant, my companion and I followed the maitre d' across the room past a score of well-dressed older gentlemen sipping brandy or barley soup and feasting on freshly baked bread and ham as we made our way to the opposite side of the room.

We approached Mycroft who was wedged between the back wall and a table that was dwarfed by his size. I could only compare him to an Eastern potentate holding court. Next to him sat a man dressed in an immaculate black-striped suit, and by the fit of his clothes, seemed to be in good physical form.

"Good morning, Mycroft."

"Yes, it is still morning, Sherlock. It is good to see you up and about around noon time. Some of us are up and hard at work at the crack of dawn every morning." The inference that the detective's chosen profession didn't call for regular hours to be maintained was a point that Mycroft often chose to bring up to chide his younger brother. The elder Holmes motioned for us to take the two vacant green velour seats at the table.

"Sherlock Holmes, Dr. John Watson, may I introduce Lord Alistair Grayson Swain, recently appointed Associate Chancellor of the Exchequer and a distinguished member of Parliament. Lord Swain and I are now in the habit of meeting for lunch every day here to discuss matters of state."

"Sherlock Holmes, consulting detective." Holmes turned to his right, extending his hand to greet Lord Swain. I could see the detective begin to size up the man, approximately in his early forties, tallish. I took note of his heavily greased, curly hair and his mutton chops. I'm positive that my companion already had all the information that he presently needed from his initial observation.

"A pleasure to meet you, Mr. Holmes. Your brother has spoken about your deductive abilities and your ability to work outside official channels. Quite impressive. I look forward to discussing our situation with you and your colleague. Although, I confess, it will be rather confusing from here on out to distinguish between the two Holmes' in conversation."

"It shouldn't be too difficult," the detective said, "you may refer to me as Sherlock, and as you will soon learn, there are very few traits that will cause you to confuse me with my brother."

Ignoring my companion's remark, the elder Holmes said, "You may continue to call me Mycroft, Alistair."

Just then the waiter appeared at the table with two bowls of barley soup and placed them in front of the other two men. "I hope you don't mind that we ordered while waiting for you," Mycroft smiled.

"Not at all," my friend said," I do believe that the good doctor and I will have a bowl of the same. What say you, Watson?"

"A capital idea, Holmes," said I, having missed our light repast at Baker Street and knowing how good the soups are at the Club.

As Mycroft reached for his spoon, the detective said, "Please, go right ahead and start without us. You look famished."

After blowing on the first sampling of soup and consuming it, Mycroft put the spoon back next to the bowl, dabbed his linen napkin to his lips, and pushed his bowl away from him. "To finish up our discussion, Alistair and I were just concluding our conversation about the Naval Defense Act."

"It must be very important, Mycroft, if it causes you to forgo your food," my companion said.

Mycroft simply ignored his brother's comment. "We need a Royal Navy stronger than the navies of France, Spain, Russia and Germany combined, as well as Japan in the Far East. And that is why Sir John Fisher has called for ten new battleships and thirty-eight new cruisers."

"Isn't Sir Fisher the one who said, 'When you are told that a thing is impossible, then it is the time to fight like the devil to do it?'" Sherlock Holmes said.

"Yes," said Alistair, "he did. But the new Defense Act will put a very serious crimp in the royal coffers. Prime Minister Gascoyne-Cecil and I are against it. But I don't feel that he will be able to hold out much longer. Parliament's Act to make another significant program of navel construction has much support."

"Spoken like a true Exchequer," Mycroft said. "But I must still disagree with you and the Prime Minister."

The waiter appeared with our soup, which I found quite tasty as Holmes said to his brother, "Quite fascinating, but it must have occurred to you that I have no interest in discussing sailing ships and sealing wax. I still have no idea why you summoned me here."

"It has fallen upon me in my duties for Queen and Country to take charge of a very important affair," Mycroft began.

"And what exactly do your mysterious duties for Queen and Country entail?" the detective interjected.

"I see your younger brother has a keen sense of humor," said Lord Swain. "I trust his deductive skills are just as sharp."

"Certainly sharper than the butter knife that my dear brother is using to carve up that scone."

"Sherlock," Mycroft slammed the handle of the knife down on the table causing many of the diners to pause and glance in our direction. "Do not make me regret having called you in on this matter. Your childish petulance will not be tolerated."

I have been witness to many verbal skirmishes between these two brothers become heated at times; but this was one of the strongest protestations I could ever recall by Mycroft. A silence, like a shroud, settled over the table.

"I apologize. We have been working closely on a situation of great import to the Royal Family. This is not a matter to be taken lightly," Mycroft huffed. The elder Holmes paused so that the gravity of his statement could take hold. "This is a matter of international significance and must be handled judiciously."

My life-long friend leaned forward, giving his elder brother all of the attention that he now commanded. I know not if it was in response to the reprimand or to focus on the words that would follow.

"What do you know about the history of Henry the Fifth?" Mycroft resumed.

"Well," said the detective, "as one of Shakespeare's historical plays I feel it is overrated."

"I mean Henry the Fifth, King of England," Mycroft said. "It is an historical fact that he was the Second English Monarch of the House of Lancaster who asserted his claim to the throne of France resulting in the Hundred Years War."

"Which in reality lasted one hundred and sixteen years, as we both know," my companion said. "And he conquered Norway and died in France. Is this to be a history lesson, brother?"

"Will you please..." Mycroft's voice raised a few decibels, and then went back to a more hushed tone. "It concluded with the marriage of France's King Charles IV to Catherine of Valois of England, Henry's youngest daughter. The dowry was said to be six hundred thousand crowns and a jewel encrusted tiara. This invaluable tiara was lost to time until recently. Now it is rumored to have returned and it is a priceless object that is desired not only by unscrupulous elements, but by France as well as the Queen herself. It is a matter of national pride."

"Not to mention great value," the detective said. "As you have mentioned."

"National pride," Mycroft asserted. "It belongs in Britain where it originated. It is part of our heritage. A national treasure. We have several investigators working on this tirelessly, and the most promising lead has been supplied to us by my best man, Tobias Bailsford. He has been keeping under observation a certain Mr. Herbert Cullenfox, a dealer of imports and exports here in England. We are not yet sure if Cullenfox has the tiara in his possession or is handling the transaction for the French or for vile scoundrels. One of the rumors is that a disreputable Englishman might be in the hunt for the tiara."

"Then what do you need from me, brother? It appears you have the situation well in hand."

"We do not want to get too close. If he gets any suspicions that we are trailing him it might cause him alarm and he may flee, causing us to lose what may be our only lead in this pursuit. We need someone who can investigate unofficially with no ties to her Majesty's Secret Service. Someone who can get close to him, such as a shady character in one of your dreadful disguises and many false identities might do. You will, of course, receive your usual fee and be compensated all expenses. We need someone with above average deductive abilities." There was the slightest hint of sarcasm in Mycroft's tone.

"Oh, I see that my many skills are now of use to you, dear brother," Holmes paused and brought his hand up to his thin pointed chin. "Since it is her Majesty who has need of our services, Dr. Watson and I will, of course, be most eager to offer our services to investigate in the name of Queen and Country."

I looked up steadying my spoon which was paused in mid-air and quickly nodded my acquiescence. We had taken many cases before for the very well-off and for the poorest of supplicants, but never for the Queen of England. Plus it must have given my companion the warmest satisfaction to have been asked by his elder brother to take a case of such import.

"After we finish our lunch," the detective said, "we would like to visit with your man, Bailsford, and gather up all the information that he has on your Mr. Cullenfox."

"A capital idea, Sherlock, that is where I would start also," Mycroft spoke. "He is currently in residence in a deserted loft almost directly across the way from Mr. Cullenfox's office at 43 Fleet Bend Way in north London. And may I suggest the duckling for lunch. It is excellently prepared in a light plum sauce."

My friend smiled slightly, letting his older brother have the last word on the subject and we finished our lunch with light conversation about the unrest in Bavaria, Lord Swain's recent elevation to his new post and the unusually warm weather.

It was slightly after half-past twelve when we took our leave from Lord Swain and Mycroft and secured a carriage to head for Fleet Bend Way in the lower north end of London. The carriage ride was slow but steady in the warm afternoon sun, made tolerable now by a slight breeze that had taken hold of the city.

As the trip proceeded, Holmes said to me, "We must enter the loft of Mr. Bailsford as surreptitiously as possible, Watson, so as not to alert this Mr. Cullenfox. I would suggest we enter from the alley or a side door if one presents itself."

"Quite right," said I. "But I say, sitting in a deserted loft keeping tabs on a man doesn't sound like the most glamorous use of one's time."

"Detective work is sometimes rather tedious, my friend."

After a while we arrived at our destination and had the driver pull well past the building, a dilapidated hulk in a row of neglected old structures. We spotted a small passageway between shabby configurations and moved down to a narrow alleyway behind the buildings. Coming up to the warehouse in question, we found the back door bolted shut.

"I'm afraid my shoulder won't be of much help to you in breaking down the door," I said, "due to the Anglo-Afghan War."

"Allow me, Doctor." With that Holmes withdrew his small leather case of picking tools from his coat pocket and proceeded to work the old lock which gave way in scant moments. "Shall we?"

We entered cautiously, not knowing if Mr. Bailsford might be armed and wary of any sudden noise and intruders. As we moved through the dimly lit interior towards the window over by the street side of the edifice we saw that Mycroft's agent was in no shape to greet any guests. There before us was Bailsford tied to a chair, slumped over, unmoving. We cautiously moved around the support pillars to approach him. Suddenly, we heard a shuffling noise from the other room.

"I don't think that we are alone, Watson. Stay here and see if you can do anything for this man. I'll check out the next room." With that Holmes darted into the darkness and made his way toward the black maw of the cavernous right side of the loft. I turned to administer what aid I could to Bailsford. I worked as quickly as I could to loosen the constraints that bound him to the chair. He slumped forward into my arms when I had sufficiently untied him. His head snapped back as he regained consciousness.

I tried to diagnose the many bruises about his neck and face. "Bailsford, that's your name, correct? Where are you injured? Try to take a deep breath and tell me where you hurt the most."

His eyes were glazed over, a steady stream of blood poured from his mouth. Through swollen lips he whispered, "The crown…in the frog…the woman behind…" It was then I heard the floorboards creak in back of me. I felt a sharp blow between my shoulder blades as if struck by a blunt instrument or a huge fist, stunning me momentarily and sending me slumping to the floor. When my vision began to clear and readjust to the dimly lit room I saw a very large figure moving ponderously away from me and toward the doorway that Holmes had just entered.

At first, I thought it was a circus bear, hulking and swaying away from me. As I regained my wits, I realized it was a shaggy Russian coat with a sable collar and matching cuffs. I then realized that he was about to ambush my friend as the detective returned to this room.

"Holmes," I cried out, "Holmes, you're not alone."

Instantly my companion burst forward to my aid. Looking down to me on the floor he called out, "Watson, are you all right?"

It was then that I came to the realization that I was being used as bait to lure my friend to his death. "Holmes, duck, man."

With that, the detective quickly bobbed his head down in a move that gave him a slight advantage over the thug. The Russian leapt from the shadows and attacked him from behind, slipping a garrote over my companion's head and coiled it around his throat. Holmes managed to slip his gloved hand between the deadly wire and his neck, momentarily thwarting the assassin.

Now I could see the wire cut into the detective's throat and gloved hand as Holmes' awkward position no longer worked to his advantage. Struggling, my companion's knees began to buckle as the assassin bent him backwards. Holmes' face began to take on a crimson shade and his hands began to tremble as he reached behind himself for any purchase. Suddenly, the detective reached down into his coat pocket and his fingers tightened around the stem of his cherry wood long-stem pipe. Gasping for air, he summoned all of his strength and cocked his arm, brought the pipe upwards and slammed it into the brow of his attacker. The Russian's head snapped back slightly. Holmes' continued with a second attack, banging the bowl against the man's head again. On his third thrust he hit the assassin squarely in the eye. Holmes matched that move with suddenly jerking his head backwards and slamming the crown of his head into the Russian's bulbous nose sending a spurt of blood gushing out. The thug instantly released his right hand from the garrote and brought his palm to his face.

My friend, now freed, dropped to his knee and forcefully slammed his elbow into his assailant's groin causing the Russian to bend over. The detective rolled over, scurried forward and brought his knees to his chest. With a powerful thrust, he kicked the assassin in his midsection and sent him stumbling past me towards the window overlooking the street.

Because of the Russian's size and weight, the scoundrel continued to stumble backwards on his heels and crashed through the thin window pane sending him, arms flailing, into the air and out of the building.

"Watson, are you hurt?" my companion's voice was a mere croak.

"I'm more worried about you," said I as I pulled myself to my feet.

"Nothing cold ale would not relieve," he rubbed his throat. "How is Bailsford?"

"I'm afraid there is nothing more I can do for him. But he did manage to whisper some words to me before he died. Something about the 'crown in a frog.' And 'a woman behind.' That was all."

"Very curious and cryptic," the detective's voice was still hoarse.

Both Holmes and I moved to the window, and, not surprisingly, the burly Russian was nowhere to be found outside.

"Perhaps his bulky coat also helped cushion his fall through the window," said I.

"Watson, one thing is for certain, someone knew we were coming here. Someone knows we are on the trail of Cullenfox. Let's find a Bobbie and report this. I'll prepare a detailed message for Mycroft laying out our encounter with Bailsford and the Russian and Bailsford's cryptic last words, then dispatch a driver to deliver that message to Mycroft at Whitehall."

"What do you think they mean?"

"The 'crown in the frog' obviously means that the tiara is in France. As to the rest, that is what we must find out."

"And then what?"

"Early tomorrow we shall pay a visit to Mr. Cullenfox and force the issue as I feel that a direct approach is our best course of action now that they know we are onto them. Come, the game is afoot."

Early the next morning we sat for a quick bite of scones and jam and a cup of coffee prepared by Mrs. Hudson before we hailed a carriage out in front of our stoop. There Holmes motioned for three of his Baker Street Irregulars to attend to him. They seemed to appear out of nowhere, as they always do, and he huddled with them a short while. The conversation ended with the detective handing each lad a coin from his pocket and he watched them scamper

He kicked the assassin and sent him stumbling towards the window.

off. We secured our cab and were immediately off to Fleet Bend Way.

It appeared that we were up before the morning breeze had time to fade away and there was a slight early autumn chill in the air giving London town a respite from the warm spell that had temporarily held it in its grip. We made our way north to the office of Mr. Herbert Cullenfox, Esquire, Importer and Exporter of Fine Goods. There we parted with our cab across the street from the deserted warehouse that had been witness to our encounter with the surly Russian the afternoon before. We paid our Hansom driver and climbed the stairs to the second floor office and entered through the door with a glass window which simply read *Cullenfox*.

Once inside, the outer office was rather large with a wooden desk, coat rack next to the door, the near wall lined with filing cabinets and wire baskets overflowing with stacks of papers. A slender and quite attractive red-haired woman was busy on her typewriter attacking a small mountain of papers piled up in front of her. It looked like a very thriving business.

"Good morning, gentlemen," the woman said looking up. "How may I be of service?"

"Good morning, Miss," Holmes nodded his head slightly. "I am Sherlock Holmes. This is my associate, Dr. Watson, and we are here to speak with Mr. Cullenfox."

"I'm Miss Goff," she tilted her head slightly.

The detective held out one of his cards and the secretary took hold of it tightly and didn't let go for several seconds. Holmes then loosened his grip on the card and smiled down at the woman. "If you would be so kind as to inform him it is about a matter of some urgency."

She returned his smile, stood up, revealing herself to be a woman of tallish stature, straightened her deep blue flowered dress and knocked on Cullenfox's closed door. After the voice inside bade her entry, she slid inside closing the door behind her. Several seconds later she exited the inner office, and brushing back a few loose strands of her hair. "Mr. Cullenfox will see you, gentlemen."

Holmes again gave a quick bow and proceeded past her with me in tow and we entered Cullenfox's inner office. His office was much smaller than I had expected and nowhere as organized as the outer office. His desk looked like a summer storm had just blown across it, papers strewn about everywhere. The morning sun shone in through the dusty, unwashed windows.

I glanced over my shoulder as the lovely secretary walked past with the matted sunlight accentuating her reddish tresses.

"She's a real beauty, my Miss Goff, ain't she?" Cullenfox said.

"Quite," Holmes replied. "Apparently, she's very austere and professional, and spends her wages wisely. Her only vice is smoking."

"Why, how would you know that?" Cullenfox exclaimed.

"Elementary, my good man. She is very tastefully dressed, very professional, not trying to call attention to her obvious good looks. Her only extravagance is the money she paid for her lovely red wig. She wears only the lightest shade of lip color. A shallow pink, I believe, and no rouge on her cheeks. And she wore a simple eight-beaded strand bracelet on her wrist and an inexpensive silhouette pendant around her neck. I noticed the nicotine stains on her forefinger and thumb from her cigarettes."

I have witnessed Holmes put many an adversary back on his heels and stunned by the knowledge that he possessed about the business and information of his rival. It kept the detective holding the upper hand and the strategic advantage from the start.

"Why, that was extraordinary." Cullenfox said.

"I am Sherlock Holmes, a man of means whose time is valuable and have no patience to be trifled with. And you, sir, are an importer and exporter of many things. Both legal and not entirely legal. I am interested in the latter. I wish to employ your services in procuring a certain piece of antique jewelry of great value, both monetary and historical. And I am prepared to pay handsomely to obtain it."

There was a palpable silence in the room. The air was still except for the sound of a solitary fly buzzing at the window sill.

"I know not what you speak of, sir. I—"

"Do not toy with me, Mr. Cullenfox. I know what I know. That is why I am here in person. If I do not get any satisfaction my associate and his associates will be the ones who you will have to deal with next."

I immediately took that as my cue to broaden my shoulders and make my athletic frame even more imposing so as to play my part.

"I assure you, sir, that I do not have—"

"How can you assure me that you do not have what I need when you haven't even heard what I am in pursuit of yet?" Holmes' tone was menacing, harsh and threatening.

Beads of sweat began to trickle down Cullenfox's forehead and channel around his eyebrows. "What is it that you are inquiring about?" he stammered.

"A tiara from the time of King Henry the Fifth; priceless in value both in a nationalistic and monetary sense. And my contacts have told me that it shall pass this way. And either my contacts are mistaken or you are mistaken. And I do not tolerate mistakes. Someone will pay dearly if there is a mistake made. Isn't that correct, Dr. Watson?"

I quickly decided that it was called for me to accentuate my part in this ruse, so I placed my palms together, intertwined my fingers, and loudly cracked my knuckles.

"Dr. Watson is an expert with a surgical blade," the detective continued.

It was then that I felt that the cracking of my knuckles was uncalled for at that juncture but hoped it had the proper effect.

"Gentlemen, I can assure you that I don't deal in such things. It is unlawful to—"

"The law will be the least of your worries, Cullenfox," Holmes said in his clipped way, now leaning in very close to the trembling man. "It would be unfortunate if you are not forthcoming with the information about the tiara, and when I can procure it. Now, how quickly can you see it delivered into my possession?"

"I can't…I mean I don't have the item."

"Well, at least we've established that you have had or will have the item in your possession soon. Now, which is it?"

"I mean, I didn't mean," he stumbled over the words like a child playing with a hoop on a cobblestone street. "The tiara is, what I want to say—"

"What you want to say, and quickly, is that you will produce the tiara or Dr. Watson here will return shortly with his bag of scalpels and show you why he graduated top in his medical class."

Cullenfox gulped once, the sweat now rolling down his face onto his collar. But from somewhere, probably desperation, with a shaky voice he said, "I need to talk to my confederates. Until then I have nothing further to say about the matter."

"You will have plenty to say about it, Mr. Cullenfox, if you value your health. My associate and I will call upon you at eight tomorrow morning here at your office and you will either produce the tiara or the location where we can obtain it. I trust you understand my meaning?" Holmes then stood erect and said, "Let's be on our way, Dr. Watson."

I immediately opened the door and stepped out into the reception room, finding the secretary moving away from the inner office door and over to the coat rack. I opened the door to the hallway and stepped out when Miss Goff leaned into Holmes and whispered, "Sir, there is much more happening in this office that you should know, but it is not safe for me to speak here. I work until sunset, but after I leave work I can meet you at the London Bridge. Shall we meet around eleven o'clock? I'll have the information you seek, but I must take great pains that I am not seen by anyone."

With that she moved quickly back to her desk and sat down behind her typewriter and returned to work. Holmes nodded slightly and joined me in the hallway.

"It seems our direct approach is paying off, Watson. I'll have three of my Irregulars follow Cullenfox from here on out and have one report his every suspicious move to me while there are always two others there to keep tabs on him. Now that he knows we are on to him, he will most likely make a move to alert his fellow conspirators. And we shall be ready."

"And that's why you spoke to your boys this morning?"

"Yes, Watson, the players are in motion already. Let's return home and wait on Mr. Cullenfox's next move. In the meantime we have an appointment to keep on the London Bridge tonight. Who knows what helpful information we can obtain from Miss Goff."

We returned to Baker Street where Mrs. Hudson prepared a delightful supper of kidney pie for us. Holmes settled in with two evening papers that he had picked up at a corner news stand to pore through after we ate, while I took the time to read several of the discarded morning newspapers that Mrs. Hudson had gathered from the floor earlier. The time flew by quickly rather like the ebbing of the evening tide on the Thames, our eventual destination. Before I knew it the mantle clock struck ten.

"We should be off, Watson," Holmes announced. We gathered our coats and hats. I checked my pocket out of habit to see that my trusty Webley was safely tucked away and followed the detective out the door. Outside we hailed a coach and began our trip to the London Bridge.

A short while later we arrived at the Bridge and exited our cab on King William Street a ways from the train station. The bridge was a noble structure, its arches considered the best ever constructed in the world. It was described as the handsomest bridge in all of London by Charles Dickens, but its strength and beauty was obscured by the late night fog that had settled in, restricting our view. As we rounded the corner to enter the bridge we could make out a figure approximately thirty meters in front of us standing lit by the soft glow of the twin gas lampposts. As we took a few steps closer we could barely make out that it was a woman, now leaning over the parapet smoking a cigarette. The mist swirled around her as she grabbed her wide-brimmed bonnet. Slowly she withdrew the cigarette from her lips and exhaled a ribbon of smoke when, suddenly, I could make out a hulking figure emerge from the shadows behind her.

Holmes cried out, "Miss Goff," as he bolted forward.

But it was too late. It was the Russian, wrapped in his fur coat. He grabbed her securely with one arm in a bear hug around her chest. She struggled in vain. Suddenly, he withdrew a pistol, put it to her temple and fired a shot, point blank, into the side of her head. The sickening sound resounded in the cool night air as her body went limp. He cradled her in his arms, lifted her up, and threw her over the parapet into the Thames.

Holmes continued forward as the ruffian then lowered his weapon and fired two shots at the detective. Holmes dropped to the ground as I fumbled in my pocket, then withdrew my revolver and returned three shots at the assailant. The Russian flinched, fired two shots back in my general direction and disappeared into the night.

Holmes picked himself off the cobblestone and gave chase, only to be greeted by another shot erupting from the darkness. The detective slowed down slightly and then hearing no more shots proceeded to the spot where the woman was killed. Blood was splattered on the pavement and the stone railing, her purse and still lit cigarette lay on the sidewalk. I reached his side a few seconds later.

"Are you all right, Holmes?" I said still catching my breath.

"Yes, quite, Watson."

"That was our Russian assassin, wasn't it?"

"Yes, it was," he answered looking down at the remains of the grisly scene. He bent down and picked up the purse.

"Are you sure that the woman was Miss Goff?" I inquired.

"Even in this dim light I could see that the overcoat and bonnet of the woman matched the one on the coat rack from Cullenfox's office. Here on the ground is her scarf and the silhouette pendant she was wearing earlier. The cigarette was the last clue." Holmes picked up the cigarette and turned it over slowly in his gloved hand. "Curious," he muttered.

"Now we'll never know what she wanted to tell us," said I. In the distance I could hear the shrill wail of a Bobbies' whistle getting closer.

"Come, Watson, let's depart. There is nothing more we can do here. Our description of a large man in a fur coat will not be of much use to Scotland Yard. And I am sure that Mycroft will want to be apprised of this development and not wish any police connection to Cullenfox in this affair while he still has him under surveillance. We shall keep our eight o'clock appointment tomorrow morning at Mr. Cullenfox's office to see his progress with the tiara."

With that we retraced our steps back to King William Street and walked to the train station where we found a sleeping Hansom driver awaiting any passengers from a late arriving train. Shortly, we were back at Baker Street. We bade each other a good night and parted ways to enter the embrace of Morpheus to mull over this night's events. Holmes had suggested that we rise early to be at Cullenfox's office at the stroke of eight.

I was up at the crack of dawn, shaven and dressed and entered the study only to find him seated in his usual chair reading the *Daily Mail* with his breakfast of a hard-boiled egg, a muffin and a half-eaten orange on the plate in front of him.

"Good morning, Holmes," said I, seating myself across from him and unfolding my napkin.

Before I could take one sip of my coffee he said, "We must proceed with all haste, Watson. There is a new stop we must make before we visit Cullenfox at his office."

"Where might that be?" I asked as I quickly grabbed the muffin to get a bite in.

"This article here on the Police Court Report with the two latest items that just happened before the paper went to press. The first one of a missing horse is of no consequence. But the second one speaks of the body of a woman found washed up on the shores of the Thames downstream from the London Bridge. That might be of immediate interest. Come, Watson, you can finish your muffin and orange in the carriage." He folded the paper and sprang to his feet.

I took one last, long sip of coffee and swallowed the egg whole, gathering up the muffin and the orange in my napkin and popped into my room to grab my coat and scrambled down the stairs. We were off into the morning fog.

Holmes bade the driver to make haste to get us to St. Bartholomew's Hospital. The cabbie was able and his cab proved nimble, depositing us there swiftly. Holmes showed his gratitude with a generous tip.

"That was rather generous of you," I remarked.

Holmes smiled. "So it was and the man deserved it."

We moved quickly through the hospital to the stairwell and descended to the basement and along a dingy corridor of white tile that led to the double doors of the morgue. Passing through the doors we came to an abrupt stop as we were suddenly face to face with Inspector Lestrade and a uniformed patrolman.

"Good morning, Chief Inspector," Holmes said.

"Holmes, what the devil are you doing here?" His eyes were wide as saucers.

"Paying my respects to the recently departed."

"You're here to interfere with official police business, aren't you?" Lestrade stammered.

"Which official police business might that be?" the detective asked.

"I'm too smart for your tricks, Holmes. Cunningham and me ain't leaving here until we know what you want down here."

"Very well, Lestrade, again you are too clever for me. I am here to inquire about the woman found in the Thames this morning."

"So, you ain't down here about the accountant who was murdered a fortnight ago and had his fingers cut off? I've got that one wrapped up now. It was his accounting partner who caught him embezzling and cut off his fingers as a sign of his transgression with the money."

"Yes, I read about that in the papers. Actually, it was the night watchman who murdered him for having an affair with the man's wife. He cut off his fingers in a fit of pique because the accountant dared to touch his wife. Dreadful business."

"How could he know that as the truth?" Patrolman Cunningham said.

"Because he's Sherlock, bloody, Holmes," Lestrade muttered.

The detective turned to the attendant and asked, "Might I please see the woman's body?"

The man stood there dumbfounded, shifting his gaze between Holmes and Lestrade.

"Well, show him the bloody corpse," the Inspector grumbled.

The attendant guided us over to the last metal-topped table in the dank room and slowly pulled back the sheet from a swollen body whose face was barely there. It was the woman on the bridge. The left side of her skull was caved in from a gunshot to her face. Her flesh was torn and mangled, exposed down to the musculature due to having been gnawed away by rats. The rest was swollen from being submerged in the Thames. Her red wig was now matted red strings chewed on along with chunks of her natural auburn hair and scalp.

Holmes reached down and slowly lifted the sheet further to observe the tattered overcoat and blue dress. Around her wrist was an eight-beaded strand bracelet. Holmes began to pull the sheet back up when he suddenly stopped at the neck. He dropped the sheet, removed his glove, and pinched the neck of the disfigured body. He rolled his fingers around then wiped them on the sheet.

"You may cover her up now." Turning to Lestrade he said, "This woman was shot at close range and then dumped into the Thames. The river rats then had their way with the body. It will be nigh impossible to make any identification, Inspector."

I took a short breath at that last pronouncement, half expecting Holmes to reveal the body as that of Miss Goff to astound and confound Lestrade. Then I remembered how we didn't want any mention or connection on this case to lead back to Cullenfox or to surface while Mycroft's investigation and search for the tiara was ongoing.

"So what was your interest in this woman, Holmes?" the Inspector asked, still suspicious of Holmes involvement.

"I thought she might be involved in our current case of a missing piece of jewelry we have been retained to locate. But she, obviously, has nothing to say about the matter. Good day, Lestrade."

And with that we were off to Cullenfox's office, wondering how he might react to being a secretary short, or if he was somehow involved in this grizzly affair. We could still make it across town to arrive at eight o'clock, assuming that Cullenfox would be there. If not, one of Holmes' Irregulars would be there to report on his whereabouts.

It was approximately eight in the morning when our carriage pulled up to the Fleet Bend Way office and we were greeted at the stoop by a scruffy young lad in a tattered coat. Holmes immediately went over to him as the youth bade him a good morning. After a quick exchange, the detective reached into his coat and placed a coin in his hand and returned to me.

"It appears that Mr. Cullenfox has not arrived and is not to be expected this morning. According to our informant, Cullenfox hurriedly left his apartment in the early morning hours with a large carpetbag and is being pursued by our Irregulars even as we speak. This fine lad has given us the address of Cullenfox's domicile, so if you would be so kind as to flag down a coach, we will be off, taking our young ward with us to catch up with his partners."

I managed to secure a carriage in minutes and we were off to the apartment of Herbert Cullenfox. It was not far from his office and in several minutes we alighted at a row of rather smart apartments in an upscale area of London. Across the street we located one of our small spies crouched in a stairwell. Upon seeing us he sprinted to our side.

"Mr. Holmes, we sees him leave about three hours ago with his bags. He took a coach and headed down towards the east end of town. Billy, he's following him, but it will take him some time to spots where he stops and then get back to you. We will lose him then. We are so sorry." The lad bowed his head to hide his face.

"There, Sylvester," Holmes said, "you've got nothing to be sorry for. You've done an admirable job. We wouldn't have gotten this far if not for you boys. Here," he continued, reaching into his pocket. "Head back to Baker Street and wait there."

The boy looked up with a timid smile and tipped the brim of his cloth cap and scampered off.

"Shall we go in, Watson?"

I followed Holmes into the building, glancing at the board posted next to the door where the inhabitants of the apartments were listed. Our Mr. Cullenfox was on the first floor in apartment 1 C. We approached the door and Holmes nodded to me. I immediately withdrew my pistol and held it at the ready as he then knocked on the door. There was no answer. The detective then knelt down taking his small leather case of lock picking tools from the inside of his coat and inserted one of them into the lock. Within seconds, the door gave way and we cautiously entered into the apartment. It was nicely appointed, fastidiously arranged, and immaculately cared for. That was until we entered the sleeping quarters where the room was disheveled and clothes tossed about as if a child had run rampant in it.

"Judging by the indentation on the bed covers," Holmes began, "a large bag was placed upon the bed and filled recently. Every drawer has been opened in search of what to pack in haste. There are clothes hangers strewn about the closet floor where suits and coats were pulled out. I'd say our Mr. Cullenfox has left in a bit of a hurry."

My companion then stopped at the dresser and shuffled through some papers that had been left haphazardly next to an extinguished oil lamp. The detective held the papers close to his face to read them in the dim light. There was a train schedule from London to Dover and a pamphlet of Paris, France with an area circled. Holmes slammed these down on the table.

"Come, Watson. We've got to get to Mycroft and alert him of our findings and then be off with haste." With that he bolted past me and headed out the door and into the street to hail a cab as the morning sun crept above the easternmost rooftops.

He inserted one of the lock picking tools into the lock.

Holmes had commanded the Hansom driver to speed across London with all the swiftness he could muster. There was a marked difference in the tone of his voice and demeanor. I have witnessed the detective consumed in the chase many times before, but this was an extraordinary effort to cross London in the early morning congested traffic. The coach swayed and bounced through the heavy traffic on its way to Pall Mall. It must have been a near record time for such a trip when we pulled up to the Diogenes Club. Again, Holmes was most generous in his tip to the driver. I know not if it was because of the swiftness of his getting us to our destination or the fact that Mycroft was reimbursing all of our expenses. We bounded up the stairs and into the lobby, pausing at the front reception desk and whispering, "Mycroft Holmes."

The front man, startled, recognizing Holmes, whispered back, "Stranger's Room," and pressed his finger to his lips and made a shushing sound.

My companion nodded his head in acknowledgement and quickly turned away. I hurried to keep up with Holmes as he charged up the steps to the second floor to the Stranger's Room, the only room designated in the Diogenes Club where silence wasn't mandatory.

There, seated in the back corner of the room, dwarfed by a canyon of books stacked to the ceiling on deep walnut shelves, was Mycroft Holmes and Lord Alistair Grayson Swain, sipping on tea.

"Ah, little brother, just in time to interfere with the digestion of my breakfast," the elder Holmes said.

"Good morning, Lord Swain," my companion said as he took the chair opposite Mycroft. "I have news on our investigation."

As I took the chair next to the detective I felt that his was an understatement to be sure. Mycroft set his tea cup down on the table to his right and then shifted his ample frame in his chair and folded his arms.

"For your sake, Mycroft, I shall begin at the beginning. You have no doubt received the information that your agent, Bailsford, has been dispatched by an assailant we shall refer to as the Russian. I made the tactical decision to proceed to Mr. Cullenfox's office and laid our cards on the table and let him know that we were on to him and that we knew he was involved in the tiara scheme."

"Yes," Mycroft said. "Not what I would have necessarily done, but not a bad move being as they knew that Cullenfox was under surveillance. But what of this secretary being murdered? And weren't you supposed to be seeing Cullenfox this morning?"

"Yes, but Cullenfox is gone. He's taken a runner," the detective continued.

Mycroft slumped back heavily into his chair.

"As you know, his secretary, a Miss Goff, set up a meeting with us at the London Bridge where we were witness to her demise by the Russian that we had encountered before."

"How ghastly," Swain interjected.

"Early this morning, we were informed that Cullenfox had not showed up at his office, so we detoured to his apartment where I discovered that he is on his way to Dover by train to catch the ferry to Calais and then onto Paris."

"Good lord," Swain interjected, "you've had a remarkably busy morning, Sherlock. Are you sure about this Cullenfox's destination?"

"Most assuredly, Lord Alistair."

"Then shouldn't we telegraph ahead to the ferry and have him detained at once," Swain demanded.

Again shifting his weight in his chair Mycroft said, "I do not think that is the wisest course of action. If Cullenfox is indeed the mastermind, or the go-between in this affair, it is best to let him lead us to the tiara. If Bailsford's information is true, then the tiara is still in France. If Cullenfox is on his way to procure it, then perhaps we can intercept it there. He should think that he escaped our grasp cleanly. He has no idea that we are on to him and know of his destination."

"Precisely," the detective said. "Watson and I will take the next train to Dover and catch the ferry. But tailing him will be difficult from there as that gives Cullenfox the advantage of a good head start on us. And my connections in France aren't as copious as they are here in London."

"Then, perhaps, I can aid you in that arena, dear brother," Mycroft suggested. "I can put at your disposal the *Queen's Bishop*."

"I don't know how the clergy is going to be of any service to us in this matter?"

Mycroft simply continued, "It is a ship recently commissioned by the Royal Navy under the Secrecy Act. It has a two-story engine, steam powered with screw propellers. Instead of the usual eight hour ferry crossing, the *Queen's Bishop* can cross the channel in three hours. It is the longest, narrowest and fastest ship that the Royal Marines have in the channel. I can have it positioned in Dover before you arrive there by train."

"Splendid. That should give me enough time to contact an old friend in Paris to set up a network of informants to make inquiries about the tiara. They are all disreputable enough to be connected with other unsavory types who might cross paths with our sought after prize."

"A decent enough plan. And, dear brother, try not to aggravate the Royal

Navy as you did the last time you encountered them. And, Sherlock, be careful," Mycroft cautioned. "This mad Russian sounds like a man not to be trifled with."

"Brother, if I avoided everyone who wanted to do me harm, I might never leave the confines of my study."

Mycroft smiled. "I was more worried about the safety of Doctor Watson."

The detective ignored Mycroft's remark. "Well, gentlemen, Dr. Watson and I have a train to catch and, thanks to my brother, a quick trip to Calais. We bid you good day."

On the way out of the club I turned to Holmes and whispered, "Is this trip going to include a lot of chasing, fighting and shooting?"

"Yes, I'm certain it will," he answered.

"Well, I could do without the chasing part, if you don't mind."

And with that we were off.

In less than three hours we had packed and arrived at the port northeast of Dover in Kent at a quaint station done in neo-classical style, very well appointed for a destination at the end of the line at such a prestigious port. Shortly, we boarded the *Queen's Bishop* and left for France. I had spoken to the first mate before we shoved off and he told me that the ship had a top cruising speed of twenty-three knots, but its only drawback was that its narrow hull design made it susceptible to heavy rollers and the danger of tipping in rough waters, such as encountered in the channel. I supposed that to achieve its speed there had to be some sacrifice, but stability was not the one that I would have chosen.

I found Holmes aft watching the White Cliffs of Dover recede into the distance as I approached him.

"I never tire of that sight," I opined.

"Yes, unique in all the world, Watson. Like the walls of a castle standing as a sentry for Britain's shore. And right now we are the sentries and guardians of Britain's history; the recovery of the tiara of Catherine of Valois has been entrusted to us."

"Quite a responsibility, wot?"

"Quite, Watson. An adventure of some gravitas." He reached into the pocket of his Inverness and withdrew his long-stemmed cherry wood pipe and clenched it between his teeth. "And I pray that we will be up to the task."

As he reached into his other pocket for his tin of tobacco, I could catch his steely gaze as he looked back at England. There was no doubt in my mind that Sherlock Holmes was up to the task at hand.

The Royal British steamer glided into the long pier sending the sailboats scattering for safety before its rapidly approaching bulk. The French dock workers scurried about catching lines tossed from the ship to guide and anchor it securely to its moorings. The steel giant slowly kissed the huge sea wall fifteen meters high on the south side of the channel with a soft thud and we were officially in Calais. The end of the pier held the obligatory lighthouse, an imposing structure. Further down the wide strip of concrete were three massive buildings, three stories each housing the official quarters of this busy port. A princely spire rose up from the center building with an impressive clock that slowly began to chime the hour. I pulled out my time piece, checked the time, and muttered in a low voice, "Four minutes slow. Typical for the French."

We waited for the porter to catch up to us with our trunks and we crossed the freight tracks to the long portico and entered the office of the Port Master. Walking up to the counter, Holmes inquired of the young uniformed gentlemen something to do about 'le chariot.' The response came quickly in French. My friend waited until the man was finished and offered a reply in their native tongue.

"I see your French is as good as ever, Holmes."

"I little bit rusty in conversation, I'm afraid, but I'm sure it will get us through this trip."

We made our way to the far end of the colonnade past dock workers in pea coats and officious men in short boot jackets buttoned up the left side carrying briefcases and rolled up papers under their arms. The sun made minimal efforts to break through the clouds as we approached a two-horse carriage. After tipping the porter, we climbed in while the driver secured our luggage to the rear of the coach.

It was a twenty minute ride to Calais proper through a rugged coastline, then a stretch of long sandy beach with rows of brightly colored beach cabins for vacationers. The area was sparsely populated with bathers due to the overcast weather. Behind the recreational area stretched booths and small houses for concessions and a hotel for lodgers. Spread out around them was the beginning of a small village, the outer touches of Calais, homes and shops haphazardly placed. The cab pulled up a narrow street that gradually widened into a pleasant square with an imposing two-story building with a sign that read *Calais Gare*.

"Ah, we are here, Watson. The train station."

We got down from our carriage and gathered our trunks, secured a porter, and made our way into the station. It was an impressive vestibule with a spacious seating area, well kept and inviting. I thought it best if Holmes went to secure our tickets to Paris as he was fluent in the language; my only French being phrases that I picked up in the Fusiliers and those were forgotten like many other memories of that campaign. Having gathered up our passes, Holmes and I wandered around the station proper, stopping to look at the many colorful posters plastered on the walls advertising and announcing local shops and attractions. Even without being able to read French, I could appreciate the artistry of the form and design of the placards, some being so obvious that I could decipher what they were meant to portray.

One was a train schedule; Calais to Paris. Starting in Calais with a stop in Boulogne and another in Amiens and then onto Paris. There were times listed underneath the cities names.

"That must be our schedule," I announced.

"Right you are, Watson. It says The Calais—Paris Express. One of the Finest Trains in the World."

"Hurump," I snorted, "Just another bit of French hyperbole if you ask me."

On the next wall was a three meter square public notice in the most pleasant colors with words in cursive across its top. I recognized the word *Boulogne* immediately. Underneath was an ornate full color drawing of a three-story peaked edifice with a perfectly manicured beach in front of it, bordered by rows of bath houses and umbrellas. This led to pleasant blue waters filled with tourists in bathing costumes looking outward at a small sailboat under a brilliant sun. In the bottom left corner was a train schedule.

"This is quite eye catching, Holmes. Is this for Boulogne?"

"Very astute, old friend. It reads *chemin de fer du nord*, the northern railway. Boulogne *mer iete*—by the summer sea.

"Rather charming, don't you think?"

"Very charming, Watson. Perhaps someday you and Mary can return to the continent and partake of Boulogne's charms."

Our conversation was interrupted by the high-pierced shriek of the approaching train. "I see our conveyance has arrived. Let's get a porter and prepare to depart."

I reached down for my pocket watch, removed it, glanced down and said under my breath, "Ten minutes late. Typical."

We found an empty compartment and made ourselves comfortable, hanging our jackets on the provided hooks and depositing our hats on the top shelves. We settled into the red velour seats and drew back the shiny gold-gilded black curtains with their gold draw strings revealing the bustle of the station as it readied for departure. We were soon under way pushing out of the city and into the countryside. Rolling hills filled with swaying trees, narrow dirt roads and dotted with thatched cottages flew past.

Truly pastoral scenes, I thought.

Both Holmes and I had withdrawn books from our small bags prepared to take advantage of the peaceful quietude to catch up on our reading when I remarked, "Trains are one of the miracles of our century. Such a wonderful way to travel."

"I couldn't agree more."

"Thank you, Holmes. And what book are you reading today?" I inquired. "I'm going to review *Brown's Study of the Human Reconstructive Condition as Applies to Severe Trauma*. Never know enough about that, can I."

"I sincerely hope that you have no need of it during our journey, Watson. I'm finally getting around to this small study of make-up and wig application by the official costumer of the Royal Shakespeare Company. I've admired the man's work in person."

So the next hour passed in silence, each of us involved in the literary pursuit of knowledge of our chosen profession. I found myself jostled awake several times by the train's whistle to find that I had dozed off and my book had dropped safely into my lap. Glancing over I observed my companion either deeply concentrating on his own book or staring contemplatively out of the window, his hand cradling his chiseled chin.

It was while I was involved in another short nap when the trains cry jostled me out of my slumber to announce that we had arrived at our first stop, Boulogne by the sea. It was a pleasant enough station ringed with more colorful posters advertising the splendors and attractions of the seaside resort. I could only assume that we would get something to eat in our next stop and I would be very rested by the time we arrived at our final destination.

The rest of the trip was uneventful with me trading short welcome naps with boring bouts of reading. Holmes had pulled another small book out of his valise, this one *The Life and Death of Rotting Flesh; A Scholarly Study in Decomposition*. I could only wonder how my friend could stay awake while reading such an uninteresting book as that. After a couple hours we arrived in Paris.

The Paris train station was quite elegant and opulent, its iron structure now a fine patina. Its giant massive steel arches engulfing four sets of tracks and supporting huge skylights allowing the afternoon sun to send beams of light streaming in illuminating all of the platforms. The sides were made up of magnificent borders of elaborate doors and windows exiting to offices and shops. Above them were rows of thin partitioned windows stretching to the vaulted ceiling allowing more sunlight to cascade in.

Our engine was parked, billowing smoke and steam like an exhausted iron horse in his stable. Between the sets of tracks was approximately ten meters of concrete walkway for the disembarking passengers. Intricately formed metal lamp posts held signs marking the track numbers, and *Paris*, our destination, plus other French directions with convenient arrows, topped by ornate globes waiting to be lighted when evening arrives. I felt that, for France, it was very well done.

A porter gathered our bags and we flagged a coach in the bright Parisian afternoon and made our way to our hotel. I looked out of our carriage as we wound our way down the crowded streets. Paris was like any other large metropolitan European city; yet it was unlike any other city on the continent. It had a flavor all its own. Once you got past its outer portions with its poorer inhabitants and crowded streets with buildings leaning against each other for support, you came upon broad boulevards rung with noble buildings, each seemingly more historic than the next. The architecture was resplendent, every structure calling out to be noticed and appreciated. There was an elegance waiting to greet you around every corner, a grandeur that made the ride enjoyable; almost regal. Paris was a beautiful city. I could not deny that.

"Here we are, Watson. *Le Grand Chateau.* This shall be our headquarters for our stay in Paris. I suggest that we check ourselves in, freshen up and meet down in the lobby in two hours. First I have to rush off a telegram to Mycroft alerting him of our current location and our meeting this evening with a certain Mr. DuBois, an old acquaintance of mine, who I have dealt with on several rather questionable ventures in the past. DuBois has set up a meeting with a Mr. L'Strange who might be of some help to us in our quest."

"Ah, the curious Mr. L'Strange. I'm familiar with him by reputation. He is an author, poet and lecturer of some note. I would characterize him as a ne'er-do-well. I have read some of his books in my spare time during evenings before my marriage. I can tell you right now, Holmes, I do have some reservations about the man."

"Well then, old friend, we are already forearmed in our endeavor. You can share your concerns with me on our way to meet with DuBois tonight."

In a little over two hours we were in a two-wheeler and were bouncing along the cobblestone streets of Paris as the afternoon sun began to stretch over the city.

"Lest I forget, Watson, we are not going as ourselves tonight. From here on out I am Franklin Stone, a gentleman who deals in imports and exports, specializing in antiques; not always on the up and up. I have dealt with Mr. DuBois several times in this guise. He is possessed with extremely poor eyesight, making my visage hardly recognizable to him. He has no inkling as to who I really am. And you are now my confederate and keeper of the purse, Mr. Jonathon Periwinkle. I may or may not have mentioned you to Mr. DuBois in the past, but that is of no concern. You are well equipped to play the strong silent type. As you are a proper Englishman, you are not expected to know any French."

"Periwinkle?" I said.

"Yes, I find the odder the name the easier it is to remember it while undercover. Besides, you look like a Periwinkle in this case," he smiled. "And what were you going to tell me about our Mr. Auguste L'Strange?"

"What I know of the man by his reputation is not encouraging," I began. "He is a novelist, and raconteur. I was made aware that his first book featured a protagonist described as a young, handsome, nobleman with dark luxurious hair that flowed down his neck like a waterfall. The novel carries on about a tragic love affair between this aforementioned viscount, a beautiful young widowed heiress and an interloper, a prominent misunderstood poet who comes between them. Though it rather hints at times that the mutual attraction of the two male suitors for each other seems very strong."

"Why, Watson, you really are quite the literary chap," he said with a grin. "That was a breathtaking description."

I chuckled. "I do write up our adventures in *The Strand*, you recall."

"Ah, yes," Holmes continued smiling," those quaint works of fiction. At times hardly recognizable as the truth."

"See here, Holmes," I continued half in jest, "I never fabricate any of our adventures. They are always based on fact."

"True, Watson, based on facts that are oft times embellished."

"Sometimes I have to make the truth more interesting."

"Nevertheless, do continue on about this L'Strange fellow."

"I have read his next translated extremely popular novel, it being a high adventure tale that was the account of the quest of a French soldier of fortune racing against an English big game hunter in the search of a rumored treasure hidden deep in the heart of the Dark Continent; both groups fighting their way through vicious head hunters, ferocious African beasts, savage pygmies, and, perhaps, the spirit of an ancient witch doctor who guards the treasure of the Golden Python."

"Watson, you really do have a way with words. So, you obviously approve of the novel."

"I never said that." Now it was my turn to smile. "Though, what brought him to the forefront of literary criticism were his works that have made him, to some, the current darling of Paris, and to others, the object of derision and scorn. They are his two volumes of salacious and scandalous poetry supposedly based on actual figures in Parisian society that gave rise to a public outcry calling for the burning of his tomes along with the demand that the author serve a period of time in prison for his indecent and offensive publications."

"So, Watson, I take it that you did not enjoy those two poetic works which you read," Holmes raised his eyebrow, his piercing gaze now focused squarely on me.

"What little I did read of it in the English first editions was, in my opinion, at times vulgar. It is poetry that no self-respecting gentleman of good breeding should ever come across in casual reading. Of course, I only read it to make my own literary judgment."

"Of course."

"Apparently, Mr. L'Strange makes quite a fine living off his poetry readings and his lectures. He is in high demand in certain royal and high society circles. Do you really think that our meeting your friend DuBois set up with this libertine Auguste L'Strange will be productive in our current pursuit?"

"We shall never know until we meet with him, will we? DuBois feels that L'Strange is connected with enough shady characters to possibly provide an avenue of possible information to the tiara," Holmes said looking absently out the carriage window.

Presently the cab pulled up in front of our destination in the Montmartre neighborhood where we found Mr. DuBois waiting at the curb. DuBois was an impeccably dressed little man with a pencil-thin moustache. His attenuated face was home to a pair of the thickest glasses that I had seen in ages. He carried himself well for a man in his late fifties. He bowed respectfully as the carriage stopped. As I exited the coach behind my friend, I looked up and took in the building for the first time and was momentarily stunned by its audacious nature.

Before me loomed a three-story building, more a garish castle from a twisted fairytale than an edifice belonging on a Parisian boulevard. Its facade resembled an Egyptian tomb or an East Indian temple with towering figures, pillars, garish demons, grotesqueries of all sizes attached to its lintels and sharp spiraling cornices. Its dull grey outer surface resembled melting wax, dripping lugubriously downward. One-story tall alcoves, cut into the drab stone, housed merrily deranged demons as if designed by Hieronymus Bosch; their tongues lapping suggestively from twisted grins, their jagged wings folded like broken branches behind them. Huge indecent figures, frozen like Medusa's victims, resembling the seven deadly sins, leered and lurched with arms outstretched and stony visages peering down in judgment.

Flanking the entrance were two bedeviling satanic horrors, resembling Pan himself, half-man and half goat, weirdly compelling and perverse at the same time, beckoning one to enter. The actual entrance to the inner sanctum was the most grotesque sight of all. It was a large gaping maw framed by sharp jagged teeth that hung down like stalactites forming a cavern-like entrance to Hades itself. Above them lurked a depraved, demonic face starting with a bulbous flat nose bridged by two piercing cold dead globes which cast its blank pupils downward at anyone who dares enter there. It was a nightmarish face with twisted ram's horns protruding from its unruly shock of matted stone hair. A club surely inhabited by the devil himself. The structure positively resembled the very gates of Hell as Dante must have envisioned them.

We exchanged greetings with DuBois using our false identities. "Welcome to *Le Trou Noir du Diable*. The Devil's Hole," he said.

"And aptly named," Holmes replied. "Shall we," as he gestured for DuBois to lead the way.

Holmes followed him across the sidewalk with me bringing up the rear. I felt that I was being swallowed up as I passed through the open mouth and between the jagged fangs at the entrance. Two small torches opposite each other lit up the short entrance to the doorway. The double doors were intricately carved in relief with vines and spiked branches with menacing carved thorns entangled throughout. In the center of both doors were Baroque angels with the most sinister visages imaginable perhaps right out of *Paradise Lost*. As I stepped inside it took several seconds for my eyes to adjust to the darkened interior.

We passed through the entrance that opened up to one grand room, its outer edge ringed with ionic pillars cutting the corners of the space giving it an amphitheater-like appearance. Along the balustrades were

...grotesqueries of all sizes attached to its lintels and sharp spiraling cornices.

perched white statues with heavenly robes, outstretched alabaster hands and framed by gently encircling wings, only to be topped off by grotesque, satanic gargoyle visages totally incongruous with the graceful bodies below. Scattered between them were statues of naked men kneeling as if in agony or supplication to their vile masters. Hanging from the second story were three large electrical chandeliers dropped from the vaulted ceiling giving the vast expanse a soft unworldly yellow glow. Tables were strewn haphazard across the floor, filled with old men in proper suits, middle-aged men in the latest Parisian fashions and younger men in the best garments that they could probably afford. The wait staff were all dressed in Greek togas, an odd choice of garments for a cabaret; but this, indeed, was an odd club both inside and out.

We wound our way through the maze of tables like Persius in the maze of Minos, gradually approaching the center of the noisy interior which served as the hub for the thick acrid plumes of tobacco and other unnamable columns of smoke. We were surrounded by the revelers of all sizes and shapes. I noticed a few patrons tugging uncomfortably at their shirt collars or fiddling with the bow of their cravats. It was then I became aware that everyone in the large room that I could see was male. But not quite everyone. It was just then I spied a rather tallish woman of sharp features stride towards me, wearing a sweeping pink gown with, shockingly, her white-boned corset on the outside of her dress. Her shining, blondish hair twisted down the side of her head in tight ringlets as was the style of the day and her face was hidden by an Oriental fan that she waved constantly. As she approached me she spoke in a falsetto voice, "Would you care to join me at my table?"

"No, Madam," I stammered. "I am perfectly content to sit with my companion here."

She glanced over at Holmes and sighed before saying in a baritone voice, "You certainly are a lucky man." The creature then sashayed away, and I was sure that I had avoided a rather embarrassing situation.

We stopped suddenly as DuBois leaned into Holmes' ear, "That is Mr. L'Strange over there."

Even without having my friend's astute powers of observation, I immediately formed my own very clear impression of the man. I judged him to be in his mid-forties. He wore a frilly paisley vest, black evening coat with a handkerchief tucked in the left cuff of his sleeve. Many rings adorned his long thin fingers. His curly auburn hair was parted in the middle and cascaded down past his ears and framed his rather droopy eyes. I swear

I detected a hint of white make-up and dark eye shadow in the dim light.

We crowded around the small table. Holmes seated himself on the right of L'Strange and I sat directly across from him.

DuBois began, "Auguste L'Strange, may I introduce my two good friends from England, Monsieurs Franklin Stone and Jonathon Periwinkle."

L'Strange removed his cigarette from his mouth and placed it into a sea shell-shaped ashtray in the center of the table and extended his hand. It hovered limply as if he half expected Holmes to bow and kiss his rings. "*Il me fait plaisir de faire votre aquantance.*"

Holmes reciprocated the hand shake. "*S'il vous plait*, would you mind terribly if we *palez-vous Anglais* for the benefit of my companion, Mr. Periwinkle?"

"Of course, the pleasure will be both yours and mine," he grinned.

And then L'Strange reached across the circular table to shake my hand. His nails were well manicured and his hand was soft, limp and he possessed a very weak grip.

"I see you like to smoke *sobranie*," Holmes observed. "Special order and rolled by hand is it not? Do yours come from Virginia or the Orient?"

One heavily made-up eyebrow twitched provocatively. "You know your cigarettes, sir."

"Yes, I can identify almost every type of cigarette. It is important in my trade." Holmes paused, then continued, "My business being import and export."

"So, what do you think of our little establishment, Monsieur Stone?"

"Well, the decor is unique and it certainly has a very diverse crowd," my friend said over the din.

"*Oui*, it is filled with the idealists, the insolent, the insolvent, the nihilists and the anarchists."

"You speak very good English, Mr. L'Strange," I complimented loudly.

"*Merci*. And please call me Auguste. I will try my best to speak your English as well as I can. But I find it to be such a harsh and guttural and unpredictable language. Almost unpronounceable at times."

"Unlike a language so sibilant and nasal," I replied. "At times it sounds like you are talking with a mouthful of soup." I was not going to let this dandy get the upper hand on my companion and me.

"Is that like a backhand observation, Monsieur?"

"No," I responded. "I consider it an undisputable fact."

L'Strange frowned slightly. "But French is the language replete with music and poetry."

"Well, it certainly isn't music to my ears."

"Periwinkle, it is truly music," he grinned devilishly. "And those who dance to the sound of their own music were once considered mad. That is until someone else heard the same sound. Then they are said to be a genius. And I am always the first one to hear that music."

"Mr. L'Strange," Holmes interjected. "I sincerely hope that you continue to hear your own symphony."

"Oh, I do. I live every day of my life to the fullest, as if tomorrow may never come. Unfortunately, after a hard night of drinking, it always does."

"Then your life must never be boring," the detective added.

"*Non*, most people just see what is in front of them. I see what is beyond that. My grand imagination is a gift from the gods. Everyone is divine; some of us are just so much more divine. There is a silent joy in being me. It is my legacy."

"Shakespeare said, 'no legacy is so rich as honesty,'" Holmes quoted. "And that is what I seek tonight."

"Ah, but the night can be so full of truth and of lies." L'Stange picked up his cigarette and placed it between his lips.

"I have no time for lies, Auguste. The night is when I do my best work."

"Sir, I begin to come alive as night approaches also, as I see you do, *Monsieur* Stone."

"Then, Auguste, let us get down to business. As Mr. DuBois has undoubtedly told you, we are importers and exporters of rare and valuable items. We operate with the utmost discretion, I can assure you. Recently, we have received information concerning a priceless tiara that has turned up after being lost for centuries. You might have heard of its pedigree. It was once part of a very large dowry presented by English King Henry the Fifth to Catherine of Valois. Their marriage was only short lived, but the silver diamond-encrusted tiara outlived them both and has been lost throughout the ages."

L'Strange smirked slightly and blew twin plumes of smoke from his nostrils.

"Until now, "Holmes continued, "it is said to be in the possession of persons here in France. We were hoping that you might be able to point us to these persons who may have it in their possession. We wish to proffer most generous terms to make it ours. And, of course, you will be generously compensated for any information that you might be able to supply that aids us in procuring said tiara."

I observed L'Strange lean forward in his chair and slowly bring his right hand upwards, stopping just below his chin and rub his finger and thumb together as if deep in thought. There was a slight grin, exposing a set of horrible yellowed teeth.

"I assume that since you are of the acquaintance of my bad friend DuBois that you must be men of, how do you say, ill repute," he chuckled at his presumed jest. "He also tells me that you are very *outré* business man. Composed under pressure, very *sang-froid*."

"Very *sang-froid* and of ill repute indeed," Holmes smiled.

"Well, *Monsieur* Stone, I have heard whispers of such an item just a few weeks ago. But I have no *certain mua* information beyond that. In your line of business, you are certainly aware that words are a valuable commodity."

"Yes, they indeed are," Holmes leaned in closer to our new friend.

"So, *Monsieur* Stone, we can now take the time to exchange words. Words are my trade and commodity. I only wish to exchange them with worthy men."

"Then I can make it 'worthy' for you, dear Auguste, if you see my meaning?"

"Ah, *oui*, I can see. But it is said that the secret to conversation is about opening one's eyes."

"And Plato said," Holmes countered, "'conversation is not directing one's eyes, for they already exist; but giving them the right direction.' If you have nothing further to offer about the object in question, then our business here is concluded. I apologize for taking up your time. Then I'm afraid we must be off."

"*Monsieur* Stone, please, all of my acquaintances are, how do you say, 'off'. Normal is so *ennui*, so boring."

"Further, I did not come here to be bored, Mr. L'Strange." Holmes leaned back in his chair.

"*Monsieur*, you use words like a rapier to prick your opponent."

"And you waste your words like someone trying to tell fairy tales to a pig. It does a disservice to both the fairy tale and the pig," said the detective. "There is nothing more to learn here. Come, Periwinkle, we shall take our leave now."

"Don't leave now, *Monsieur* Stone. You are such a man of interest. This is but the opening gambit of our game of chess. I love a challenge of words. Are you of the fear that I will win and remain the king?"

"I doubt that would ever happen. The most important thing in our game of chess, as is in life, is your next move. Apparently, you have none. The best that you could ever hope for is to come out as the queen." Holmes then pushed his chair away from the table.

L'Strange reached over to his left and grabbed DuBois's sleeve. "My, your friend is a most exquisite soul and a man of infinite wit. I like him." Turning to Holmes he said, "Sir, I would be happy to share a drink with you and truly discuss any topic that you wish."

"Like the tiara?"

"*Oui*, the tiara."

I watched L'Strange snap his fingers over his head and suddenly a thin, young waiter appeared wearing an immaculate white toga. Then I happened to look down and immediately noticed that he wore only a thin silk wrapping around his waist that hardly concealed his prodigious manhood.

"*Champagne, si vous pla'e*," L'Strange called out as he ran his bony hand through his unruly shock of wavy hair. "And the usual for me." The waiter immediately disappeared into the crowd.

"You seem to have a very comfortable lifestyle, Mr. L'Strange," I commented, hoping to gain a foothold back into the conversation.

"*Oui, mon amie. Comfortable, oui.* I have made my fortune by preying on the gullibility of the simple and mad populace."

"Then they must be very gullible," I proclaimed loudly as the volume around us had just increased.

"*Oui*, Periwinkle. The only difference between me and a mad man is that I am only half crazy. I sow chaos out of still embers." He smiled a wicked crooked smirk.

The same thin waiter brought a bottle of champagne and three flutes to the table. The young man turned to L'Strange and with a telling grin placed a bottle of absinthe next to his empty glass. Then as quickly as he appeared, he disappeared into the smoky haze.

"I observe that you drink absinthe with some abandon," I said. "And I, as a man with some knowledge of medical science, know that you are tempting the Grim Reaper with every sip."

"Dear Periwinkle, the depth of my absinth addiction will probably be the death of me. But I will *certain mui* die a happy man."

"Then to a happy death, my friend," Holmes toasted raising his champagne flute and taking a sip.

"To a happy death, *mon frer*." L'Strange said lifting his glass, "How do you say it? Bottoms upwards?"

"I believe that you speak better English than you let on, Auguste," my companion said.

"But I jest. And to jest is a form of art," he said.

"A very low form of art," said I.

"Any form of art is art," he smiled through his crooked teeth. "After all Paris is the art capital of the world. Take my friend over there." He turned to his left and raised his glass in a toast to a very short man in a derby hat seated two tables over from us flanked by two very young boys who must have been in their early twenties. "My friend Philippe is a true artist. His paintings are very abstract. A talent ahead of his times. He also does advertisements for this *magnifique demoniaque*. This garden of carnal delights. Is one piece of art better than the other? They are both art of the highest kind. To know the artist is to know the art."

"Do you mean those posters that I saw on the way in?" I countered now sure that I had the upper hand on this irreverent man. "They are gaudy, highly suggestive, bordering on immoral."

His nostrils widened and he emitted a snort. "You know nothing of true art."

His insouciance infuriated me. "Can you actually consider them art? How does drawing posters compare to the artistic works of a Michelangelo?"

"Why my good Periwinkle, all art is immoral. Take your Sistine Chapel. Two naked men in repose touching hands suggestively."

"One of them is the Lord God," I said loudly.

"Only if you believe him to be such," he answered. "Or how about *Lido and the Swan*? A naked woman and that long suggestive neck on the fowl. Or *The Rape of the Sabine Women*? Not a very moral subject at all."

"You, sir, are impossible."

"*Merci beaucoup.*"

The detective sat there, observing, obviously feigning interest to stay on the man's good side to obtain the information for which we came, leaving me to uphold what was decent and moral in the world from the insufferable attacks of this Philistine.

Suddenly, what passed for lights now dimmed and a flickering spotlight shone on a raised platform in the center of the room several tables to our right. From somewhere in the shadows came the sound of shrill, wheezing flutes and beating drums, trying their best to imitate the music of Morocco. An incredibly fit youth, who appeared no more than sixteen years of age, jumped up onto the wooden circle, naked except for a short, flimsy well-worn and frayed white skirt hanging from his waist. He began executing complex undulations with an increasingly violent swaying motion of his hips that revealed with every movement the fact that he was uncovered underneath the opaque cloth. As he continued his sensual dance, his taunt muscles moved suggestively, accentuating his hips and belly. The spectacle was at the same time mildly erotic and totally repulsive to me.

"What do you think about the *danse du ventre, Monsieur* Stone?"

I glanced over at Holmes. As his eyes met mine he correctly surmised that I didn't comprehend L'Strange's last words. He cocked his head and said under his breath, "Belly dance."

The belly dance continued, the music making any further conversation impossible. Finally, several minutes later, and not soon enough for me, the show ground to a halt to thunderous applause and the din of voices once again filled the room.

"I hope that you are not offended by my opinion, Mr. L'Strange," I said, "but while I am sure that most men in this establishment admired that dance, I must say that, at times, I found it rather boring."

"No offence taken, Periwinkle. But the dance is, like me, an acquired taste." He again smiled that crooked, self-assured smile.

I told myself that, surely if a man says something over and over again, he must start to believe it himself.

He lit another cigarette. "Now that we can talk again, *Monsieur* Stone, let us discuss the mysterious tiara once more. I believe that I can be of service to you. You must come to my soirée tomorrow evening at my home. The information might be obtained there. My house, it is a proper salon guided by the most inspirational host in Paris—me. I am considered the *importances*, how do you say, 'literary lion', of France, *n'es pa*? There, we simply amuse one another discussing *politesse*, scandals and petty intrigues. It falls to me the burden of defining what is in the good taste, what might be art or which falls below my standards as simply rubbish." He hoisted his glass in a toast to himself.

I watched with growing revulsion as he set the glass down and blew out a plume of smoke before continuing.

"There will be a collection of the *crème de la crème* of the newly rich bourgeois, old blue bloods and simple artistic rabble who are not above dealing in all sorts of, how you would say, mischief. They are a fountain of information. A garden of gossip. And I the gardener. I will ply them with champagne, cigars and intoxicating powders to loosen their tongues. We will most likely find your information there."

"And what will this cost?" Holmes gestured at the both of us.

"For you, my handsome friend, I will do it for the excitement alone. For him," gesturing to me, "forty francs."

Before I could protest the obvious insult and exorbitant price, Holmes reached over and shook L'Strange's hand. "Then I shall see you tomorrow night. At what time?"

"Around eight of the clock in the evening." L'Strange's bony fingers rummaged around in his vest pocket. Slowly he withdrew a small card holding it between his thin fingertips. On it was etched his name in the center in a most elaborate cursive style. Below it was his address. He handed it to the detective.

My companion took a small sip of his champagne and set his glass down. I grabbed my flute, took the largest swallow that I could and placed it firmly back on the table. Then after excusing ourselves from the table, we slowly wound our way through the crowd of men who now seemed even more raucous than when we had first entered. The tallish woman with the blonde curls waved and blew me a kiss from the corner of the room, which I tried to ignore. We exited the club into the approaching sunset; DuBois chose to stay behind at the table with his friend and with the large bottle of champagne. There was a slight chill in the air as night began to fall and we hailed a cab and climbed in.

"Holmes," I began immediately, "have you ever seen a place quite like that in your life?"

"My dear Watson," he turned towards me, "in my many evening travels under my ubiquitous disguises I have found myself in many odd and unusual places. I neither approve nor disapprove of any establishment. Rather, I observe."

I could only shake my head trying not to imagine what other unsavory places that my friend had to frequent in pursuit of the truth. Being a consulting detective must certainly have its drawbacks.

"All in all," he continued, "I thought that it went rather well."

"I certainly don't think so. That man was an utter bore and the most obnoxious Frenchman I have ever met. And that is saying something. How could anyone find such a repugnant conversationalist at all interesting is unimaginable as I found the man infuriating with his flippant, irreverent and caustic responses to every decent sentence that I uttered?" I turned to completely face my friend. "It's a man like that who would never be trusted to hold his own in battle with my regiment. He would not have lasted long in the Fifth Northumberland Fusiliers."

"My dear Watson, I am of the opinion that he might have rather enjoyed being in close quarters with all those men."

I huffed at his irreverence. "Holmes, I really don't like depending on that insufferable man for anything. It's like making a deal with the devil."

"Come, Watson, if that is so, than the worst that can happen is we'll have hell to pay."

I had to grin at his splendid jest. "Then we are going through with attending this ridiculous party?"

"He may prove useful, Watson. DuBois thinks he can be and that is good enough for me at the present time. So, let's try to enjoy ourselves tomorrow at his soiree. But before we return to the hotel, let's make an evening of it in Paris, enjoying its charm and the grand monument, that exhibit that marks the one hundredth anniversary of the storming of the Bastille; what's being hailed as the Eifel Tower. It's been a while for me since I have taken in the sights of Paris and I hear that the 1889 *Exposition Universelle* has added much to its beauty."

I sat back and looked out the coach window as night began to fall and the shops were illuminated by the soft glow of the electric street lamps that were still being installed to replace the gas lights on the boulevards, making Paris truly the City of Lights. We passed many closed and open air horse drawn trolleys and scores of men on all shapes of bicycles pedaling their way pell-mell between the carriages.

We joined the procession of carriages like ducklings in a row slowly making their way down the crowded tree-lined boulevard. Abruptly we turned down Champ-de-Mars in central Paris to cross a splendid bridge whose stone arch supports were adorned with magnificently carved angels, wings unfurled, standing guard over the river Seine as we passed above. There we were let out by our carriage driver as cabs were not allowed to cross the bridge; only foot traffic was permitted from this point on. We crossed the bridge with the throng of Parisians and tourists who were taking in the lovely evening and the wondrous sight of the *Le Tour Eifel* as Holmes had told me the French called it. I found it a truly inspiring feat of modern engineering, not a controversial centerpiece of the Paris Exposition Universelle, this exposed lattice tower, a one thousand foot tall construct of wrought iron, the tallest structure on earth, referred to by the French as the Eighth Wonder of the World, reaching like a needle pointing towards the stars that slowly tried to break through the Parisian dusk. It has been criticized as a 'truly tragic street lamp' and a 'high, skinny pyramid of iron' by French critics. I found it rather exhilarating.

Two appropriately gigantic mythological statues greeted passersby on

We joined the procession of carriages like ducklings in a row

either side of a huge rectangular clear pool, flanked by cascading water features spouting streams of water through large urns.

We walked slowly past the pavilion of Nicaragua with its unique native carvings embossed on the building's facade. Then we encountered a truly remarkable sight, four restaurants set side by side between the base supports of the tower, seating five hundred patrons each. If the crowd outside hadn't been so thick and teeming we would have considered stopping there to sample their offerings, but we decided to pass up that opportunity.

We made our way to the side of the tower where an lift, attached to the outside of the support brace of the tower took passengers up to an observation deck some three hundred meters, about the length of two rugby pitches, above the pavement to afford people a magnificent view of Paris. We got into the line to wait our turn to partake of this once in a lifetime opportunity.

"I dare say Paris is beginning to grow on me, Holmes."

"Yes, it is a unique city with a flavor all its own. It holds its own mysteries like every other city. Secrets that we must unravel starting tomorrow evening. Until then," he smiled, "we shall make time to take a ride to where angels fear to tread, Watson."

The populous craned their necks to take in the sheer height and scope of the structure and to watch the ingenious lift inch its way up one the support sides of the magnificent edifice and view the ascending winding corkscrew stairway that allowed visitors who did not trust the lift to bring them safely up to the observation platform. All around, the tower was gradually being lit up by lamplighters accompanied by the hiss of their gas lamplights. As nightfall took hold of the city it became a magical sight to behold. The view from the observation platform was even more spectacular. From our perch we looked out the large open windows at the city below. We could see the Seine winding its way through the city, then the Central Dome at the end of the manicured park that stretched out from the opposite side of Mr. Eifel's tower. Off in the distance we could make out the lights of the Louvre and Notre Dame Cathedral.

But our revels were abruptly interrupted by the sudden appearance of two thugs pushing their way through the crowd, armed with a cudgel and night stick. My eyes locked with one of them and his sinister intentions suddenly seemed clear.

It was evident to Holmes as well, for he said, "Brace yourself, Watson. We've got trouble approaching. "

As I was the closest to the first attacker, I was first to be assaulted. I had to pull back quickly as the burly ruffian swung his wooden club at my head. The stick barely missed my face. I raised my right fist and delivered a blow to his head sending him reeling backwards, momentarily stunned.

Out of the corner of my eye, I spied the second attacker, a tall man of medium build, brandishing his truncheon at his side, attack Holmes. The detective quickly shot his left foot out and kicked the weapon out of the attacker's hand. His assailant quickly assumed the same sideways stance as the detective, as he was also apparently versed in *l'savatte*, the French art of kick boxing.

I had to return my attention to my attacker as he regained his composure and lumbered towards me, his club now raised over his head, ready to strike a heavy downward blow. I put my left arm up in a defensive posture. The billy club struck the muscle on my raised arm, stinging me, but my overcoat absorbed most of the blow, causing little damage. It was then that I unleashed a powerful straight right-handed punch directly into the face of my attacker that sent him stumbling backwards and slamming into the wall behind him. His head hit the embankment squarely and he slumped to the ground, unconscious.

I turned to Holmes, where I saw him trade round kicks with his assailant, each striking the other in the side. Then they threw kicks outwards that met in midair which stopped in front of each other. They immediately tried the same maneuver, this time when the kicks met, Holmes moved forward and threw a strong right hand to the thug's chest, catching him when he was standing awkwardly on one foot. It sent the ruffian reeling back towards the window where he caught his midsection on the railing, flipped suddenly, and plummeted down to the pavement below, his scream echoing in the lighted darkness.

It was only by the grace of God that he missed the people down below. As Holmes and I looked over the edge of the railing I spied a familiar sight on the ground. The Russian glared back at us. The burly Cossack turned and fled the scene as Parisian gendarmes came running quickly to the scene, blowing whistles and pushing their way through the crowd.

Holmes turned back to the thug lying against the wall, bent over, and shook him back to consciousness. He held his fist cocked in front of the man's face and barked out, "Tell me, who sent you?"

"We were told to follow you," the felon said in halting English, fear etched on his face as his right cheek and eye began to turn purple and swell from the blow that I had delivered.

"For what purpose?"

"Our job was to kill you."

"Interesting choice of occupation. Who sent you?" There was a growl in Holmes' voice now.

"I do not know. We were hired by a big man in a fur coat. He found us at our saloon. We followed you from Montemarte. That is all I know."

"The Devil's Hole," Holmes muttered. He lowered his fist and threw the thug hard back against the wall. "Come, Watson, we can learn no more from this man. He has served his purpose. He is of no further use to us. It is the Russian we are after, once again. I suggest that we return to our hotel and retire for the evening, being careful that we aren't followed again."

We then returned to Le Grand Chateau by a circuitous route, having the cab driver stop every so often and check that no one was following us. Returning to our hotel, we consumed a light dinner at the corner cafe and retired for the night. I was sure that Holmes had plans that would occupy us during the next day, plotting how to keep one step ahead of the crafty Russian, and preparing for the party at the L'Strange domicile that awaited us that next evening.

The next morning after tossing and turning all night, I awoke, prepared myself and finished my continental breakfast, and then sojourned to Holmes' room across the hall from mine. After being bade entrance, I found my friend seated by the window having his morning pipe, his breakfast hardly touched, reading several newspapers in French. "Good morning, Watson," he greeted glancing over *La Petit Lune*. "I see you had a fitful night's sleep."

"How the deuce would you know that?"

"Elementary, you are standing rather slouched and you missed several spots while shaving this morning." His head was already buried back in the paper.

"Amazing, as usual. So what is our itinerary today?" I took a seat across from the detective.

"There is an exhibit on knots at the French maritime museum that I would like to take in. Then, perhaps, a trip to the Louvre to absorb some culture. After spending an evening in the Devil's Hole I feel that we deserve some time amongst more heavenly artistic surroundings. Afterward, we can have a late lunch at some charming bistro to fortify ourselves for our evening affair. A rare day off, as long as we aren't being followed," he lowered the paper once again and tapped his pipe in the nearby ashtray.

And thus our day did progress. Mr. Stone and Mr. Periwinkle, two men of leisure, taking in a clear, sunny day in Paris. We returned to our hotel about six in the evening, retired to our rooms and prepared for our evening's sojourn. Both Holmes and I chose to wear our black evening suits with plain white pleated shirts, white bow ties and top hats, appropriate for the affair. A carriage was procured for us at the hotel entrance and we were off through the glittering streets of Paris.

The ride took a good thirty-five minutes to reach the outskirts of the city and into the lush countryside where tall majestic trees separated large domiciles from each other with manicured hedges and stone walls. Our carriage turned up a cobblestone drive to the portico of a grand house of recent construction. Torch lamps had been lighted all along the driveway to illuminate the entrance. A coachman opened our cab door and ushered us towards the huge ornate gilded double doors.

Once inside, a pair of men-servants took our gloves and hats and we proceeded into the marble-tiled foyer. Straight ahead was a magnificent double staircase that wound its way up both sides of the walls to a second floor. At the bottom of the opulent stairway were two nude cherubs with puffed up lips and wide eyes affixed to the newel posts holding electric light globes in their outstretched arms as a symbolic offering to anyone transcending the grand staircase. The steps were lined with Axminster carpet, the finest Persian carpeting that I had ever seen.

Past the foyer we encountered the first of many fireplaces, this one made of white hewn stone with a black hearth, its sides carved into the figures of Bacchus, portly God of wine, holding grapes up to his open mouth and his other hand tucked inside his toga.

In the center of the room was a pedestal base about two feet off the ground that supported three life-size marble sculptures of nude athletes, back to back, arms upraised supporting an opaque globe lit by a large electric light bulb inside its confines. It was Atlas times three burdened with the world. The walls of the grand room were covered with ornate oriental rugs and paintings of notable scenes from mythological lore and legendary tales, never missing an opportunity to present the heroes and heroines in the nude wherever possible. It was a mixture of classical and erotic, obviously done to the peculiar tastes of this singularly peculiar man, Auguste L'Strange.

Around the spacious room were tables set up with champagne and crystal wine decanters, plates and glasses, pastries, hors de oeuvres, and food stuffs, more than enough to feed a regiment. Mingling about were small crowds of revelers dressed in their evening finery, the men in black and white only, with their hair slicked back or plastered down on the sides. Of course Mr. L'Strange's guests were the height of Parisian fashion, adorned in dark tail coats or gray coats with covered buttons and floppy four in hand ties or proper Ascots. There was a smattering of the recently introduced tuxedo jackets worn with dress studs and cuff links, with black wool trousers in straight cuts. Patent leather two-toned side-buttoned shoes were definitely in style.

The women wore shades of black, the fashionable color for evening soirees. Then there were others wearing gray with black trim and many stylish hats. And there were a few tempting fate adorned in *Paris Green,* a green-tinted pigment infused with arsenic dye that has been responsible for the death of many young ingénues absorbing the poison through their skin. I again wondered about the prudence of the French commitment to fashion.

That was especially true of our host. As Holmes and I passed the champagne table well stocked with *Bollinger* 1888, I spotted L'Strange holding court in a small circle of guests. I shall try my best to accurately describe the appearance of the master of the household. He wore a light gray waist coat with a paisley vest over a frilly white shirt and sported a lavender beret. I was sure that he was the living embodiment of the word 'dandy'.

As we got closer, I could see that the object of the group's rapt attention was a handful of French postcards that were being passed around in the company of several men and women. By this early point in our evening I was becoming inured to any unease brought about by the behavior of L'Strange. My friend and I had entered a Wonderland of excess created by this twisted fellow who Holmes was counting on to garner information about a priceless tiara that already had intrigue and murder attached to it.

Holmes had suggested that we split up and engage several small enclaves of guests in conversation by introducing ourselves as our undercover guise as merchants of import and export looking to procure fine silver or jewelry for a royal English buyer of some means. I was more than capable of engaging strangers in conversation and putting people at ease, as my many years of practice as a physician made me quite adapt at small talk with patients. It was a task that my friend entrusted to me many times in the past. Plus, in my role as party guest, I might partake of the many fine hors d'oeuvres that were in abundance as one never knew when one would get a chance to eat a tasty morsel again as the evening progressed. But to imbibe while on a case was frowned upon so as not to dull the senses.

I was again struck by the gross sensibility of L'Strange when I reached the pâté table and found it guarded by a small statuette of three monkeys walking in single file, tails upraised so that the head of each trailing monkey was firmly affixed in the hind quarters of the preceding monkey. I had hoped it wasn't a comment on the food.

The first cluster of party goers I approached were mature fellows. I felt it might be easier to start out with sensible gentlemen. After introductions, and their graciously deigning to speak English in my presence, the conversation gradually got around to what each one did for an occupation. I found myself in the company of a bank manager, a candle shop merchant, and a wine exporter. The last man gave me an easy opportunity to push the topic to my feigned vocation and to my interest in acquiring any fine silver pieces for my employer. Alas, no useful information was to be had.

Excusing myself after a short while, I moved to the next assemblage, a mixed group indeed. A young, immaculately dressed barrister, whose broken English, though far from perfect, was nevertheless greatly appreciated, a fetching female poetess from what I could gather from her French, and an elderly, bewhiskered Admiral or some such higher commander of the French maritime branch, and an under-dressed bohemian artist judging by the paint stained cuffs and hand which I very tenuously shook. The jaunty lawyer translated my profession to the gathering along with my query pertaining to their knowledge of where I might be able to acquire any precious jewelry. To my amazement, it was the disheveled artist who immediately spoke up and rattled off rapid French sentences leaving me totally in the dark. I turned to my barrister friend, anxiously waiting for his translation.

He began in halting English. "Andre says that to him…he has heard spoken of several silver, how do you say, things not legal, being, ah, sold in the underground most recently. But it is just the talk."

"Can you ask him where these items might have been sold?" I asked slowly and loudly as if that would help the young lawyer translate my words easier.

The question was hopefully given to the artist. I observed the puzzled look on the man's unshaven face, wondering if something was lost in translation or if he was having trouble calling up the information that I so desperately needed. The answer was short and low pitched.

"*Non, Monsieur,*" was the answer.

"He said, no, he do not have that informations."

Confound it, I thought silently. I was so close. But at least I had some kind of confirmation that our tiara might indeed be near here in Paris. I quickly excused myself after thanking the group for their kindness and went off in search of Holmes. I wound my way through the throng of merrymakers, careful to avoid the ones who were already teetering precariously due to their overindulgence of too much alcohol, finally spotting the detective in the far corner of the room speaking furtively with a small group skulking in the shadows to be out of earshot from any prying guests. Upon seeing my approach, he bowed politely and departed the small circle of five gentlemen and moved to meet me.

"Any news, Watson?"

"Only spurious confirmation that the tiara might be in Paris according to a disreputable source." I reported.

"Yes, I have not fared much better. Only vague rumblings that a valuable silver item was being proffered several days or so ago. Very disheartening," he stroked his firm jaw. "Let's hope that L'Strange has better luck."

We spent the remainder of the evening engaging several other persons in small talk, always steering the conversation to our fabricated occupation and our actual interest in the silver object. But, alas, there was no other information to be gleaned. Other than the multitude of *amandes, salees* with olives, dates and figs in great abundance, the evening passed uneventfully.

It was slightly after midnight when we spotted L'Strange descending the stairway. Slowly we made our way over to him, catching him at the bottom step.

"Ah," he said with his crooked smile. "*Mon frere*, we meet *mis en scene*."

"Yes, very dramatic at the bottom of the grand staircase, my friend. *Parlez Anglais*." Holmes said, his voice sounding more like a command than a request.

"*Oui*, Yes, of course. *Excusez moi*. You found the *soirre grande*?" he waved his hand about as if he were flagging down a carriage.

"Quite elegant, I assure you," said Holmes. "But not very enlightening. Mr. Periwinkle and I did not encounter anyone with much knowledge about the tiara or anything else for that matter. I trust that you have had better fortune that we had."

"*Certain moi*. Did I not tell you that I knew the best and the basest of society? And with my *e'lan, pardon moi*, style, I can get the tongue to speaking better with my Bordeaux and cocaine. Such a sweet drink."

"And what did these tongues tell you?" In the yellowish glow I could detect my friends eyes begin to narrow and focus on L'Strange's face like a predator gazing upon its prey.

"There was such a silver tiara on the market approximately *huit*, how you say, eight days ago. It went for many, many francs. An impossible number of francs by their accounts." He snapped his fingers above his head for emphasis and again puffed out his chest flashing his silly grin, obviously proud as a peacock of his pronouncement.

"Excellent," Holmes proclaimed. "Now, my evening will be complete if you can tell me where this transaction took place and with whom?" The detective's hawk-like eyes narrowed even more.

"*Mon ami*, he is not one to be trifled with. He is *bete-noirs*. To be avoided at all the costs."

"Mr. L'Strange, in my line of business I make it a habit in dealing with men who should be avoided at all costs. This time shall be no different. Now, tell me the particulars of this man and his location." This time there was no mistaking the commanding tone in Holmes's voice.

"Well, it is your death," our host said somewhat rattled at the shift in my companion's demeanor. "His name is Pierre LeBlanc. He has a warehouse at 412 *Rue des Colombes*. The street of the doves. Is that what you needed?"

"Indeed it is, Mr. L'Strange. I will have the francs wired to Mr. DuBois and he will send them to you. You have been very helpful and a man of your word. I hope that we have the good fortune to do business again in the future." My friend's voice was now most cordial."*Merci, bon ami.*"

"*Au revoir, Monsieur* Stone. The pleasure was truly mine." The crooked smile once again twisted across his face.

I nodded my good-bye to L'Strange, none too glad to be taking our leave of him. I then followed Holmes to the entrance where we retrieved our hats and gloves and the footman hailed a waiting carriage. We climbed in and gave the driver the address of our hotel. When we approached the end of the long driveway I turned to Holmes and said, "Do you trust that what he told you was the truth?"

"I have little reason to doubt him, Watson. There is nothing in it for him to lie. To tell us the truth of the matter only makes him more significant in his own opinion of himself and that seems very important to him." A slight smile crossed my friend's lips. "And, besides, I think that he rather liked the idea that he could impress me, what with his obvious infatuation with me."

I returned Holmes' smile, glad this time that it was he who was the object of the infatuation instead of me. Idle chatter about the odd decor and guests at the soirée occupied a part of the long trip, but most of it was spent in quietude, the kind of unaffected silence that can only be shared between friends.

We arrived at our hotel around two in the morning, startling the clerk with our appearance and proceeded to our rooms. Holmes suggested that we retire and meet in the downstairs cafe in the morning for a late breakfast. It then dawned on me that my friend had been awake almost twenty four hours having gotten very little sleep the previous night; but that was not unusual for Holmes, as sleep was something he would forgo when wrapped up in an engaging case.

I awoke, prepared for the day, and met Holmes down in the outdoor cafe a little after nine in the morning. There was still a slight chill in the air, a portent of a cool day to follow. He was seated comfortably with a cup of piping hot tea in front of him which he was totally ignoring as he perused yesterday's English copy of the *Times*.

"Good morning," I cheerfully greeted him, taking the seat across from him.

"I can tell from your jaunty salutation and brisk step that you enjoyed a good night's sleep, Watson," he said, moving the paper only a few inches.

"Very observant as usual." The waiter appeared and I ordered a continental breakfast with two helpings of toast and honey and extra fruit to go with my customary coffee. "Positively famished after the light repast I got to enjoy last evening."

"Don't eat too much. You don't want to get sluggish for today's adventure in search of the tiara." He began to flip from page to page at a much quicker pace, obviously finding nothing of interest there in the morning's news to store away in that magnificent brain of his. The large, sensational political stories that dominated the front page were of little interest to him. It was the smaller stories, the lesser tidbits, which might get only a passing glance by the casual observer that drew his attention. How he chose what to read and what to store away will always be a mystery to me.

After our breakfast, we returned to our rooms to don heavier coats as the chill and cool breeze might last well into the day. I wore my ulster and billycock and Holmes, of course, in his familiar Inverness and cap. We both had safely stowed our pistols; my Webley Mark III was in my right pocket while Holmes' revolver was tucked snuggly in his, as agreed upon, so that we were prepared for any situation that might arise. Shortly, the detective flagged down a carriage and we were off to *Rue des Colombes*, hopefully getting one step closer to the elusive tiara like Jason on his quest for the Golden Fleece.

The closer we got to our destination the more we were jostled along the Parisian boulevards like a stein of ale being carried by a drunken sailor. It was very obvious that the maintenance of the streets was not a high priority in this run-down section of the city. Even the buildings seemed to sway and touch one another with the clouds casting ominous and odd shadows across the landscape and pushing the pungent odor of long unattended alleyways to assault our nostrils. Though the environment had changed and taken on a more sinister appearance, it didn't seem to affect Holmes. His face now adopted that familiar taunt look, like that of a fox, its full attention and focus on the hunt before it, eyes narrowed and steely, allowing nothing to avert them from the intended prey.

We departed our carriage at *412 Rue des Colombes*; a boarded up, long neglected factory that had apparently outlived its usefulness many years past. We made our way to the small door facing the street and pushed it open as it gave little resistance.

"Someone has been using this entrance recently. See how the dirt has been disturbed from the door sweep," the detective said in a hushed tone. "Let's proceed with caution from here on out."

Cautiously, we made our way through the dusty large open space lighted by the now creeping mid-morning sunlight sneaking in through the slats of the boards nailed haphazardly across the windows. At the far end of the first floor of the open expanse, broken up by scattered crates and piles of straw, we found a rickety staircase leading to the second floor loft. Holmes motioned for me to follow him up the dark wooden planks; the only illumination now the light pouring in from the uneven window slats above us on the upper floor. The old steps and shoddy railing creaked beneath our combined weight like ghostly moans announcing our every movement. I thrust my hand into my pocket, feeling a little more secure with my grip filled with the security of my revolver.

Suddenly, as we almost reached the middle landing of the stairway, from below and to our left, a man of medium height with a case underneath his arm bolted out of the door that we had just entered and raced out into the street. As I turned to holler to Holmes, a slender figure appeared in front of us peering down menacingly. We stared at each other for seconds, neither one moving. Then the man reached into his jacket pocket and fumbled around. Holmes took this as his advantage to spring forward

The detective flagged down a carriage...

trying to close the gap between them. The man's arm was suddenly outstretched and in the semi-darkness I could barely make out the gun in his extended hand. I scarcely had time to dodge to my left as the thug above us fired off a shot that whizzed above my right shoulder. The bullet had obviously missed Holmes.

The detective instantly leapt forward, flattening himself on the stairs anticipating a second shot from our assailant. Holmes grabbed the man's ankles and pulled the attacker toward him, twisting him forward for all he was worth. The man lost his footing, teetered, and gave out a short scream, crashing through the rotted wooden railing, falling one story to the floor beneath. The sickening sound of his body slamming against the floor boards below signaled that he had, indeed, received the desired effect of my companion's maneuver.

"Please check on our thug, Watson. And search him for anything that might be of use." Holmes said standing upright once again. "The other man has well escaped us by now. I'll search the loft above."

I did as my friend bade, finding that the ruffian had cracked open his skull upon hitting the floor rendering him in a doubtful state to answer any prolonged queries. The search of his ragged cloth coat revealed over two dozen franc notes, a few bullets, several unsmoked cigarettes, two pieces of crumpled paper, and a broken comb. Nothing out of the ordinary except the odd fact of the large amount of money upon such a scruffy person. Presently, Holmes joined me and related that he had found nothing out of the ordinary on the second floor.

The detective bent down over our semi-conscious assailant and began to question him. "Sir, you've had quite a nasty fall and you are in need of medical assistance. We can go for aid presently if you will quickly answer a few questions for us. Do you understand?"

It was obvious even to me that the man did not understand a word that my companion spoke to him. Holmes immediately recognized the same and switched to French. "*Repondez-moi et nous vous aiderons,*" the detective repeated. "*Monsieur LeBlanc?*"

The man shook his head slowly. His pain was abundantly obvious. I could see that this was a desperate ploy on my companion's part as the ruffian had little chance of survival due to his steady loss of blood. There was no medical attention that could now save him in time.

"Are you Mr. LeBlanc? *Monsieur LeBlanc?*"

"*Non,*" came the reply.

"Who sent you here? *Qui t'a envoy'e?*"

"*C'etait... LeBlanc,*" he said haltingly.

"LeBlanc," Holmes repeated. "What do you know of the tiara? Where is it? *Ou est la tiara?*"

"*Il a ete vendu.*" The man coughed fiercely, blood spurting forth violently.

"It was sold. When? *Quand?*" There was urgency in the detective's voice.

"*Ila ete vendu... aujourd'hui...*" the injured man spit blood across his matted coat as more crimson poured out of his head wound.

"He hasn't got much time, Holmes." I warned.

"Damn it, man. Sold today. Today. To whom? *Vendu a qui?*"

"*A un Anglais connu... sous le nom de... champ de corbea,*" he whispered. And that was the man's last breath.

"What did he say?" I inquired.

"Sold to an Englishman.'Field of the raven' I believe he said."

"Field of the raven. What kind of name might that be?"

"A strange one indeed. I can't be sure if he meant it as a name or a place, Watson. We will get no more out of him," Holmes said brusquely standing up and turning away from the lifeless body of our one-time assailant.

His tone was rather terse as there was no further chance of gaining any more information from our now deceased attacker. "Another lead now snuffed out. And the man who fled earlier must surely have been LeBlanc. And for all we know it could have been the tiara he carried in that case."

"Hullo," the detective exclaimed looking down at the pile of items strewn across the floor from the ruffian's pockets. He bent over and retrieved the two crumpled pieces of paper and slowly unfolded them. He quickly discarded one piece and then stared intently at the other, tilting it to catch the sliver of light shining on his face.

"This might prove quite helpful. It simply reads *Livres du Monde.* That's *Books of the World.* Let's have our good friend DuBois fetch us the location of this shop. It's as good a place as any to go next." His timber was back to the familiar one, stout and resolute. I recognized it as my companion's voice being the one signifying that we were back on the hunt.

We departed the warehouse, stopping to alert the nearest gendarme of the situation and assuring him that we would report to the police office later that day and give our complete report of the incident, only leaving him with two more false aliases. We walked a ways through the dilapidated section of *Rue des Colombes.* It took time to secure a carriage and went slowly through the streets of Paris directly to the office of DuBois, which was on the other side of the city where we found him dictating a rather long correspondence to a business associate in Bombay. After apologizing for our intrusion upon his business, Holmes laid out our situation and inquired as to the location of the *Livres du Monde*. DuBois went to his well-stocked bookcase and withdrew a large tome with addresses of shops around Paris and shortly located the *Books of the World.*

After Holmes inquired if the sum of money promised to L'Strange had indeed been forwarded, and he was satisfied with the affirmative reply, we thanked him and we took our leave. We had little problem acquiring a cab and we were off to our new destination in the still breezy Parisian afternoon.

It took us a little over half an hour in the congested evening traffic to arrive at the book shop in an alley off a main boulevard. It was an unassuming small shop shaded by the two buildings. We paid our driver and proceeded into the shop, the tiny bell over the transom announcing our arrival. The interior had several flickering gas lamps giving the shimmering dust motes the appearance of tiny specters floating over the shadowy shelves of dusty tomes, as if resting uneasy on literary tombstones. A smallish, bespectacled man stood hunched over a counter that was piled high with books giving me the impression that I had walked into a Charles Dickens' novel.

"Parden moi," Holmes began, "Parles vous Anglais?"

"Oui, Monsieur," he answered peering up over his thick glasses.

"Splendid, my good fellow. This is quite a wonderful shop you have here. Do you have any rare books by Emile Zola about?"

"No. Of that I am sure. But there are many more antique books on my shelves. I have an old book by Dumas. But it is not in a very good, how you say, conditions."

"Thank you, but I have never been a fan of Dumas. Too overblown for my tastes."

A chuckle escaped the shopkeeper's lips as he pushed his glasses up on his face.

"But I do have another question for you. Do you deal in objects besides rare books? Like jewelry? Rare jewelry," Holmes inquired.

The clerk was momentarily taken aback by the question. I could observe his lips quiver. He immediately readjusted his glasses, even though he had done that just seconds before. "I can assure you that I do know nothing of which you speak. Such an accusation. Please leave my shop," he demanded.

"I can see by the set of scales tucked discretely behind that pile of books that you have a need for a weighing machine in a book store. Perhaps you sell books by the pound. Plus, I have been told differently by my acquaintance, Pierre LeBlanc." Holmes dredged up the name supplied to him by L'Strange from the party and by the dying man earlier. The detective's steely eyes narrowed, piercing the dim light with his blazing intimidating stare.

"Who is this Pierre LeBlanc? I know him not."

"Do not play coy with me. LeBlanc is the middleman who is involved in the transaction of a tiara in which you have had your part to play. I am certain that in obtaining rare books you have several men of ill repute in your employ who, for money, will take any course of action to acquire a book from its owner who might not be receptive to your offer to purchase it from them. These ruffians could come in handy to obtain or guard or transport a tiara once it has been located, making you an invaluable part of this transaction either by securing it from whomever had it in France, or by passing money, and by helping it find its way to the highest bidder." Holmes was now concocting a tale of the tiara and its journey the best that he could from the clues available to him, hoping that he had all the pieces correct so far as we have progressed.

"Again, Monsieur, I know not—"

"Yes, you do," his tone was strong, commanding, unmistakably menacing; one not to be trifled with. "My patience goes only so far. I assure you that the deal that he is pursuing is not the most profitable one available. I represent an interested buyer who will offer twice whatever the agreed upon price was that he has secured for the tiara, thus making him rich beyond the dreams of Midas."

The small man's face had a blank stare and was now devoid of color. He appeared both intimidated and interested at the same time.

"I am sure for your part you received substantial compensation. Perhaps you understand that, for aiding me in this affair, you will get much more than what you have agreed upon now that I have doubled the sum for the tiara."

My companion was so forceful that even I began to believe his tale for a second.

"Now, man, for the sake of your own purse, where is the object in question so I might conclude this transaction to the benefit of all involved?"

The shopkeeper gulped down a large swallow of air and his eyes began to water as he tried to push his spectacles even further up his nose. "It has probably left the country for all I know. It will be sold to an *Anglais. Je recois mon argent demain.* I get my money tomorrow."

"Damn. How will it leave France?"

"I was not supposed to know, but I overheard them say it was on a ship. The *Dame Solitaire.*" The clerk was now sweating profusely and seemed to be hunched over even more than when we had first entered. His heavy breathing was deafening amid the quietude of the bound books.

"The *Lonely Lady,*" Holmes translated. "To whom is the tiara going?"

"I do not know. I only heard *eglise des corbeaux.*"

"*Eglise corbeaux.* The raven's church? Where is that?"

"That I do not know. They did not tell me anything. I was not supposed to hear that, Monsieur. I only help... how you say, 'procures' the tiara."

"I want a complete description of this man, LeBlanc, and be quick about it," Holmes ordered.

"But, sir, I thought you said that you knew him?"

"I want to be certain you do, as well."

"He is rather average, has a small scar on his cheek and is without hair on the front of his head. They will cut out my tongue if they knew I told you that much."

"And I will have my associate Mr. Butcher cut your tongue out if you tell anyone of your conversation with us. Right, Mr. Butcher?"

"Ah, yes, right," I quickly nodded, assuming that Holmes had just assigned me another new identity in our present situation. The shopkeeper eyed me nervously and then nodded his head in agreement. With that, we took our leave of the little shop and quickly made our way out into the cool evening darkness and flagged down a carriage at the end of the alley to take us back to our hotel.

It took a while to return to Le Grand Chateau. Holmes went into the hotel to dictate a telegram to Mycroft asking for the royal naval transport to be ready to disembark as soon as we could reach Calais the next morning. Holmes remembered from the train schedule that he observed when we had arrived in Paris that there were no further trains running from Paris to Calais after nine in the evening. There was no possible way that we could catch that one in the time allotted us. He knew that the first train to Calais would depart Paris at six the next morning and that we were close enough to get to the station from our hotel in plenty of time to catch a cab and make the train. He asked that the Royal Marines also be on the watch for the ship, the *Lonely Lady.*

I went to the corner cafe to procure a table for a light dinner after which we retired in anticipation of an early morning departure for the train station. Time was of the essence if we were to catch up to the elusive tiara, find this raven's field and the ship, the *Lonely Lady*. Truly the game was afoot.

Early the next morning before the sun rose, we loaded our trunks into a cab and were off to the station to catch the first train to Calais to our waiting ship to close the gap between Mr. LeBlanc and ourselves. Holmes was quite sure that the *Lonely Lady* would not put into any port on the English coast, but rather drop anchor somewhere off the coast of Britain and row ashore with LeBlanc and the tiara in his possession.

It was several hours until we arrived at Calais, where we hurried to the dock to find the *Queen's Bishop* waiting for us. But first Holmes and I headed for the Harbor Master's office and found an official to whom he spoke in French and inquired as to the whereabouts of the *Lonely Lady*. The Harbor Master informed us that the ship had left the port around three o'clock that morning to make the treacherous voyage across an angry channel in a waning moon. Figuring in the longer time that the trip would take with the rough seas and going against the current, that gave the ship an approximate arrival time in Dover of eleven in the morning. If we could push the *Queen's Bishop* across the channel, which was now as smooth as glass, we could also dock in Dover at around the same time. We informed the ship's captain of the importance of the situation and he sternly replied that he would make it his duty to get us there as quickly as humanly possible.

Our crossing of the channel was smooth and effortless with Holmes and I ensconced in the wheelhouse of the royal ship keeping our eyes peeled for the first signs of the White Cliffs of Dover. It was slightly less than three hours that the *Queen's Bishop* pulled into the Dover port. As soon as it was securely tied, Holmes and I jumped off and quickly made our way to the coach station, leaving our luggage behind, where we would gather a cab to take us to the station to catch the train to London.

Imagine our surprise when we secured a driver of a two-horse four-wheeler that we also happened to catch a glimpse of a man of average height with a small scar on his cheek and balding pate carrying a case underneath his arm. It had to be LeBlanc. Standing very close to him was a man of stocky build with a pock-marked visage and the look of a ruffian. What I was not prepared for was the sight of two other familiar persons. The first was the elusive Mr. Cullenfox. The second being our Russian assassin in his large fur coat. They also spied us at the same moment and quickly entered their four-wheeler commanding their driver to leave with great haste.

Holmes and I quickly boarded our coach and instructed the driver that it was a matter of Royal importance that we apprehend the men in that carriage. With that, the chase began. The dust rose up from behind the two cabs as they tore out from their respective spots, the horses whinnying loudly, their hooves clopping madly. Since our coach was lighter, it didn't take long until we were immediately behind them. The detective leaned out the window and exhorted our driver to overtake them and force them off the path. The driver cracked his whip above the heads of our steeds and steered his charges to the right of the lead coach and began to overtake it. As we began to pull up alongside, the ruffian leaned out the window of his cab door and aimed his revolver at our carriage.

"Watson, take cover," Holmes shouted.

I barely heard his admonishment in time as the bullet passed only inches from my left ear.

The thug slowly cocked his weapon as I recovered and brought my own revolver up and fired a shot out of my window. It struck the assassin squarely in the forehead. He slumped forward, forcing his carriage door to swing open and his body dropped heavily to the ground outside the coach. Both carriages jumped slightly as each passed over parts of his body with a sickening thud.

The coaches were now racing at breakneck speed along the narrowing country path, almost colliding with each other. It was then that LeBlanc leaned out the back window of his cab and took aim only several feet from my head. As I brought my pistol around to get off the first shot, our coach hit a rut in the road jostling us severely, slowing our cab slightly. LeBlanc's carriage was jostled forward and he had to adjust and lean back to take aim once again when, suddenly, Holmes threw open our carriage door smashing it into LeBlanc's hand, dislodging his weapon and sending it tumbling to the road.

The detective barely had time to pull the door shut when both coaches slammed into each other, the wheel hub of the villain's cab nicking the spokes of our carriage and cracking two of them. Our conveyance wobbled mightily and tilted to the right, narrowly missing the other cab and then slowly grinding on its broken spoke. A resounding crack sounded as the wheel gave way, causing the side of our carriage to smash into the earth before grinding to a halt. Holmes and I were tossed about like two leaves in a strong wind.

It took a little effort for us to extricate ourselves through the other carriage door of our upturned cab. The driver had been thrown from the coach and was slowly gathering himself off the hard ground as we all came together.

"Are you all right, man?" my companion inquired.

"None the worse for wear, gov'ner," came his reply. "Can't say the same for my cab, though, but at least the horses are all right."

"Well, Watson, we know where the tiara is and where it is headed. Now we must find a way to get there." Holmes looked around for several seconds. "Good sir, is it possible that we might borrow your team of horses and ride them the rest of the way to the train station. It is only a short way from here. We will make sure that they are tethered and waiting for you when you arrive there. And Dr. Watson will pay you a handsome sum for your trouble."

The driver wiped his hand over his forehead. "I suppose that would be all right wif' me."

"Fine. I'll unhitch the horses while you are recompensed. And Watson, remember to save some money for our tickets to London."

"My," I commented. "You're certainly generous with your brother's money."

It took several minutes to unfetter the two horses and produce makeshift bridles for us to ride bareback to the train station. We bade our driver farewell and were off the short distance to hopefully apprehend the elusive Mr. Cullenfox, Mr. LeBlanc and the Russian.

We must have been a queer sight riding into the Dover train station. We found a stable as quickly as possible where we could leave the horses, again having to dip into the now dwindling purse. Holmes was rather anxious that this was taking so long and half way through our transaction suggested that he go ahead to the station to see if he could apprehend the trio by himself. A few minutes later I found him at the entrance to the station leaning up against one of the neo-classical white pillars, his chin buried in his long thin fingers.

"I have walked this station thrice and could find no sign of the scoundrels nor could I locate the carriage they were riding in," he said dejectedly. "And the London train is at the platform ready to depart at any moment."

It was then that we both spied the dastardly trio scampering up the far end of the station platform closest to the engine, the Russian still cradling a half-pint of ale in one hand. LeBlanc had the briefcase holding the tiara in his arms. It was now obvious that the detective was so intent on guarding the station that he dared not leave his post and scour the surrounding area and search the local pub for his quarry. And it was obvious that the felons had spotted him also.

We immediately darted into the station and exited onto the platform as the mighty engine belched steam and passengers moved about boarding the train as it blew its whistle. The scoundrels were coming towards us from the front of the train. When we were less than thirty meters away from us Holmes shouted out, "Stop right where you are."

It was Cullenfox who first pulled a revolver out of his coat pocket and sent two shots in our direction, both whizzing by wide of our shoulders. Holmes flattened himself against the side of the station while I moved quickly and took cover behind a pair of barrels. The Russian dropped his pint and withdrew a small bore pistol from his long coat pocket and began firing wildly. I had my revolver drawn and took careful aim at the gathering.

It was just then that three passengers, intent on not missing their train, scampered between me and the villains. I raised my Wembley, holding my fire just in time. The engine blew another blast of steam and put forth a shrill whistle signifying its intention to depart from the station.

It was the Russian and LaBlanc who immediately boarded the nearest carriage as the Russian leaned back and kept up his barrage of bullets. As I returned fire, Cullenfox, too, hopped onto the train as it began to pull out.

Holmes jumped up as Cullenfox suddenly reappeared out of the steps of the train carriage, leaned out, and fired off three shots at the detective. Holmes ducked behind one of the wooden pillars as two of the bullets tore into its side sending a shower of slivers flying past the detective's face as the train cars passed him by.

It was then that I carefully fired off a single shot which hit Cullenfox squarely causing him to fall forward and land flat on the farthest end of the platform. As the train left the station, Holmes and I rushed to his fallen body.

"Good shot, Watson. Your steady hand and eye has not deserted you."

"Thank you," I said, wiping my brow.

He slowly turned the body over. It was lying in an ever-widening pool of blood. "Cullenfox, can you hear me? Is the tiara in the case? Where is it headed?"

The man's eyes were glazed over. Blood poured from his chest with

"Good shot, Watson. Your steady hand and eye has not deserted you."

every breath that he took and began to trickle from his mouth. His voice made a gurgling sound like a tiny brook in the spring.

"Yes, the case. Miss Goff," he began. "The tiara." His voice was now barely audible. "Import—paid in silver."

It was obvious that the man was delirious and in the throes of death.

"Where is the tiara going?" Holmes continued. "This is your last chance to do something good, Cullenfox. Clear your soul."

"Tiara," was the last word he said.

Holmes stood up slowly with a look of frustration on his face.

"And we are no closer than when we were when we started." There was disappointment and disgust in his voice. "Let's telegraph Mycroft and have him post men at the London station and all the other stations along the way. But who knows when that crafty Russian will somehow exit the train. Watson, I swear he will not escape me next time."

It was two hours before the next train brought us back to London. Holmes was as agitated as I had ever seen him. He spent half the trip pacing up and down the corridor outside of our coach and the rest of the time sitting and smoking his long-stem pipe somewhat furiously, filling our compartment with smoke. Once we arrived at the station, we made haste to secure a cab and immediately raced to Whitehall. Holmes was silent all of the way, a mere frown on his aquiline features about the congestion whenever our coach slowed to a crawl. After what seemed like an interminable ride, we arrived at the royal building. The detective bounded up the steps and headed immediately down the long marble hallway to the office of Mycroft Holmes.

My companion ignored the secretary as he stood up to inquire who was wanting an audience with Mr. Mycroft Holmes and what the nature of their business was. The detective threw open the doors and marched right into the spacious office, interrupting a meeting between Mycroft and three Lords of the Parliament.

"Mycroft," Sherlock Holmes began, and then paused, realizing the audacity of his intrusion.

"Gentlemen, "Mycroft Holmes said, "you'll have to excuse this intrusion, but apparently I have an urgent meeting on a matter of important business of the Crown to attend to. If you would allow me this boon, I would appreciate your indulgence."

The Lords mumbled and nodded their heads and slowly pushed themselves out of their chairs and began to shuffle out of the room past my companion and me. I closed the door behind them, nodding politely as the last one left the room.

"Now, "Mycroft's eyebrow arched upward as he glared at his brother, "What is it that is so important that you interrupted a crucial meeting about an issue concerning the so called veiled protectorate of our empire over Egypt? This had better be good news about the search for the tiara."

Holmes moved over to the recently vacated chair directly across from Mycroft's massive desk and sat down. I followed suit, though not as determinedly.

"I am confounded at every turn, Mycroft. The tiara has been dangled before me tantalizingly, but always right out of my grasp. It is somewhere here in London in the possession of a man called LeBlanc and that surly Russian. Every clue has led me to them, but they remain one step ahead of me. And I am sure that you have not had any luck in capturing them at any of the train depots or else you would be stating your triumph most emphatically right about now."

The detective paused for effect.

"You are correct," Mycroft answered somewhat dejectedly. "They slipped through our net. The conductor reported that a large man in a fur coat and an accomplice forced him to stop the train just outside of the first stop from Dover so that they might depart safely. One can only assume they have found their way to London. He does seem to be one step ahead of us as well."

The detective pushed himself up from his chair with both hands and began to pace the room. "I have tracked the tiara to the thieves who currently have it. I know that it will soon be delivered to a buyer in London. And time is running out."

"There must be something else, Sherlock. What are we missing?"

My companion threw himself back into his chair and raised his thin fingers to tightly grip his chiseled chin. He closed his eyes to cut off all contact with the room and his surroundings. He had now retreated to that special place where he was alone with his exceptional mind and his exquisite thoughts.

"Unless this Russian is a man of exceptional wit, he is most surely not the mastermind of this plot. He serves only the purpose of being the muscle and messenger in this affair," Mycroft began. "And this other person, LeBlanc, seems to be yet another mere accomplice whose only purpose is to carry the tiara to its final destination."

"Yes," Sherlock Holmes replied. "That is all plain and obvious. What is still left unsolved is the apparent murder of the secretary Miss Goff and the mysterious *Englise des bois de corbeaux.*"

"What could Miss Goff's death have to do with solving the case," I interjected.

"The cryptic words of Bailsford, 'the woman behind,'" Holmes said. "And Cullenfox mentioned her right before he died. She was the one who was going to reveal some information as to what she had overheard concerning some business having to do with the tiara? She was obviously silenced to prevent her from divulging that information to us.

"I'm still not certain about her role in this affair. There is something that still disturbs me about her death on the bridge."

"Of what good is the information that a dead woman might have passed along to you since you will never know its content, Sherlock?" Mycroft queried. "You can't waste time on speculation."

"It might all tie in with the words overheard by the book shop owner,' *englise des bois de corbeaux*,'" Sherlock Holmes continued. "But its translation still baffles me."

"Well," the elder Holmes said, "it translates literally into 'church of the crow's woods.'"

"But who or where is the 'church of the crow's woods?'" said I.

"But what if it's not so literal." the detective suggested. "*Englise* is a church. *Des bois* are the woods or a forest. And *corbeaux* are crows. Perhaps the original translation from English to French is much looser. 'Church' could be chapel or monastery. 'Woods' could be forest or trees. 'Crows' could be black birds or ravens."

"Exactly," mused Mycroft. "We might have a poor translation from the French."

"And the words could be slightly mixed in their order," continued the detective. "Where do we know crows from? Or ravens? Edgar Allan Poe? The bible, where Noah sent ravens out first in search of land? Now take 'woods'. It is not too much of a stretch to put 'raven' with 'woods' together to get 'Ravenswood.' Very British. But Ravenswood is a common name around the countryside," he paused.

"Not when you add in 'chapel,'" Mycroft added. "As in 'Chapel Lane'. There is a mansion, Ravenswood on Chapel Lane, less than ninety minutes ride northwest from London that just became the property of the widow Geoffrey after her husband, Lord Gilbert Geoffrey, died in a mysterious hunting accident in southern France. The Secret Service was asked to look into it as a favor to a Member of Parliament, but the inquiry was cut short."

"And why was that?" I queried.

"The Mistress Geoffrey was quite upset with our inquiry into her husband's death and took serious judicial action against us. She is, it turns out, a very intelligent and formidable woman. She did not appreciate our taking an interest in the case."

"I would venture a guess that there might be something of interest to us there, dear brother," said the detective. "Then Ravenswood at Chapel Lane it is."

It was truly remarkable to watch two of the greatest minds of our generation working in tandem to figure out the answer to a conundrum at such lightning speed. There is nothing that I could imagine that would stump Sherlock Holmes or his brother.

"Let me put a carriage at your disposal and you could be there by mid-afternoon, Sherlock. I'll send some of the Royal Marines to accompany you."

"Aren't you coming, Mycroft?" my companion asked.

"Alas, no. I still have that urgent matter of Egypt to attend to. Not as important to me personally as the tiara, but one that must be attended to immediately. And I can be sure that the case of the tiara is now in the most capable hands."

"Why, thank you, Mycroft."

"I meant Dr. Watson, of course," he smiled, and rang a bell resolutely on his desk.

It was nigh three in the afternoon when our double horse drawn four-wheeler pulled through the gates of stately Ravenswood manor in the countryside northwest of London. Its exquisitely manicured lawns and pastoral settings gave no indication of the treachery hidden behind its walls. But its inhabitants knew nothing of our arrival with two more four-wheelers filled with Royal Marines with special instructions from Sherlock Holmes. They stopped approximately thirty meters beyond the gates. The detective was sure that he would have the business of the tiara cleared up quickly and then the soldiers would be able to enter, perform their duties and take the perpetrators away after the tiara had been appropriated for the Crown.

We proceeded up the long drive where a coachman greeted our carriage at the main portico and accompanied us into the main foyer of the mansion. I was hoping that we were not being led into the lion's den like

Daniel in the Old Testament. I felt somewhat better that I still had my trusty revolver tucked safely in my coat pocket. Holmes showed no outward sign of apprehension and strode confidently into the immaculately appointed mansion. There a butler asked our names and the nature of our visit with the lady of the house. My companion boldly announced us as the Reverend George MacDonald and Deacon David Flynn, much to my amazement. But I immediately recognized the name of the well-known and respected religious preacher Reverend MacDonald. It was a clever ruse to gain entrance to the home.

Presently, the butler returned and asked us to follow him into the parlor where the Lady Geoffrey would be down presently. It was when she and another gentleman entered the room that I was momentarily dumbfounded. There standing before me was Mr. LeBlanc and a dark haired woman who resembled Miss Goff.

"Miss Goff, you are looking extremely well for someone who has recently died," Holmes noted.

Before I could catch my breath, the doorway was filled by another familiar figure, the Russian.

"I see that we are all together at last. No more chasing you, my Cossack friend," said the detective. "Miss Goff, or should I say, Lady Geoffrey, I've come for the tiara. I'd like to see it safely in the possession of Her Majesty the Queen."

I was now in shock at the revelation that the woman standing in front of me was actually Miss Goff, the secretary that I had witnessed being murdered before my eyes on the London Bridge. But Holmes seemed unflappable. I only wish that I had felt as confident as my companion was as we again faced the burly Russian.

"Holmes, how can this be?" I stuttered.

"It is convoluted, my dear Watson. Mistress Geoffrey stands before you as the mastermind of this escapade. She has the means, money and intelligence to pull this off."

"Why thank you, Mr. Holmes. How very kind of you," she spoke through a coy smile.

"You knew that Dr. Watson and I would be calling on Mr. Cullenfox that morning, so you concocted a sly conspiracy to masquerade as his secretary in order to introduce yourself into the scheme."

"Very astute, Mr. Holmes. I knew of your reputation. I already knew from my Russian assistant, Pietor, that you were probably informed by Mr. Bailsford before his death about a woman being involved in this tiara affair, as Pietor had already gotten that same information out of him. I thought that I'd set you off the trail by throwing you a false suggestion that there were other people involved, and Miss Goff might have information to aid you. That gave poor Mr. Cullenfox time to leave immediately on his trip to Paris to speed up the acquisition of the tiara. Miss Goff served her purpose. So I removed her from the equation."

The detective moved slowly into the room away from me. I stood in the open space at the parlor door, slowly, imperceptivity moving my hand into my jacket pocket to seek purchase of my revolver.

"Yes, rather inspired," Holmes admitted. "You set it up so that you had two most credible witnesses to the demise of poor Miss Goff."

"Mr. Holmes, you are too modest. You are surely the most credible man in all of Britain."

"Yes, I did observe your bracelet, your pendant, your cigarette stained fingers that you conveniently showed off by gripping my business card so tightly and not releasing it to give me time to take in all the fine little distinctions of your presence. You even made sure to stop me by the coat rack to make sure that I observed your coat and bonnet before I departed. All of which I did."

She smiled demurely. "You are so clever, mister detective, but it was that cleverness that I was counting on."

"And then you needed a substitute for Miss Goff to be murdered on the London Bridge. I suspect that a prostitute was procured who matched your stature and weight. Her part in this deadly charade was to dress up in the very clothes and wig that you wore that day and wait on the London Bridge for Dr. Watson and myself to show up. You planned everything, including that she had to be observed smoking."

There was a taunt, wicked smile on the woman's face as she was obviously enjoying my companion's explanation. "It is said to be a dangerous habit."

"Yes. Quite true. And little did she know that the cigarette she smoked was the last thing that she was going to do on this earth. But your plan was not perfect. You may have dressed her up as you and planted your purse in her hands, and even gave her one your cigarettes to smoke, but you didn't change her lipstick. The lipstick I found on the cigarette butt was a deep red, not the pale pink shade that you were wearing that morning. I found that disquieting. Then you had your accomplice, the Russian, sneak up behind her, and force his pistol to her head, firing to make sure that identifying her would be almost impossible."

There was a wide grin on the big Cossack's face as he was now included in the narrative.

"Lastly, he tossed her into the Thames for good measure, where you were not worried if her body might be discovered the next morning."

"Please go on, Mr. Holmes," she urged. "This is so fascinating."

I could see my friend's eyes narrow at the last remark as he surely found nothing to be fascinating about the murder of an innocent woman.

"You made doubly sure that when her body was inevitably found that her face would be unrecognizable to me. So you took extra measures to be sure that the river rats would eat off her features, and this proved a fatal flaw in your plan. Upon inspection of the body I found that lard had been applied to her neck and face. Lard and rats, Watson, a deadly combination."

By then my hand had slipped into my pocket and was gripping the handle of my Webley, waiting for the proper moment to brandish it.

"And the assassin's bullets on the bridge were meant mostly as a warning. You needed us alive to identify the woman who was thrown off the bridge as the woman whom we had gone to meet that night."

There was a look of disappointment on the Russian's face as he heard the detective explain how he figured out the ruse.

"Quite good, Mr. Holmes. I applaud you on your powers of observation and deduction."

"But you, on the other hand, are not so observant, as you failed to notice Dr. Watson secure his revolver in his pocket."

With that, I pulled out my revolver and pointed it at the Russian, the largest target in the room.

"Excellent, Watson, but might I suggest that you keep an eye on the archway to the next room behind the Russian, as we might be joined by one other guest."

"Another guest?" said I incredulously. "Don't we have enough people here to wrap this up?"

"No, there is one other problem with this case that must be resolved. And that is how the Russian knew that Mr. Bailsford had Cullenfox under surveillance and how he knew where Bailsford was hiding while he was spying on him. How did they find out at the very moment that we were going to speak with Bailsford?"

Holmes paused, took out a cigarette, and lighted it. "And how did they know that we were going to come to Cullenfox's office that very day to confront him about the tiara, giving them time to set their plan in motion? Plus, how did the Russian know to follow us to the Devil's Hole when we were going to meet Mr. DuBois and then lie in wait for us and eventually overtaking us at the Eifel Tower?"

He blew a plume of smoke into the air.

"Then he knew that we were following him and the tiara back to Calais and back to England, giving him a head start that we were able to cut short and almost apprehend him, if not for his departing the London-bound train just ahead of us."

Holmes drew deeply on the cigarette once more as he stared from one to the other of our adversaries. "How was the Russian able to keep one step ahead of us in France? It was clear to me that only Mycroft, you Watson, and I knew of our whereabouts and our planned movements by our conversations and the telegrams that we sent. But on further reflection, there was one other person who had this knowledge. Someone who was present with Mycroft every time we spoke, or when Mycroft received one of our telegrams."

He paused and inhaled on the cigarette once more. "You can come out now, Lord Swain."

"Bravo, Mr. Sherlock Holmes" Alistair Swain said as he stepped into the room with a revolver drawn and pointed at us. "You are every bit the detective that your brother claimed you to be. When did you first realize that it was I who was passing along the intelligence on your movements?"

Holmes shrugged. "When I last saw my brother, Mycroft, I went over all the possible scenarios as to how the Russian was always anticipating our movements with such accuracy. Then I eliminated the impossible, and what remained, however improbable, had to be the answer."

Swain canted his head in compliment.

Holmes smiled as he brought the cigarette to his lips once more. "I know not if you have gambling debts or you have run short on inheritance funds or are simply greedy that made you throw in with this scheme to cash in on the tiara, but it had to be you who were passing along our next moves. That's why I made sure that you were nowhere around when Dr.Watson, Mycroft and I formulated our next step."

"Quite brilliant, Holmes," Swain's smile broadened. "I have been bleeding money for several years trying to keep up the family estate on ever dwindling incomes. And it takes coin to facilitate one's rise in the Parliament. My share of the profit of the sale of the tiara will set me up comfortably for life."

The Russian took advantage of Swain's appearance and drew his pistol from his trouser pocket and pointed it at me. He motioned for me to drop my revolver, which I did, setting it down gently on the carpet.

"You seem to be out gunned and out witted, Mr. Holmes," Swain boasted. "More the pity. Now, Doctor, if you would be so kind as to join your friend over there." He wiggled his pistol to the right and I moved over to stand next to my companion.

Swain crossed the room, slowly picked up my revolver and tucked it into his waistband. "Why don't we all sit down and enjoy the last little tale that Mr. Sherlock Holmes might have the opportunity to tell."

We made our way over to two over-stuffed chairs flanking the fireplace while Swain and Mistress Geoffrey sat on the settee immediately across from us. The Russian took up his post like a sentry at the end of the sofa, the wide grin now returned to his broad face. LeBlanc pulled a chair from the corner of the parlor and positioned it to the left of the settee.

"Now do continue, Mr. Holmes," Swain directed. "I'm most interested in what led you here, to this final destination."

"Mycroft was kind enough to inform me that Ravenswood is one of the most prosperous Houses in all of the surrounding countryside," Holmes complied. "Perhaps in the north shires, making her one of the only people with enough capital on hand to purchase the tiara from the French at what must have been an exorbitant price. And Mistress Geoffrey is a woman of great cunning and exceptional intelligence, judging by the clever way that she mysteriously disposed of her late husband while he was on a hunting trip in the south of France, making her the Lady of the manor. A partnership between Lord Swain and Lady Geoffrey was only elementary."

"You are truly amazing, Mr. Holmes," said Mistress Geoffrey. And while you rambled on I have worked out a perfect little plan that even the great Sherlock Holmes won't be able to foil because you shall be dead at the end of it."

"I am all ears, madam," my companion said. "Do go on."

"Sherlock Holmes and Dr. Watson will be shot dead while breaking into Ravenswood Manor with the intent of assassinating the Honorable Lord Swain and Mistress Geoffrey because of Holmes' and Watson's allegiance to Mycroft Holmes, who is known to be opposed to many of the policies of Prime Minister Gascoyne-Cecil; whereas Swain and I are both known as staunch supporters of Gascoyne-Cecil. So, Mycroft Holmes sent his brother and his companion as assassins to kill us. But they failed. It also implicates Mycroft in an intrigue that will besmirch his reputation and ruin his career."

"Brilliant, darling," Swain boasted. "And we still have the valuable prize, the tiara of Catherine of Valois. All due to the wealth and cunning of Mistress Geoffrey."

"I shall wear it proudly around the manor. The dowry fit for a queen." A smirk crossed her lips. "Then, when I tire of it, Swain knows of a baron in West London who will pay a king's ransom to possess it. Thus making the two of us among the richest personages in all of England."

"Well, as interesting as this has been," my friend removed his time piece from his vest pocket, "I feel it is time to end our little chat."

"Oh, I agree, Holmes," said Swain." If you will be so kind as to follow Pietor," he glanced at the Russian, "out to the garden, he will set the stage for your demise. Too bad you were better detectives than you were assassins."

The Russian moved out from behind the settee and lumbered to the French doors leading to the garden. Holmes got up slowly, again checked his pocket watch, and shook it. "It must be running slow," he muttered.

At that very moment, the front doors flew open and several Royal Marines stormed into the vestibule, guns drawn and the captain shouting at the top of his voice, "Everyone stop right where they are. Do not move. Put your hands over your heads."

It was Lord Swain who made the first move. He stood up and fired two shots at the group of soldiers, one bullet hitting a corporal in the right thigh. The captain of the guard returned two shots striking Swain square in the chest, dropping him to the floor. Lady Geoffrey let out a blood curdling scream. LeBlanc immediately dropped to his knees, arms raised, pleading for his life.

The Russian turned and leveled his pistol at the group of Marines, but before he could fire, Holmes was on him like a jungle cat. He grabbed the trunk-like arm and yanked it downward, sending the shot straight into the Persian carpet. With one sweeping motion, the huge Cossack swung his arm and flung Holmes back into the air. The detective slammed hard into a teak end table, upsetting an oriental vase. Holmes grabbed the teetering vase and flung it at the behemoth, sending it crashing into the side of the massive head. Shards of porcelain flew everywhere, some embedding themselves into the huge face. The Russian roared in pain and swung his arm towards the detective, all the while trying to focus his aim. Holmes ducked underneath the outstretched arm and delivered a sharp kick to the knee cap of his assailant. The Cossack roared again in distress and bent forward grabbing his knee. It was then that the detective locked both hands together and delivered a devastating underhanded uppercut to the jaw of the Russian. There was a slight hesitation, and then the massive frame dropped to the carpet.

By then I had recovered my revolver from the waistband of Swain and now stood over the Cossack's fallen body, offering a hand on Holmes' elbow to steady him. "Are you all right?"

"I do believe I've scraped my knuckles," he replied.

The Marines had clapped irons on Mistress Geoffrey and LeBlanc and were now struggling to force them around the wrists of the fallen Russian. The captain stood over the dead body of Lord Swain and turned slowly to the detective and me. "It looks like we timed our arrival exactly as you requested, Mr. Holmes."

"I dare say your timing was impeccable, Captain. Another few seconds and you would be informing my brother that I wouldn't be troubling him ever again. Might I suggest that you cordon off this manor and let no one enter or leave until Mycroft arrives. I am sure that he will want his own men to conduct a thorough search of the premises. He will most assuredly be arriving after he concludes his meeting back in Whitehall."

The captain nodded his acknowledgement and moved over to where his men were still struggling to place the irons on the burly Russian. Lady Geoffrey moved past Holmes and me, escorted by a soldier, then abruptly stopped and turned to face the detective.

"Damn you, Sherlock Holmes. Why couldn't you have stopped scratching away at the surface to uncover the truth of this matter?"

"When it comes to matters of the Crown," Holmes replied, "it is never allowed to stop until the truth is uncovered."

"Curse you," she yelled. "Until the day that you die."

Holmes raised an impervious eyebrow and smiled at her.

"Madam, it appears that we would all have been better off if you would have had perspicacity to remain among the dead."

THE END

THE STORY BEHIND THE STORY

After taking a short hiatus from writing, a mystery worthy of the great Sherlock Holmes himself, I was pressed by my best friend, Michael A. Black, to set down and revisit the world of the great consulting detective. One of my visits to Chicago found us sitting in our favorite coffee shop near Chicago's south side when I mentioned an idea that I had for a Sherlock Holmes's story involving an adventure taking Holmes and Watson to Paris and back in pursuit of a treasure of great value to the Crown and France. And that's as far as I got. Talk about a vague idea.

Mike, in his best Holmesian way, said that he would ponder the situation and get back to me. After completing our day's agenda, trips to various book stores and comic book shops in search of our own treasures, we parted ways for the day. The next day at breakfast, he presented me with a slip of paper that had notes on it with the words 'Henry the V, Charles IV, Catherine of Valois, marriage, dowry, tiara.'

If not for the brilliant mind of my life-long friend there would be no Adventure of the Queen's Tiara. He also spent hours editing, adding brilliant dialogue, formatting, and encouraging me to keep on course.

There are no words that can ever express my gratitude for the lifetime of his always being there for me.

I am sincerely indebted to my Victorian Historian, Carl Wayne Ensminger. From procuring an 1880 map of Victorian London to tireless research on Parisian fashion, he is a fountain of information and true friend.

My eternal love is always there for my beautiful wife, Susan Marie Koss Lovato, for her encouragement and support. She is my beacon in stormy seas.

Special thanks to my saintly mother, Elaine Mary Michels Lovato, for starting this whole thing.

This story is dedicated to my friend, Michael A. Black.

172

RAYMOND LOUIS LOVATO - was born on the south side of Chicago, Illinois, the oldest of eleven children. He has a Bachelors of Arts degree from St. Xavier University in Chicago where he was editor and wrote a monthly column for the university newspaper and had several poems published in the university's literary magazine. His varied careers have included: English teacher, designing a college credit course in Popular Culture; a hospital administrator; a resort owner in Palm Springs, CA.; wrote a monthly column for an Antiquing magazine; advertising and marketing; and newspaper columnist. His tourism articles have appeared in prestigious magazines in Australia, England, Germany, as well as the U.S. While in Palm Springs, he helped establish and was president of the Desert Screenwriters Guild.

Ray has written several short stories for independent publishers and co-authored an e-book, DARK HAVEN. As co-creator of Doc Atlas, Ray has collaborated on and written parts of various Doc Atlas stories with his life-long friend, Michael A. Black. For Airship 27, Ray and Michael have collected several Doc Atlas stories and reissued them as DOC ATLAS VOLUME 1.

Also for Airship 27, Ray has had the privilege of writing the adventures of the Great Detective, Sherlock Holmes. He has authored and co-authored five short stories, one novella: THE CHARWICK GHOST, THE SINGULAR TRAGEDY, THE LOST GOSPEL, THE INDEFATIGABLE SPIES, THE QUEEN'S TIARA, and THE RHYMES OF DEATH. He has also co-authored a full-length novel with Michael Black, SHERLOCK HOLMES AND THE ADVENTURE OF THE IRON CROWN.

Ray's long-time hobbies include photography and collecting old books. His real passion is traveling the world with his inspiration, his lovely wife, Susan.

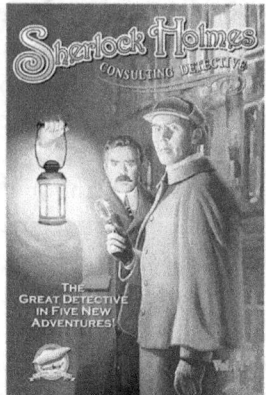

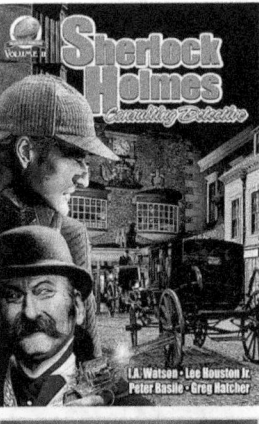

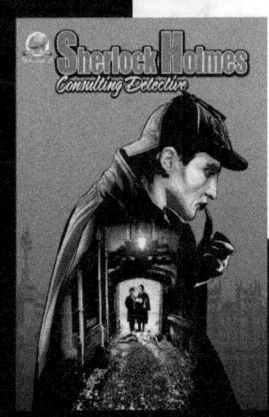

HUNT FOR THE IRON CROWN

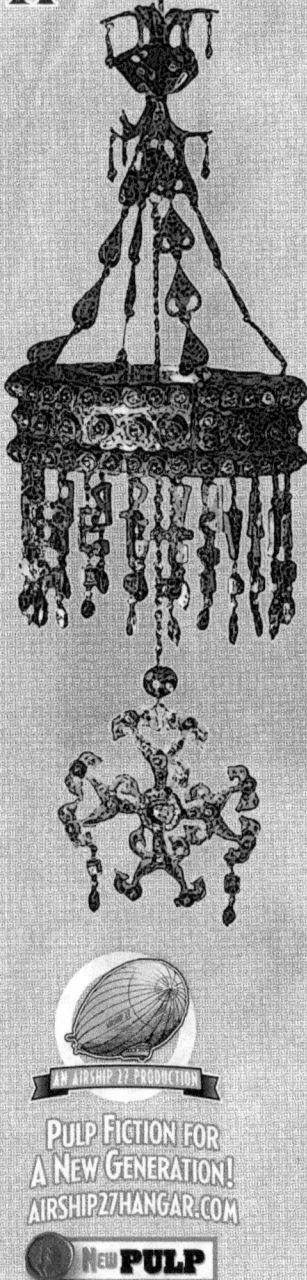

One of the most cherished religious artifacts in history is the Iron Crown of Constantinople, supposedly containing the nails that were used to crucify Jesus Christ by the Romans. A fire at a London Mason Lodge reveals the murdered remains of one of the Temple Officers. At the request of a Scotland Yard inspector, Sherlock Holmes is brought into the case and learns that four groups are involved in the crime, all revolved around their search for the lost crown. The agents of the Masons, Templars and the Illuminati are involved in the hunt as well as the vicious Thieves Guild controlled by the mysterious mastermind known only as the Hawk.

But none can decipher the Latin poem handed down through the ages which reveals the hidden location of the prized relic. When a second murder is discovered, the Great Detective and his loyal companion find themselves racing against time to solve the puzzle before further blood is spilled. Yes, devoted Holmes readers, the game is most certainly afoot!

SHERLOCK HOLMES AND THE ADVENTURE OF THE IRON CROWN

RAYMOND LOUIS JAMES LOVATO & MICHAEL A. BLACK